IN THE EYE OF THE STORM

DEBORAH E. HAMMOND

Susan
I hope you will
enjoy. This was
my first.
Debbie
Hammond

Copyright

DEDICATION

To the People of Wilmington, North Carolina – You were my first love and to Bill; with you all things are possible.

CHAPTER ONE

August, 1865 – Wilmington, North Carolina

The day was warm with the promise of another scorching late August heat wave as Elizabeth walked down Market Street to the Cape Fear River. With the words of her aunt ringing in her ears, she thought of the many times that Aunt Felicity had warned her against contact with the wharf area. "No lady ever sets foot beyond Front Street, Elizabeth. Do not ever think of going to Water Street for any reason. The only thing that you will find there is rough men and trouble. If there are any dealings to be made with the Captains of the seagoing vessels, let your father make the arrangements through respectable agents. Water Street is no place for a lady!"

The war had taken all of the respectable agents, just as it had taken her father, she thought. As there was no remaining family members left to make arrangements for her, she had decided to take matters into her own hands. Even her father's Wilmington attorney, Herbert Hill; had decided to return to his family's lands upstate, and had left Wilmington shortly after the reading of her father and aunt's wills. With the City in chaos after the Union occupation and the matter of her inheritance left unresolved, she had decided to set off to make arrangements for a voyage to London to settle her financial affairs. The war had left communication lines as destroyed as the farmlands that surrounded Wilmington. With no way to assure that her correspondence with the London solicitors would be received and answered, she had decided that a trip to London was the only way to settle the matter.

As she headed beyond the infamous Front Street boundary area, the courage that she had felt so strongly in developing her plans began to waver. She had the sinking feeling that all eyes were on her as she approached the Custom House and turned towards the harbormaster's office. The sight before her made her temporarily forget some of her fear. Docked along Water Street were seven vessels with sails wrapped and men busily loading cargo and passengers. Shirtless men turned, stopped their chores and ogled her as she walked on to the harbormaster's office, but she remained spellbound by the sight of the tall ships and the thoughts of the many lands that they had visited and the adventurous journey that lay ahead.

Her mind wandered to thoughts of the war as she watched the blockade running ships from the cupola of the DeRosset House. Her reoccurring fantasy was to board one of the blockade runners and set sail with the crew to Bermuda. That she would actually be sailing on one of these vessels, made her head reel.

As she mused on these recollections, she was rudely interrupted by fierce hands grabbing her around the waist and the stale smell of whiskey. "Here's one straight from the farm. This one is fresh as a spring morning; how about a kiss lass, for a sailor about to return to the sea."

Elizabeth was horrified by the encounter and barely able to speak, but she did gather her wits quickly enough to swing her small purse in the rough sailor's face. At that same time his equally repugnant partner grabbed her from behind and proceeded to draw her back in an embrace. "Give us a kiss lass," said the drunken sailor. At that moment she feared fainting and wished that she had had anyone make the arrangements for her voyage rather than setting foot beyond Front Street.

As the sailor's leering face came closer, she heard a booming, masculine voice call out and suddenly found herself swept away from the rough handling of the two sailors. When she opened her eyes, she found herself being propelled away from the sailors by the iron grip of her rescuer. Having placed her behind him, he quickly dispensed with her two attackers. She watched amazed as he struck both sailors with a leather bull whip and shouted "That's the last time I accept such behavior from the likes of you. Collect your wages from Mr. Pearson and be glad that I don't throw you in irons. Can't you see that she's a lady and not one of your fancy women? Get out of my sight now before I change my mind about your fate!"

Elizabeth watched as the two sailors shrank away from the large man and found the courage to fully look at her rescuer for the first time. What she saw temporarily took her breath away. He was one of the most handsome men that she had ever seen. He had dark, almost black hair and eyebrows, with the bluest eyes that she had ever seen. He had high cheekbones, and a perfectly straight profile. His physical build was equally impressive. He stood at least six foot three with a powerful physique, as evidenced by the ease in which he removed Elizabeth from the sailor's grasp.

He wore a neatly trimmed moustache and beard and the perpetual tan of a man of the sea. His dress consisted of a white open necked shirt and a black jacket and slacks that accentuated his rugged good looks. Both his height and his bearing made him a man to contend with and his rough booming voice and handling of the bull whip showed him to be a man of authority.

At that moment he turned to Elizabeth and she tried to find her voice to thank him for his courageous intervention. Before she could open her mouth however, her rescuer began to lecture her as though speaking to a child.

"Don't you know any better than to come to the docks unescorted? You have no business in an area like this. Do you know what might have happened to you if I had not been here? Now run along home to your mother before you get into any further trouble young lady!" The mockery of his words stung her as badly as the rough handling by the sailors, especially since she knew that he was partially correct. She did then find her voice to respond to him and to her horror, her voice shook with the emotion of her attack and his quick rebuke.

"I am only here, sir because I have business with the harbormaster. If I had not been accosted by your men, I would be in his office now and making the necessary arrangements for my voyage. As for running home to my mother, she has been dead since I was ten years old and I have managed since then on my own!"

With that, Elizabeth drew herself up to her full five foot two inch height and proceeded to walk quickly away to the harbormaster's office. Had she remained, she would have seen the quick smile and the twinkle in the blue eyes of James O'Rourke. He stood, hands on hips, smiling at her outrage. He admitted to himself that she may be a slip of a thing, but at least she had spunk. In an instant he had caught up to her and grabbed her arm in his iron grip.

"If you must proceed with this errand, child; at least let me escort you to the harbormaster's office so that you avoid further trouble," he said mockingly.

She noticed then the soft Irish brogue as he spoke and the second reference to her as a child. That mockery was enough to stir her anger a second time.

"I am not in the habit of speaking to strange men, sir. You seem as determined as your men to accost me and prevent me from my task. If you will kindly unhand me, I will not bother you further," Elizabeth replied heatedly.

Captain O'Rourke smiled gently this time and really noticed for the first time her dark shining eyes and the hint of blush that had come into her fair face with the angry exchange.

"I should apologize for my behavior, lass. My name is Captain James O'Rourke of the ship Alliance and I would be honored to escort you to the harbormaster's office." The statement had been made with a great show of mock respect and gallantry and only served to anger Elizabeth more.

When she did not respond, he took her arm and propelled her on to the harbormaster's office. Once there, his burly frame muscled past the men in the doorway and led her to the harbormaster's desk.

"This lass would like to make arrangements for a passage. She has been accosted twice so far this morning, so please be gentle with her," Captain O'Rourke stated smiling.

The man was absolutely maddening, Elizabeth thought and staring at her in a way that made her very nervous. To cover her embarrassment, she turned to the harbormaster and requested information on the earliest passage to London from Wilmington.

"Why that would be by way of Captain O'Rourke's ship the Alliance, young lady. The ship leaves in two days for Bermuda and would be your earliest passage to London," he stated.

Elizabeth turned slowly to face Captain O'Rourke who she knew was mocking her with his sunny smile. At that moment, she considered cancelling the trip altogether, or at least taking a later passage; but the matter of her inheritance and the adventure which lay ahead made her quickly change her mind.

James tried to look very serious and failed at the attempt. "I'm not accustomed to transporting children on my ship, young lady; but if you can bring your nanny with you and promise to stay out of trouble, I'll consider the proposal."

Elizabeth chose to refrain from the quick retort that rose to her lips, and with all of her dignity intact, turned to the harbormaster to book her fare. She finished by requesting an escort back to her home to avoid further encounters with the riffraff of the wharf. The latter statement she specifically directed to Captain O'Rourke.

Captain O'Rourke chuckled at the insult and offered to walk her back to Front Street. The harbormaster appeared relieved to be rid of the young lady and only too anxious to allow Captain O'Rourke to escort her while secretly wondering why a young lady would be traveling out unescorted on Water Street and planning a trip abroad in the bargain. He shook his head as he watched them leave and put the whole incident down to the evaporation of decency since the war.

Once outside, Elizabeth lit into her escort, angry for a third time to be in his debt. "I suppose I should thank you for saving me from your men and for agreeing to take me to London. I assure you, however that I will be no trouble to you or to your crew during the passage and will be quite content to stay in my cabin until we reach London."

Again she met his distractingly blue eyes and quickly looked away as she realized her anger had brought that mocking smile again to his face.

James had studied her closely as she completed the transactions with the harbormaster. He had been wrong about his first impression, he thought. Damn she might be young, but she was beautiful and curvaceous beyond her years. Her eyes alone could lure a man from the sea. He put aside these thoughts however, to lecture her further.

"I will accept your gracious thanks, lass and assure you that you will be safe from my crew during the voyage. They are not normally accustomed to accosting children, although Riggs and Bellows were obviously willing to make an exception in your case. I will assume that you will be properly escorted by a relative of suitable age."

"If I had any remaining relatives, Captain O'Rourke; I wouldn't be making this journey at all. Again I promise that I will be no further trouble to you now or during the voyage. Good day, Captain, until we sail," Elizabeth replied primly.

With that she quickly walked away hoping that he would not follow. At the present she was more angry than fearful of her safety and walked away briskly into the bustling waterfront crowds.

Captain O'Rourke watched her on her way and silently thought that she would be no end of trouble to both the crew and to himself. The image of her dark sparkling eyes and young womanly figure was not one that would soon leave him. Yes, he thought sagely; this one will be a great deal of trouble.

CHAPTER TWO

The day began hot and fair as the voyage to London began. Elizabeth had asked the parson's wife next door to wake her early to make sure that she did not miss the departure of the Alliance. As it occurred, Elizabeth was awake well before the rap by Mrs. Haynes. Reverend Haynes and his wife had tried unsuccessfully to convince Elizabeth that her voyage was foolhardy and bound for trouble. Although they did not know her well, as they had recently been transferred to the parish; they feared for the safety of a young unescorted lady on a voyage of such length. Reluctantly they had agreed to help her pack for the trip and to watch over the family home while she was away.

There had been precious little to pack, Elizabeth mused; as few of the family possessions remained. Aunt Felicity had been forced to sell most of the fine furniture and silver during the war years to provide Elizabeth, Robert, Jr. and herself with the Confederate funds to survive. As port after port of the former Confederacy was occupied and closed, the goods coming into Wilmington were the only lifeline of the Confederate cause, and their price became more and more dear. With so many men at war, even food items became scarce.

The only precious items remaining to Elizabeth were her miniatures of her mother and father and her brother Robert Jr., her mother's jewelry, and the few remaining clothing items that were still in fashion. She was thankful for the beautiful turquoise silk that her aunt had purchased through blockade running contacts of the DeRosset family. As she had stated at the time, "A young lady should have some fashionable items for her dowry even if our circumstances are temporarily reduced." She believed that her mother would have understood the sale of the family silver serving spoons to provide Elizabeth with a few proper dresses to attend the remaining society activities in the occupied city. As her aunt had predicted, the turquoise was a perfect compliment for her fair complexion and chestnut hair. Most of the remaining items had been handmade or items cut down from her aunt's wardrobe after her death. Elizabeth had vowed that once she obtained her inheritance, she would buy something in the most up-to-date fashion in the London clothing shops.

As she rode in the rented buggy to Water Street, she thought about the many days of sea travel ahead of her before she saw the sights and sounds of London. Most immediately however, she thought with dread of her next encounter with Captain O'Rourke. She hoped that she could uphold her promise to keep out of trouble and out of that man's way during the duration of the voyage. She meant to keep a diary of the entire adventure and to concentrate on the necessary correspondence and visits that she should make when she reached London.

The mockery of the man and his treatment of her as a child was more that she could endure. She decided that he was a conceited, arrogant man who she would avoid at all costs. When the buggy arrived at the ramp of the Alliance, she paid the driver and proceeded to climb the gangplank to the deck of the Alliance.

Captain O'Rourke noted her arrival at the shipside and took the opportunity to thank Mr. Pearson for vacating his customary cabin for another in the passenger wing of the ship. James was taking no chances with this particular passenger. He would have no interference from the crew or from any other passengers; as she would be the only woman on board. A woman passenger was always a distraction to the crew, but especially an unescorted one as young and beautiful as Elizabeth Majors.

As her luggage came aboard, Ruggins, a surly mate came to James and asked where the young lady was to be billeted. "Mistress Majors will be placed in Mr. Pearson's cabin for the voyage," James responded gruffly.

"Do you fancy that lass then, Captain?" Ruggins asked insolently.

"I plan on keeping her out of the clutches of the likes of you. Now stow her luggage and get below," James growled.

As he watched Ruggins take the luggage below grumbling to himself, James thought silently that the young lady had started trouble already without even setting foot on the ship. He only hoped that she would keep her promise to make her presence scarce and that he could keep his promise to keep her out of the path of his crew.

As Elizabeth came aboard, she was greeted by Samuel Pearson, First Officer of the Alliance and a man of advanced years. After one look at Elizabeth, he understood the concern of his Captain for both her comfort and safety. His usual cabin was directly adjacent to Captain O'Rourke's and was the second most spacious cabin on board ship. It afforded her great privacy and protection from advances of the crew or other passengers, all of which were male.

She responded to Mr. Pearson's courteous attentions to her comfort and found that she would have an ally on board in the older gentleman. To her relief she was spared contact with Captain O'Rourke; as he was busy with last minute preparations to set sail. She took her position at the rail to watch the preparations for departure and tried to focus her thoughts only on the adventures that lay ahead. As she looked at the crowd, she thought sadly that it would have been nice to have a family friend or relative on the dock to wave her farewells; but the war, Yellow Fever epidemics and death by natural causes had taken her family and acquaintances in the past four years. She vowed to not think of the past, but to look confidently toward the future; a vow that she frequently realized was easier said than done.

Once the ship had set sail, she watched as they progressed down the Cape Fear River past the Dram Tree; historic demarcation lines for crews down the years. It was the point at which no alcohol would be allowed on ship until the return to a port and the point at which grog was distributed on a return to Wilmington. The crew as well as the passengers passed that marker with mixed emotions of the perils of sea travel and the adventures that may lie ahead.

The ship was bound first for Bermuda; a voyage of approximately three days and then on to London; a customary voyage of two weeks. The sailing date was momentous and an added concern to the crew, as late August and September were known as the peak hurricane months in the Atlantic. Although James kept his concerns to himself, he secretly dreaded a voyage at this time of year due to the dangers of the killer storms. He prayed for an uneventful voyage, yet feared that this would not be possible with his most worrisome passenger aboard even if they were spared the dangerous weather of hurricane season.

In addition to Elizabeth, the ship carried three other passengers; Jacob Wright, a merchant from Wilmington, Benjamin Whitfield, a Yankee with business interests in Bermuda and London and Zachariah Sprunt, a planter from the Wilmington area traveling to Bermuda to finance the rebuilding of his cotton and rice plantations. The three men ranged in age from mid thirties to mid-fifties and James had noticed their keen interest in Elizabeth's arrival. He had made a special effort to assure their separation from Elizabeth physically by her location in his portion of the ship's cabin area and vowed to keep her separated from them as much as possible during the voyage.

As James steered the ship under the watchful gaze of the river pilot, he briefly assessed his reasons for concern over Elizabeth's welfare. Although he mockingly referred to her as a child, it was clearly evident that she was a grown woman. At thirty years old, their age difference was not so great to justify his concerns as purely paternal in nature. He tried to assure himself that he had no personal interest in Elizabeth other than keeping his ship running in a smooth fashion and women were notorious at causing disruptions in schedules and procedures. He also assured himself that it was only natural for him to be concerned about her personal safety, thus the move of Mr. Pearson and the settling of Elizabeth in the nearby cabin. He satisfied himself that he had taken the only practical course open to him.

When the proposal was initially broached to Mr. Pearson, he had not questioned his Captain's judgment or motives. After seeing the young lady for himself, he was not so sure. He chuckled to himself that nothing would make him happier than to see his young Captain happily settled with a wife and children as he himself had been blessed; but to date James had shown no interest in a permanent relationship with any one woman. Although not wishing to see himself in the role of matchmaker, he had wondered if this young lady could be the one to change his Captain's mind. He decided that his role to Elizabeth as a combination chaperone/confidant could make him a go-between for the two.

Within hours of meeting Elizabeth however; he soon thought better of his original plan. She was a very spirited and opinionated young lady who appeared to have taken an instant dislike to James O'Rourke. Before the ship reached Southport, Elizabeth had shown a desire to solely investigate her cabin and avoid any contact with the Captain whatsoever. This attitude was going to be particularly difficult for Samuel Pearson, as he had been dispatched to invite her to the Captain's table for dinner with the other passengers.

Mr. Pearson approached his customary cabin and knocked with his Captain's errand as well as a written invitation from James. He found Elizabeth unpacking her luggage and bringing a feminine touch to the usually masculine surroundings.

"Good day again, Mistress Majors; I have come with an invitation from Captain O'Rourke to the customary first night sailing dinner in his cabin," Mr. Pearson stated.

Elizabeth read the brief note then smiled shyly at Samuel. "I thank you for your invitation and for that of the Captain, but I did promise him that I would keep to my cabin as much as possible and would therefore prefer my meal in my cabin if at all possible."

"I'm sure that the Captain would not expect you to be locked away during the entire duration of the voyage and would in fact enjoy your company, as would our other passengers," Samuel replied.

"Just the same, I would not wish to break my vow so early in the voyage. Please thank the Captain for his kind invitation, but I must decline," Elizabeth stated calmly.

Samuel did not relish conveying this message to his Captain. Since he had known James as a young lad, he had never been known for his calm temperament. As excellent a mariner as he had ever served with, he also had a fierce temper which Mr. Pearson strived to keep under control whenever possible. He guessed that Elizabeth's reluctance stemmed from their earlier meeting and he did not think it would bode well for a happy ship to allow the disagreement to fester. Arriving at the Captain's side, he relayed Elizabeth's message. He was unprepared for James' quick response.

"Go back and tell her that her presence is expected at tonight's meal in my cabin and that you will arrive for her at 8:00 p.m. sharp. I will not have her accusing me of holding her prisoner in her cabin for the duration of the voyage. Now go deliver that message to Miss Majors!" James stated heatedly.

Samuel reluctantly returned to Elizabeth's cabin to deliver the second message of the day. He decided to rephrase the message somewhat to avoid the escalation of the tension between the two.

"The Captain has asked that you reconsider your earlier decision, as you would be much more comfortable at the generous banquet that will be provided than with the simple meal that would be served in your cabin. He also stated that you would be a graceful addition to his table." Samuel secretly prayed for forgiveness for his white lie and awaited her response.

Elizabeth appeared astonished at the latest message, then sweetly smiled and accepted the Captain's kind invitation. She made a mental note to thank the Captain for his consideration and wondered if she had misjudged the man at the wharf encounter. Samuel returned to Captain O'Rourke and conveyed the fact that Elizabeth would join them for dinner. He secretly hoped that the Captain would forget his earlier anger when Elizabeth arrived for the meal and prayed that his slight exaggeration of the truth might pass undetected.

Elizabeth spent the remainder of the day unpacking, starting her diary entries of the trip and planning her attire for the evening's dinner. As she had awakened early for the sailing, she decided on an afternoon nap to prepare her for the night's activities. She lay on the bed allowing the ship's motion to gently lull her to sleep, daydreaming about her first sight of Bermuda and London that lay in her future.

When she awakened, she had slept for several hours and had only a limited time to prepare for Mr. Pearson. She had decided on wearing her good turquoise silk; as the first night's sailing dinner had been described as a special night for all. She carefully laid out the necessary petticoats and crinolines. Given the confined spaces of the ship, she had chosen to not wear the customary hoops, as she feared that she would be unable to pass through the ship's corridors with their full size. The turquoise silk dress had been designed to her aunt's description as a gown for both day and evening wear. It had been fashioned after a gown that they had seen in the spring issue of Harper's Bazaar with slight modifications suggested by her aunt. The lace collar and bib attachment used during the daylight hours obscured the décolletage more appropriate for the evening. The gown had a fitted waist, long tapered sleeves and a row of pearl buttons at the wrists. Buttoning the tiny pearl buttons in the back had always been difficult for her so she wore the gown with a lace shawl to cover buttons that she could not reach. She finished the outfit with her mother's pearl earrings and a delicate freshwater pearl necklace to remind her of Wilmington and the coast.

Her hair was brushed until it shone and coiled on her head in loose ringlets with one ringlet strand on the left side of her neck. When finished she looked in the mirror and was quite pleased with her reflection. If Captain O'Rourke expected a graceful addition to his table, she decided that she would not be a disappointment.

True to his word Mr. Pearson arrived sharply at 8:00 p.m. to escort her the short distance to the Captain's cabin. The look on his face and in his eyes told Elizabeth that she had chosen her ensemble well. He walked her the brief length of passage between her cabin and the Captain's and knocked on the cabin door to gain entry.

The other passengers were already gathered at the table sharing a glass of port with their host. James had taken the trouble to dress for the occasion in one of his better suits to signify the festive nature of the occasion. When he saw Elizabeth, the look on his face was not one that she had expected, however. Instead of the admiring glances she received from the other men, he was scowling at her with a look that was murderous. She took care to position herself next to Samuel who sat at one end of the table and Jacob Wright who sat next to the Captain at the other end of the table. She then proceeded to respond to Mr. Wright's polite questioning and that of Samuel as the meal progressed.

The banquet that Samuel had promised was no exaggeration. For a woman who had lived in an occupied, war torn city, the amount of food before her was more than she could recall since Christmas feasts before the war. There was She Crab soup for the appetizer, Crab Imperial for the Fish course, sliced Roast Beef for the meat course and assorted carrot, peas and corn dishes to compliment. The dessert course consisted of pecan pie. It was explained to Elizabeth that the first night's sailing dinner was a tradition in which the finest dishes with fresh ingredients from the last port were served. From this time on the meals would consist of salted and preserved foods that would not require icing and would require minimal food preparation. The ship's cook used the opportunity of the first night out to utilize their skills and to provide the Captain, First Officer and passengers with a taste of the port just visited.

Following the meal Elizabeth prepared to leave the gentlemen to their brandy and cigars and suggested that she might take a walk on deck. James signaled to Samuel to accompany Elizabeth and all gathered stood as she left the spacious cabin. The talk immediately turned to Elizabeth and speculation circled on the fact that the young woman was traveling to Bermuda and on to London unescorted.

"I expect she has her reasons," James responded gruffly. Despite his attempts to change the subject, the three men were acting like love sick schoolboys with talk of nothing but Elizabeth.

James stopped listening and started to ask himself about his reaction to Elizabeth and the reason for his anger. He found most men's lack of self-control disgusting when it came to women. They certainly had their place as amusing companions on a temporary basis, but he could never understand the obsession some men had for their constant companionship.

The immediate issue that concerned him was his reaction to her from their initial contact. Her quick anger had amused him and then her beauty and independence had touched him. He had instructed her to stay to herself and then was angered when she refused his invitation. Never had he had that particular problem with women. Usually they pursued him, not shied away from him as did Elizabeth.

Then this evening the sight of her in that turquoise gown brought a whole new set of problems for him to sort out. His anger came from the fact that he reacted so strongly to her beauty and voluptuous figure. When she responded to his scowl by keeping her distance, he reasoned that he should have been happy; yet seeing her circled as the belle of the table with all men's attentions on her made him as angry as a jealous lover. She made an effort to speak sociably with all of the passengers and especially with Samuel, yet made no attempt to draw him into conversation and in fact avoided him completely. While this should have pleased him, it angered him that he should be ignored in this way.

He decided to leave the discussion that stubbornly centered on Elizabeth and go on deck to get some fresh air himself and clear his mind. When he arrived on deck he saw Samuel and Elizabeth by the rail and signaled to Samuel that he would assume Samuel's bodyguard role.

Elizabeth turned when he joined them and managed a brief shy smile. This time James did not scowl and returned her smile. The three quarter moon and sprinkling of stars reflected in her shining eyes.

"I wanted to thank you for your kind invitation to join you and your passengers at the meal tonight, Captain. It was the most wonderful meal that I have had in ages," Elizabeth stated. She decided that she was willing to meet the man halfway despite his scowling expression during dinner.

"Thank you for the kind remarks regarding the meal. I will pass them onto the Cook in the morning. You mentioned my kind invitation, Miss Majors; I wonder what you meant?"

"Well, Mr. Pearson had stated that you hoped that I would change my mind about my earlier refusal and join your company; as I would be more comfortable and would be a graceful addition to your table. I thought it a very gallant statement, Captain," Elizabeth replied smiling.

"He said that," James asked laughing. "Those were not my exact words, but I am glad that you joined us for the evening."

"What precisely were your exact words, Captain?" Elizabeth was starting to suspect the amused reaction to her words and was having her earlier angry reaction to James' mockery.

"My exact words were that I would not have you accuse me of holding you prisoner in your cabin for the duration of the voyage and that you should be ready by 8:00 p.m. sharp to be collected by Mr. Pearson," James said eyes twinkling.

"Are you always so accustomed to having your every order obeyed then, Captain; that you thought I would automatically obey your summons?" Elizabeth was working herself into another state of anger at James.

"On my ship, all orders are obeyed and promptly," James replied. He was coming to enjoy the flush that entered her face as she prepared for each battle with him.

"I am not one of your crew, Captain; and not accustomed to obeying orders, promptly or otherwise," Elizabeth responded heatedly.

"I am responsible for this ship and for everyone on board. Any order that I give *will* be obeyed and not questioned by you or any other member of the crew or passenger list! Is that understood?" James responded just as heatedly.

"Do you have any orders for me now, Captain?" Elizabeth responded exasperated.

"Yes, Miss Majors, as a matter of fact I do. I would request that you not wear anything quite so revealing again while on board ship. It is hard enough for me to protect your safety as the only woman on board without your further provocation in a gown like this," he stated pointing to the lovely turquoise gown.

Elizabeth's face turned scarlet at that remark. She had so carefully dressed to make a graceful and beautiful addition to the group and not as a provocative woman. This was the second time he had questioned her judgment under the guise of personal safety and she did not appreciate the reference to her beautiful dress as provocative in nature.

"Would you like me placed in irons, Captain and allowed out only with an armed escort?" Elizabeth responded.

James ignored the sarcastic tone and continued in his instruction. "I am glad that you mentioned your outings while on board. I would prefer that your outings be limited during daylight hours while the crew is working, as your presence might distract them. Evening hours would be preferred, but then only in the presence of Mr. Pearson or myself. We will be glad to accompany you on an evening constitutional of the ship to provide you with fresh air and exercise," James replied.

"Any other orders, Captain?" Elizabeth responded barely in control of her anger. She had no greater desire than to slap the mocking look from his face.

"No that will be all for now, Mistress Majors. I will accompany you to your cabin now if you are ready to go below," James replied.

"Gladly, Captain; I would not want my presence to compromise the safety of the ship by luring the men from their tasks," Elizabeth responded.

With that statement Elizabeth angrily walked away with James hurriedly walking to keep up with her on her way to their cabin passageway.

The other passengers were leaving James' cabin and warmly bid Elizabeth a good night. James glared at them and waited for their exit, then reminded Elizabeth to bolt her cabin door.

Once inside, Elizabeth exploded with pent up rage. Her beautiful dress had been scorned as a seduction tool when in point of fact it was the height of fashion. Elizabeth looked in the mirror and saw her scarlet face looking back at her. The man was impossible she decided; a brute and a prude for all of his worldly manner. She wished that she was aboard any other ship than this one and angrily threw crinolines and petticoats around the cabin as she undressed.

James returned to his cabin and pondered their encounter. What was happening to him, he wondered? Why had he acted like a jealous, possessive lover when he had initially only wanted to protect her from the glances and intentions of the other passengers and crew? He was sure that this concern had only been her safety, but when he saw the scarlet rise in her cheeks and the sparkle to her angry eyes, his only thought had been to do the very thing that every man on board must be desiring; take her in his arms for a long, passionate kiss to help soothe the ache he felt for her whenever in her presence.

Those were the very feelings he feared from the crew and worse of course and now he was feeling them himself. He vowed anew to keep his distance from her and to allow Samuel to serve as her companion. Samuel was at least one person that he completely trusted to assure her safety.

From his cabin he heard items being thrown about Elizabeth's room and laughed at the anger that he seemed to provoke at their every meeting. He reasoned that if she was always angry at him, he had less to fear than if she were to become a constant companion for the voyage. The thing that worried him most was if he really wanted her to stay away from him, or if her absence would create even more confusion.

He angrily decided to put all thoughts of Elizabeth out of his mind and try to get some sleep before relieving Mr. Pearson. To his disgust, he dreamed of nothing but Elizabeth's fair face and shining eyes until being awakened near dawn.

CHAPTER THREE

Elizabeth had slept fitfully through the night and had attributed it to her quarrel with James. If she had been totally fair, she would have attributed it in part to the heat and in part to her encounter with James. But she was in no mood for fairness.

Never had she encountered a man who could stir her anger faster than James O'Rourke. She knew that she had a fearful temper and tried in recent years to bring it under control. Aunt Felicity had continually lectured her about this flaw and her father, when he was made aware of the fact; put it down to growing up without the calm, patient hand of her mother. He had assumed that she would grow out of this trait and become more like her mother when grown.

James O'Rourke, she decided; was a man who would test the patience of a saint. His arrogance and conceit knew no bounds and she was condemned to spend over two weeks on his ship at the mercy of his commands and orders. The fact that angered her most was that she had dreamed of a sea voyage all her life and her encounters with Captain O'Rourke plus her ordered confinement would ruin her enjoyment of the experience.

Finally getting out of bed she decided that the day was too hot for breakfast. She ordered hot water to freshen up and dressed only in her chemise, sat on her bed writing a diary entry on her first full day at sea. She laughed to think what Captain O'Rourke would think of her scanty dress, but decided if she was going to be a prisoner of her cabin, she might as well be as cool as possible.

Above her on deck, James O'Rourke suffered the effects of a sleepless night also. His crew suffered as well; because every order was barked out by the Captain and every task was done too slowly for his wishes. The crew all looked forward to the mid-day break when their Captain would go below for a rest and they could escape his wrath. They didn't know the cause of his mood, but like passing storm clouds, hoped that it would soon blow over.

Near mid-day Samuel Pearson knocked on Elizabeth's door to see if there was anything that she needed. He had not seen her above decks all day and was concerned that she might be ill.

"Thank you for inquiring, Mr. Pearson; but I didn't sleep well last night and thought I might take a midday rest to escape the heat. I would like a stroll on deck after sunset, however, if your schedule will permit." Elizabeth had carried on the entire conversation through the door as she was still not properly dressed.

"I should be honored, Miss Majors, and will come by your cabin at 8:00 P.M.," Samuel responded.

How unlike his Captain, Elizabeth thought. If only Captain O'Rourke were a third as thoughtful, how pleasant the voyage would be.

Not quite a half hour later, a second rap came to her cabin door. Elizabeth went to the door still dressed only in her chemise. "Yes, Mr. Pearson," Elizabeth responded.

"It's not Mr. Pearson, lass but Captain O'Rourke. I came to see if my steward can bring you anything. He tells me that you have not eaten your breakfast or noon day meal. Are you ill then?" James asked.

"Thank you no, Captain. I will eat when I am hungry and will not bother your crew otherwise. The heat has taken my appetite for the time being," Elizabeth replied.

"You may endanger your health if you do not eat. I insist that you at least have some water with lime to keep from dehydration. I will have the steward deliver it immediately." James had decided that Elizabeth was just being stubborn and was in fact ill or seasick but did not want to admit to it.

"Oh very well, Captain; if you insist." Elizabeth would have gladly continued the argument further, but as she was not properly dressed, did not wish to argue through her cabin door. When the water with lime arrived, she had the steward sit it down outside the door and collected it when she was sure the corridor was empty.

James watched from his cabin door after the steward had left the refreshment. He noted only Elizabeth's hands as she brought in the tray and was convinced that she was in fact ill. He decided to send the ship's doctor to her if she had not eaten or emerged by evening.

In the adjacent cabin, Elizabeth was pacing. How dare he continue to act as if he was her father, Elizabeth thought angrily? One minute he was solicitous for her health and the next minute he was ignoring her, scowling at her or lecturing her. The man was a puzzle and one that she decided that she did not wish to unlock. She thought it ironic that women were always viewed as changeable in their moods and preferences, when in her limited experience; men could be just as difficult to predict.

Elizabeth decided to proceed with a nap after finishing the refreshing water and lime. Unbeknownst to her however, James had already instructed the steward to bring her water with lime on an hourly basis and to keep checking on her as he feared that she might be ill. With the constant hourly interruptions, Elizabeth was never able to completely drift off to sleep and was in an extremely foul mood by the time Samuel Pearson came to collect her. She had managed to eat a light supper and dress before his arrival.

Mr. Pearson asked after her health after they had arrived on deck. Had it been any other person on board ship, Elizabeth probably would have screamed after the hourly inquiries, but with Samuel; her response was mild.

"I am feeling quite well, Mr. Pearson; although I had difficulty sleeping last night and could not sleep this afternoon because of hourly knocks by the steward. I don't understand why he kept bringing me drinks on an hourly basis," Elizabeth replied.

"Captain O'Rourke feared that you might be ill or seasick and did not wish you to become dehydrated by your nausea."

"Now I understand. I told him at noon that I had not eaten breakfast or my noon day meal because the heat had taken my appetite. I assume now that he thought I was lying to cover seasickness." Elizabeth was starting to work herself into another fit of anger.

Samuel was quick to deflect the growing anger. "I am sure that Captain O'Rourke was only concerned for your welfare. He is not quite the ogre that you seem to take him to be," Samuel stated calmly.

At that comment Elizabeth looked quite shocked at the First Officer, but then remembered that it would only be natural for him to defend his superior officer.

Samuel continued with his explanation. "I have known Captain O'Rourke since he was a lad. His father was a sea captain before him and his mother died when he was only eight. He was reared at boarding schools and joined his father at sea when he was only eighteen. Most of his life has been spent in the company of men and rough men at that. As a result, he doesn't have the gentler touch required of dealings with ladies such as yourself. I myself have been blessed with my lady wife and four daughters in addition to my five sons. I have learned the value of gentle relations with the fair sex," Samuel stated smiling.

Elizabeth smiled gently at that remark and found herself warming to the older man. Samuel went on to inquire about Elizabeth's family and her reasons for traveling to Bermuda and London.

"My mother died when I was a child also. I was ten years old when she died in childbirth with my brother Robert. She was always a delicate person and never in good health. I don't believe my father ever recovered from her death. He carried on of course, for my brother and my sakes; but when the war came, he had no compunctions about fighting. I think he thought if he were to die, he would be with my mother again. We found out in May that he died in the siege of Richmond. His death coming after the death of my brother from Yellow Fever proved to be too much for my father's sister, Aunt Felicity. She died in early July. It was then that I decided that I must travel to London to settle my inheritance." Elizabeth's eyes had filled with tears as she told her tale, but Samuel noted the courageous way in which she pretended to be unaffected.

After giving her a moment to gain her composure, he continued with his questions. "Why must you travel to London to settle your inheritance?" Samuel inquired.

"My father fought bravely in the late war, but he did not believe that the South would be successful when the war began in 1861. To protect our family fortune for my brother and myself, he sent the majority of the family funds, stocks, bonds, etc. to London for safekeeping with our London solicitor Hilary Cross. I am travelling to London to meet with Mr. Cross and settle all matters of my aunt and father's estates."

Samuel looked at Elizabeth with new respect for her courage. He had a daughter very close to Elizabeth's age and he doubted that she could have undertaken such a trip with as much spirit as Elizabeth. He thought he would pass this information onto the Captain as it might soften his attitude to the girl.

Samuel chatted about his family and their home port in Ireland. Before they realized it, they had walked the decks for over an hour. As the Captain emerged from below decks, Samuel prepared to go below.

Captain O'Rourke joined the two by the rail. He could tell from the relaxed look on Elizabeth and Samuel's faces that they had a pleasant constitutional and conversation. Samuel excused himself when the Captain joined their company.

"Miss Majors are you feeling recovered then?" James remarked.

Elizabeth began to angrily correct the Captain, then remembered Samuel's words from their earlier conversation. She suspected that he was just trying to be overly concerned for her welfare in the only way he knew to respond.

"As I told you this afternoon, Captain; I am quite well, but the heat took my appetite for breakfast and lunch. I ate a light dinner and am feeling quite well. As I have never been seasick Captain, I did not plan to begin now," Elizabeth replied.

James smiled at that remark and went on to explain the benefits of water with lime to prevent dehydration. Elizabeth assumed that he was happiest when ordering or lecturing everyone in sight, so allowed him to continue while she gazed out to sea.

In order to change the subject, Elizabeth inquired about Bermuda and how long they would have to explore the island. She thought to end the lecture and find out something truly beneficial.

"We will be in Bermuda but a short time to take on supplies and deliver Mr. Whitfield and the others to complete their business. We will be picking up cargo of course; but should be leaving in two days time. It should afford you an opportunity for exploration. Perhaps Mr. Pearson or I could accompany you on your visit," James offered.

"Oh I am sure that you will be occupied with supplying the ship and a hundred other tasks and too busy to accompany me on site seeing ventures," Elizabeth responded.

"I am sure that I could save some time if you would like. I wouldn't advise you to travel on the island unless properly escorted," James responded.

"If your schedule permits, Captain; I would enjoy seeing the island with someone who knows it well, like you, and Mr. Pearson of course." Elizabeth gave her full smile and attention to James at that moment and he felt his chest tighten.

"I am sure we can arrange something between the two of us to keep you occupied," James responded kindly despite himself. He then offered to continue her stroll of the ship's decks and offered her his arm as they walked.

Elizabeth responded courteously, but with inward amazement that the man could manage to be so pleasant. Perhaps Mr. Pearson was right after all and he had the potential to be a considerate person. At times like these, she felt especially vulnerable to his sunny smile and beautiful blue eyes.

James for his part was amazed by his own behavior. He had never permitted himself to become personally involved with a passenger before; but then Elizabeth was no ordinary passenger. She was the first unescorted female that he had ever transported and though initially dreading it; he had now come to welcome her company, especially when she wasn't riling at his every word. He thought she could be quite reasonable at times, when her anger didn't get the best of her. She was one of the only people who did not seem to fear standing up to him and that was a very new experience for him.

They walked arm and arm chatting occasionally and enjoying the calm sea and sky. When James returned her to her cabin, he was reluctant to part with her company.

"Good night, Captain. Thank you for our chat. I enjoyed it very much," Elizabeth remarked shyly.

"It was my pleasure, Miss Majors; good night," James replied. After she closed and bolted the door, James stood in the corridor for a few moments trying to sort his feelings for the girl. Only the appearance of his steward in the hallway urged him onto his cabin. His steward smiled at the puzzled look on his Captain's face and thought his Captain may have been captivated by their female passenger.

Although Elizabeth did not sleep well a second night in a row, this time she attributed it to the excitement of reaching landfall in Bermuda. The Captain had told her that they would reach Bermuda that evening and could have dinner on shore if the weather and the authorities cooperated.

When Samuel and James met to discuss the day's assignments, Samuel casually mentioned his discussion with Elizabeth the night before. This new information did in fact place Elizabeth in a new light. James admired her for her courage and pluck and came to realize that they had a strong bond in the loss of family members at an early age. He also came to the realization, although he made no mention to Samuel, that his desire to protect her was even greater now knowing that she was alone in the world.

After several minutes silence, James noted to Samuel that Miss Majors was quite an impressive young lady and someone to admire for one so young. Samuel listened quietly and smiled at the change in his Captain's demeanor towards Elizabeth.

The hours couldn't pass quickly enough for Elizabeth. She couldn't wait to see her first sight of Bermuda. She hoped that the new thawing in her relationship with the Captain might mean that he wouldn't mind if she went above decks during the day to check on their progress and their proximity to Bermuda.

Elizabeth went above decks at mid-day and immediately sought out Mr. Pearson or the Captain with her eyes. Neither one was in view, so she decided to go below. Mr. Whitfield called out to her at that moment and she joined him at the rail.

"Miss Majors; I have not seen you since our first night dinner. Have you been ill?" Whitfield asked.

"No, I have been spending most of my time in my cabin to avoid the daily heat. In fact the heat is a bit much for me now, but I hoped to learn the progress of the ship and the remaining distance to Bermuda," Elizabeth replied.

"Perhaps you will join me for dinner in one of Bermuda's finest restaurants when we dock," Whitfield asked.

"Miss Majors will be dining with Mr. Pearson and me in Bermuda." James had come upon them unannounced and had overheard the invitation. His scowl showed he was not pleased with Whitfield's approach to Elizabeth.

"That's right, Mr. Whitfield; Mr. Pearson and Captain O'Rourke extended an invitation to me last night to join them upon our arrival, but I thank you for the thought," Elizabeth replied smiling.

"Good day then, Miss Majors, Captain. I hope that I will see you both before departing the ship," Whitfield responded.

Whitfield walked away then as much in response to Elizabeth's statement as the scowl and perpetual presence of James at Elizabeth's side.

"Thank you, Captain; I would rather walk the plank than eat dinner with a Yankee!" Elizabeth responded angrily.

James laughed at that reference. "I guess even dinner with me would be preferable," James responded mockingly.

"Oh, I didn't mean it that way, Captain. I just meant to thank you for saving me from that man. You seem to do that quite often." Elizabeth smiled sweetly at James then. "I'm sure that you didn't really mean to extend an invitation in earnest."

"On the contrary, I would be happy for you to join me for dinner; that is Samuel and I would be happy for you to join us," James responded flustered by her smile.

"I would be happy to then, Captain," Elizabeth said sweetly with her most beautiful smile.

"Well until tomorrow evening, then," James responded. "Perhaps you would like to have a mid-day rest now." He motioned then to Samuel who had just come above decks to take Elizabeth below and gruffly walked on, barking orders at an unlucky sailor in his path to cover his reaction to Elizabeth's dazzling smile.

What had possessed him to ask her to dinner, James asked himself and how was he going to keep his eyes or hands off her? He definitely needed Samuel with him or he would be looking at her like that fool Whitfield had just done. He was amazed at his reaction when he saw her with another man, especially one that looked at her like Whitfield had done. Damn, he thought, I hope she doesn't wear that turquoise gown again.

CHAPTER FOUR

Elizabeth had felt like a child anticipating Christmas for the past day and a half. Since she had received the invitation from the Captain; her worries about exploring Bermuda on her own had been dispelled. Even though she had overcome a major obstacle in undertaking the trip to London on her own, she had rationalized that it was necessary, as there were no other family members to finalize her father's estate and finances had been too short to wait for confirmation by the London solicitors. As a lady of the Old South, however she knew that she would not have been able to rationalize traveling throughout Bermuda unescorted as a tourist. What would Aunt Felicity have said, not to mention her mother! With the kind offer by the Captain and Mr. Pearson, she would be able to dine on the island and perhaps see some of the notable sites before the ship set sail for London. At the present time, London was too far away to start having the same set of worries about traveling unescorted.

The only negative aspect of the trip so far had been the unexpected heat. Born and reared in Wilmington, she had thought herself immune to heat and humidity. The past two days and nights had been so hot that she found even she was not immune to its affect. Had it not been for the cool water with lime that the Captain required be delivered to her quarters, she thought she would melt with the heat. She found that she had no appetite until after the sun went down and had had difficulty sleeping each night while on board. Had she not thought that lightning would strike her port hole, she would have considered sleeping without her chemise. Luckily for the crew; she had promised to keep below decks during the daylight hours or she would have been shocked to see the level of undress of the men above. Unable to rest in the heat of the day as was Elizabeth, the crew wore limited garments with little care that a lady was on board. They assured themselves that orders from the Captain had taken care of any unexpected appearance by Miss Majors above decks.

On the evening before their arrival in Bermuda, Elizabeth was full of questions about their docking and the expected time of arrival. Mr. Pearson was only too glad to impart his knowledge to Elizabeth.

"Bermuda is like nothing you have ever seen," said Mr. Pearson. "The buildings are painted every color of the rainbow and the people are as friendly as any you would hope to meet. There are several smart hotels, but of course you are welcome to stay onboard the ship in the evenings, as the Captain and I will be on board each night. There is a very heavy presence by the British navy on the island, so you will be able to contact your solicitors in London and make arrangements for your meetings when we arrive. I will be happy to escort you to the British consulate once our docking had been completed."

Elizabeth was once again struck with appreciation for the older man's kindness. "Captain O'Rourke has stated that I might accompany you both to dinner tomorrow night and perhaps see some of the notable sights. I am so looking forward to it. You don't think he will have changed his mind do you?" Elizabeth asked worriedly.

Samuel did his best to hide his amazement at her statement and thought that the two had not only mended their quarrel, but might be coming together without any matchmaking on his part. "You will find that the Captain very seldom changes his mind about anything and especially not an invitation to a lovely lady. I am sure that the two of us can provide you with a suitable tour of the parts of Bermuda appropriate for a young lady. As with all ports of call, there are some rather unseemly areas that we would best steer clear of."

"Oh I wouldn't want you to change any plans on my account, Mr. Pearson. I do not want to be a burden to you or the Captain."

"I can assure you that you would not be a burden to the Captain or to me. It is our pleasure to have such a lovely lady to accompany," Mr. Pearson replied.

"I believe that I understand the origins of the famed Irish charm, Mr. Pearson. You are as gallant as the southern gentlemen that I knew as a child. I thought to never experience that type of grace again. It seemed that my whole world had come to an end with the coming of the war and the occupation by the Union Army." Elizabeth's features had darkened as she remembered the horrors of the Yellow Fever epidemic, the strains of war, and the stress of the recent occupation.

Samuel's heart was touched by such sadness in one so young. "As a true son of Ireland, I can tell you Miss Majors that grace is within the individual. Regardless of station or standing in life, the true test of an individual is the manner in which they show their true colors under adversity. The highest born can become a scoundrel and the lowest born a hero when faced with true adversity," Mr. Pearson stated.

Elizabeth blinked away tears as she remembered the experiences of the past four years. "That is very true Mr. Pearson. I am sorry to be melancholy so near to our docking in Bermuda. I guess I was feeling a little homesick and longing for the days before the war. I try to stay focused on the future, but sometimes it is hard. Thank you for our stroll Mr. Pearson. I believe I will go below to my cabin now."

As Elizabeth and Samuel neared the entrance to the cabins, they were met by Captain O'Rourke coming from below.

"Good evening, Captain O'Rourke; Mr. Pearson was just telling me a little about Bermuda. I am certainly looking forward to our excursion tomorrow evening," Elizabeth said smiling.

James looked quickly at Samuel with a slightly embarrassed look. Samuel cleared his throat and quickly stated that he would leave Elizabeth in the Captain's capable hands.

"Please don't leave on my account, Samuel. I am sure that you had more to tell Miss Majors about Bermuda," James said smiling.

"Actually I was just going to my cabin, Captain, so I will say good night to you both," Elizabeth stated.

After Elizabeth's departure Samuel smiled at his Captain waiting for the explanation of this change in heart. "I know what you are going to say, Samuel and I am sorry to have scheduled your first night in Bermuda as I have apparently scheduled my own. I thought that Miss Majors should be rewarded for her uncommon good judgment in staying below and not being a nuisance to us or to the crew. I would not want her to go onshore alone, as anything could happen to her and I certainly would not trust anyone else but you and I of course to accompany her," James said firmly.

"Are you sure that you were not interested in a chaperone for yourself when you made the offer of both of our services?" Samuel asked smiling.

"Nonsense, Samuel; Miss Majors is attractive enough certainly, but she is very young and besides this is a business matter. After all, she is a passenger of this ship and we can't let her go off alone getting into God knows what type of trouble," James said heatedly.

"I am sure that Miss Majors would appreciate your concern for her welfare. I don't recall your personal attention to a passenger before," Samuel replied.

"That is because we never had a young, unescorted female passenger before. I know what you are hinting at, Samuel and I can tell you that it is the farthest thing from my mind. I am a man of the sea Samuel and too set in my ways to start becoming a nursemaid to a young southern belle of all things.

She probably would faint at the thought of an encounter with a Captain from Ireland and not one of her southern dandies."

"I think she has shown a great deal of courage in coming on this trip alone. Besides, I haven't seen her faint yet and having heard of some of her experiences during the war years, I don't think our Miss Majors is the type to experience fainting spells when encountering life. She seems to face it head on and deal with whatever she must," Samuel replied.

"If I didn't know better, Samuel; I would say that you were sweet on Miss Majors yourself. I don't understand why everyone on board this ship seems to speak of nothing but Miss Majors." James was starting to work himself into another fit of anger over the discussion. "I'm sorry now that I ever brought up dinner in Bermuda tomorrow night, but I guess that it is too late to cancel now. You can go below now Samuel. I need some fresh air and will handle the watch for now."

Samuel laughed to himself as he walked away. Never had he seen his Captain flustered over a woman before, but he was certainly showing all of the classic signs. Unless I miss my guess, Samuel thought; Miss Majors has made a very serious impact on Captain O'Rourke, perhaps even more than he realizes.

As Samuel walked away, James was left on deck staring out to sea. Why was it, he asked himself, that all he seemed to be able to think about was Elizabeth? Everyone on board wanted to know about Elizabeth, was concerned about Elizabeth, or wanted to see about Elizabeth's needs. Just this morning he had found two sailors willing to trade double shifts of watch in exchange for his steward's job of bringing Elizabeth refreshments and water. The whole crew was like a bunch of lovesick schoolboys, even Samuel. His worst fear was that he was no better than they. Just now when he had seen Elizabeth's excitement about dinner and touring Bermuda tomorrow evening he had wanted to say that he would gladly show her every inch of the island so that he could hear her honey accented voice. What was happening to him and why was he letting it happen? He decided that the best thing might be to have Samuel accompany her to dinner on the island tomorrow evening, pleading work on board and paperwork to be completed. As simple as that excuse would be, he seemed unable to face disappointing Elizabeth, as he fancied that she would be hurt by his sudden change of plans. Having thought that, James then wondered if his worst fears were true; he was not so much concerned about disappointing Elizabeth, but about the disappointment that he would feel if he was unable to accompany Elizabeth on her tour of Bermuda. Regardless of his motives, he decided to give the idea more thought before deciding to cancel the evening's plans.

The next morning dawned hot and humid, but no amount of discomfort could discourage Elizabeth given the excitement she felt about seeing Bermuda for the first time. All of her dreams of accompanying the dashing blockade runners during the war came to mind as she anticipated the evening's docking. Her mind was in a whirl with anticipation. She decided to pass the time by updating her travel diary and writing the necessary follow-up letters that she would send to her London solicitors from Bermuda. As another evening with interrupted sleep had taken its toll, she indulged in a mid-afternoon nap.

James had also suffered the effects of a poor night's sleep. He continued to argue the pros and cons of accompanying Samuel and Elizabeth to the island that night. Frustrated with his own waffling on the issue, he decided that he would accompany Miss Majors and Samuel and the devil hang the outcome. After all, Bermuda was a mariner's paradise and there would be plenty of other women who could quickly take his mind from this child that had occupied his thoughts on board. He decided that he was just suffering from too much work and not enough recreation. A short stay in

Bermuda would be just what he needed to get his mind focused and off its present obsessive course.

Spying Samuel mid-afternoon, he conveyed his plans for the evening. "I thought we would go ashore with Miss Majors around 7:00 this evening. Dinner at the Carlyle and a brief tour of the island should be sufficient to address our tour guide obligations," James said gruffly.

Samuel nodded sagely in agreement, all of the while considering his own plan for the evening. He intended to accompany the pair on shore, then pleading work; return to the ship, leaving James and Elizabeth an opportunity to spend the evening together and perhaps stop the courtship dance that they seemed to have begun from their first encounter. Although he considered the fact that his plan may be disloyal to James; his growing regard for Elizabeth and his observance of the two together led him to regard it as the right choice.

Elizabeth was dressing when the time for arrival in Bermuda drew near. She had planned on the turquoise gown that she wore the first night of the voyage and had debated attaching the lace collar and bib attachment that covered the décolletage after the comments by the Captain following the first night's dinner. She had no intention of starting a second argument about her attire. Seeing her reflection in the mirror before going above decks however, she decided that the customary evening décolletage was just the right attribute for a night in one of Bermuda's finest restaurants. She could barely contain her excitement in seeing Bermuda for the first time and alighting from the ship after all docking had concluded.

Once the ship had concluded its movement, she could see the multi-color buildings of Bermuda. The sun was starting to set and a beautiful sunset welcomed them to Bermuda. The breeze was heavenly and Elizabeth decided to go above deck to wait for Mr. Pearson and the Captain.

James noted her arrival on deck, but luckily had too many last minute orders to the guard of the watch to occupy his mind. As Elizabeth moved to the rail, the rays of the afternoon sun shone on her chestnut hair, creating a halo effect of color. James felt his chest tighten when he looked at her and had his customary feeling of protectiveness toward her. Benjamin Whitfield who would be leaving the ship in Bermuda moved toward Elizabeth to join her at the rail. James seeing this movement motioned to Samuel Pearson to join them and save Elizabeth from any unwanted *Yankee* encounters. The movement was well timed, as Whitfield was about to continue his pursuit of a dinner partner in Elizabeth.

"So what are your first impressions of Bermuda, Miss Majors?" Whitfield asked.

Elizabeth had been so deep in thought taking in the sights before her that she had not noticed his approach. "It certainly is breathtaking, Mr. Whitfield," she stated.

Whitfield continued to press his court to Elizabeth. "Breathtaking is a word that I would certainly use for you, Miss Majors. The gentleman of Bermuda will stand in awe of our own southern belle. Are you certain that I cannot escort you to dinner this evening?"

At that moment, Samuel Pearson had made his way to the railing where Elizabeth stood with Benjamin Whitfield. "Miss Majors, I was sent to find you to escort you to our dinner this evening. Hello Mr. Whitfield. I am afraid I must claim our dinner companion for an earlier commitment made to both the Captain and to me. Captain's privilege in these matters as I am sure you understand," Samuel stated.

Elizabeth looked from Whitfield to Mr. Pearson with a look of relief. "That is correct, Mr. Whitfield; Mr. Pearson and Captain O'Rourke were kind enough to invite me to dinner for our first night in Bermuda. As I have never been here before, it certainly is pleasant to travel with experienced tourists." Elizabeth had blushed under the scrutiny and press of Mr. Whitfield and was glad for the escape offered by Mr. Pearson.

"The Captain will join us shortly, Miss Majors. He asked that I escort you to the restaurant while he changes for the evening. Good evening, Mr. Whitfield and I hope your trip was pleasant." Mr. Pearson spoke the latter as he carefully moved Elizabeth from the railing and away from Whitfield towards the landing from the ship to shore. Whitfield was none too happy about the course of the evening, but watched them leave the ship and alight in one of the carriages waiting to transport visitors to the hotels and restaurants. The ship had docked in the Town of St. George, which was the most historic part of the island. Carriages were awaiting transport of passengers from waiting docks to the hotels and restaurants of the town. Elizabeth and Mr. Pearson entered one of the carriages for a brief tour of the city prior to dinner.

Back on board, Whitfield continued to stand at the rail watching Elizabeth and Mr. Pearson's departure. He was still there as the Captain came above decks from his cabin, dressed for the evening's activities. He noted Whitfield's frown as Elizabeth and Samuel departed from the dock.

"I hope that you enjoyed your voyage to Bermuda Mr. Whitfield and that your business will be successful," James stated diplomatically. He could see Whitfield's disappointment at again missing the opportunity to spend time with Elizabeth.

"I won't keep you from your dinner companions O'Rourke. It seems that you have again thwarted my plans to spend time with the charming Miss Majors. St. George is not a large city so I am sure that I will see you again before the Alliance departs." Whitfield had retained his outward finesse in speaking, but James could see he was seething at again missing time spent with Elizabeth. Giving little thought and less notice to Whitfield, James departed and took a carriage directly to the Carlyle Hotel where he would be dining with Elizabeth and Samuel.

James arrived at the Carlyle before Samuel and Elizabeth and engaged a table in the charming restaurant; ordering champagne to accompany their dinner, as well as delicacies of the island which he felt would appeal to Elizabeth. A few minutes later, Samuel arrived with Elizabeth and they found their way to the table. James again felt the customary tightening of his chest as he saw Elizabeth move towards him. Wherever she goes, James thought, she must be the most beautiful woman in any room and I have the pleasure of her company for the evening.

James stood on Elizabeth's arrival at the table. She was glowing from the carriage ride and her first impressions of the island at sunset. She sat across from James and made herself comfortable. At that moment, Samuel made his excuses to return to the ship to assume the evening watch. Elizabeth thanked him for the brief tour of the island and noted her disappointment that Samuel would be unable to join them.

"I have much to do, Miss Elizabeth to get the ship resupplied. I also need to organize the watch for our time in Bermuda. Please enjoy your dinner and I will see you tomorrow." With this said, Samuel prepared to leave the table. He noted on his departure that Benjamin Whitfield was also in the restaurant seated with two men who appeared out of place with their surroundings in the restaurant. Samuel was not observed by the party and positioning himself behind a palm tree, noted the two rough looking men leaving the table. Samuel followed and took the next carriage away from the Carlyle. He noted that the two ruffians were heading in the direction of the berth for the Alliance.

As always, James' keen observational skills as a Captain had spotted Benjamin Whitfield and the two companions seen by Samuel. His attention was there when he realized that Elizabeth was talking to him about her brief tour of the island. He stored away the information so as to not worry Elizabeth and returned his attention to his dinner companion.

"The island is so beautiful and the scent of the air is like perfume," Elizabeth stated. "I am sure that you have been here many times and this would seem old hat to you, but I thoroughly enjoyed my brief tour with Mr. Pearson."

"One should never take a thing of beauty for granted Miss Majors. I assure you that no matter how many times that I have been here, Bermuda is always a welcoming island. Because there are always so many details to sort out upon our arrival, I sometimes miss the opportunity to enjoy the islands that we visit," James replied.

"I so appreciate you taking the time to entertain me this evening, Captain. I know that you have so many things to tend to," Elizabeth responded.

"Nonsense, it is my pleasure and I hope that you will enjoy yourself this evening. Would you like some champagne to start?" James asked smiling.

Once Elizabeth had been served and tasted the chilled champagne, she instantly lost her nerves over the evening and began to talk about her upcoming visit to London and the many tasks that she needed to complete. While she talked, James kept an eye on Benjamin Whitfield. He noted that Whitfield never moved from his table, but kept a close eye on James and Elizabeth. The two rough looking companions had not returned to the dining room, so he assumed that Samuel had taken care of that little problem. The issue bombarding James was why Whitfield continued to show up wherever Elizabeth was found. He knew that Whitfield had no interest in his whereabouts, so concluded that Elizabeth was the focus of his furtive glances and apparent plotting. He decided that he would not let this mystery spoil his evening with Elizabeth, but vowed to get to the bottom of it in the morning.

Dinner was a pleasant diversion with each sharing stories of their upbringing and their respective homes. James told Elizabeth about his family home of Broadlands. "Like you I was born near the water and the sea has been my second home since I was eighteen years old. Because my mother died when I was young, my father spent most of his years at sea. As soon as I was old enough and had concluded schooling, I joined him to apprentice. We have a fleet of ten ships which transport goods and passengers across the Atlantic and to various other ports of call. The war put quite a cramp in the Atlantic transport, but since the peace has returned, our fleet will sail from Wilmington to Bermuda, Charleston to the Bahamas and Savannah to Jamaica and back again to London laden with goods," James stated.

Elizabeth shared with him that she had dreamt of a sea voyage her entire life. She used to go to the house of the DeRosset family before the war and watch the ships as they sailed into the Cape Fear River and sailed out again for ports unknown. She never guessed that she would one day sail on one of them.

"What are your plans when you reach London?" James asked casually. He was certain that Whitfield's interest in Elizabeth lie at the heart of this mystery.

"I will be visiting the offices of my father's solicitor in London; Mr. Hilary Cross. I will need to probate my father's will and make arrangements for my inheritance which he secured with his London lawyers," Elizabeth replied.

"Do you know where Mr. Cross' offices are located?" James asked again casually.

"The address that I have sent all correspondence is in Fleet Street. As I have never been to London, I will need to verify upon my arrival," Elizabeth answered.

James had determined that she would not make that trip alone, because unless he missed his guess; Whitfield had some interest in Elizabeth and her trip to London. He intended to get to the bottom of it and to make sure that Elizabeth made her visits to Hilary Cross unmolested.

At that moment, the orchestra began dance music and James asked Elizabeth if she would enjoy a turn around the dance floor before the main course arrived. Elizabeth stated that she would be charmed and James rushed to his feet to accompany Elizabeth. As he rose from the table, James noted Whitfield moving to the exit. James confirmed his determination to get to the bottom of Whitfield's ongoing interest in Elizabeth's affairs. For now, he had the pleasure of Elizabeth's company on the dance floor. The orchestra was playing a waltz and James decided to allow his mind and body to focus on the joy of the dance with Elizabeth and not on the machinations of Whitfield and his minions. His hand around her tiny waist, James was reminded again of his intense need to protect Elizabeth which had begun with their first meeting. He tried to analyze why this had become important to him as his usual contacts with women were casual and of a limited nature. In this very hotel, he had had a number of trysts with the daughters of planters here to meet a man who would take them from the island to the larger world. None of those women had moved him like he was moved by Elizabeth and her openness and courage. As they waltzed, James found himself at ease and wanting nothing more than to hold her in his arms for the remainder of the evening. Dismissing this idea as soon as it was thought, James returned Elizabeth to her seat at the end of the dance.

Elizabeth's cheeks were again glowing from the dance and the shawl that she had demurely placed around her shoulders was now on the chair following their return to the dinner. James found it harder and harder to concentrate on her face when the alluring décolletage was within view. He reminded himself to end his champagne intake at that juncture.

The food was excellent and the room lovely with its candlelight magnified in numerous mirrors. As handsome as the assembled customers may be, James believed that no one could hold measure to Elizabeth. Her smile as dazzling as always had a far more profound effect on James than she would realize. By dessert, James was feeling that a return to the ship was in order. After paying the bill and gathering up Elizabeth, they proceeded to return to the ship for the night.

James hailed a carriage from the steps of the Carlyle remembering to keep an eye out for any possible threat to Elizabeth or to him as he did so. He helped Elizabeth into the carriage and they began a leisurely ride around the island and back to the Alliance's berth. With his arm draped across the seat, he made a point of watching Elizabeth's reaction as he stayed focused on his surroundings. Shortly after departing the Carlyle, he noticed the carriage which was following behind their carriage and the passengers who were the same ruffians from earlier in the night. He changed his mind about continuing the tour at that moment and casually requested the driver to return to the Alliance; trying all of the time to avoid alarming Elizabeth to the danger which he felt was near.

When they arrived at the Alliance berth, he exited the carriage, paid the driver and all but lifted Elizabeth from the carriage, keeping her close to his side as they boarded the ship. He turned as they arrived on the deck and noticed the two toughs lingering along the dock. He motioned to Samuel who while supervising the watch had noted his Captain's return and the return of the two men. The gangplank was pulled up for the night and James gave direction to add to the watch for the night as well.

James escorted Elizabeth to her cabin. At that point in which he knew Elizabeth was safe, he managed to focus on her and allay his fears for the time being. Elizabeth looked up at James with her shining eyes and thanked him for the lovely evening. "The pleasure was all mine, Miss Elizabeth," James smiled gallantly. At that moment he lifted her hand to his lips and bid her good evening.

Once arriving at his cabin, he turned to assure that she had gone into her cabin and returned above decks to Samuel. "Those two toughs are definitely associated with Whitfield," James stated.

"Aye, Captain," Samuel responded. "I spotted them as I was leaving the restaurant and kept a close eye back to the Alliance. They arrived here before me and lingered on the dock. They seemed to be assessing the watch for the evening which I had posted before my departure. They then left and must have returned to the hotel to wait for you and Miss Elizabeth."

"I am sure that they have no dealings with either you or with me," James stated. "I believe that they are somehow connected to Whitfield and that Whitfield may somehow be connected with this solicitor that Elizabeth is to see in London. His name is Hilary Cross and I intend to find out in the morning what connection the two men have in common. In the meantime, I want the watch doubled and I want to make sure that Miss Majors does not leave this ship without one or the other of us with her. I also want a two man team to follow any carriage that contains Miss Elizabeth. There is a mystery here and I intend to get to the bottom of it. If she asks why she must have an escort, tell her that it is a service we offer to all damsels in distress." James laughed at that moment, but with no mirth. He knew that Elizabeth was in danger but needed to determine why and from whom.

James returned to the corridor of Elizabeth's cabin and his own. He checked the door of Elizabeth's cabin to make sure that it was locked and returned to his own cabin. Well James, he thought; you said she would be trouble, but had no idea the true extent. For the first time he realized that he was infatuated with her and needed to protect her against some outside sources that were beyond his reckoning at this time. Being a light sleeper, he knew that he would keep one ear focused for noise on the ship while he remembered the joy of holding Elizabeth in his arms. As always the customary tightening of his chest accompanied that memory. As he changed out of his dress clothes, the vision of Elizabeth's shining eyes and décolletage haunted his mind.

Elizabeth had closed the cabin door behind her and waltzed to her bed. She could not believe that such a night was happening to her. She was so happy and only hoped that she had not been too much of a burden to James on his first night in Bermuda. She imagined that he would have rather been anywhere other than playing host to her on such a beautiful night, but let her mind return to every beautiful moment from the time that she and Mr. Pearson had left the Alliance at sunset to the moment that James had kissed her hand in the corridor. If only he could think of me as I now think of him. He is my knight in shining armor; always there and kind and considerate tonight when I know that I must have been a bother. As she undressed for bed her only thoughts were that James would come to think of her in the same way that she was coming to regard him. He certainly was not the ogre she had originally considered him to be but something very different indeed.

Elizabeth retired to bed, but the night was not to be a restful one. Whether it was the champagne that she had had with dinner or the excitement of the day and night or the ongoing insomnia, Elizabeth threatened to be robbed again of her sleep. When she did fall asleep, she had a series of horrible dreams. First, her father visited her and asked her why she had let his only son die. Next, her brother was being torn from her arms when he became ill with the Yellow Fever and had to be quarantined with the dread disease. Her father returned in the next dream from the battlefield. She saw him die in front of her and gasped with the shock and pain. The nightmares were not yet over, however. She was next in the midst of a thick fog. She was in a carriage and someone was following her. The carriage came closer and closer and the two tough looking occupants tried to come onto the back of the carriage. As fast as the carriage was traveling through the streets of a large, congested city; the closer the two tough looking men came to her carriage. They were carrying weapons and as they came closer, she saw that they meant to kill her and to kill the other occupant of the carriage. When she looked to her side, she saw that the other occupant was James. Her fear increased at that moment not for herself, but for James. She started to scream to alert James to the peril. She screamed and screamed but could not get his attention as the assailants started to attack James.

At that moment James heard the screams coming from Elizabeth's cabin. Remembering the two ruffians on the dock below, James bounded from his bed and burst down the cabin door. He looked all around Elizabeth's cabin, but could find no one in the cabin other than Elizabeth who was on the bed tossing in her sleep against some unknown assailant and screaming for her life. James lifted Elizabeth from the bed and attempted to hold her and comfort her. She continued to cry out as he held her and gently kissed her forehead. He gently rubbed her back as he would a child waking from a bad dream. At that moment, Elizabeth finally opened her eyes. James gazed into her tearful, shining eyes then and seeing her vulnerability and closeness, kissed her gently on the mouth. He meant only to continue to comfort her; however the kiss became more intense as Elizabeth began to respond to his caress. She was so warm and vulnerable that he expanded his embrace to part her full lips and intensify the kiss. To his surprise and to hers, she embraced his neck and drew him further into the arousing kiss. He was an experienced man of the world and knew how and when to impose his self control. To his surprise, he felt his self control rapidly eroding, as the kiss became more arousing for him and confusing for her.

At that moment James broke away from the embrace in an effort to find his own self control. He could not help but let his eyes wander helplessly to the open neck of her soft white gown. Elizabeth followed his gaze only to find that in the struggle her ribbons had come undone and her gown was open exposing a significant portion of her chest. She pulled the covers to her neck and attempted to regain her composure. “I am so sorry that I disturbed you, Captain. You must have thought me mad just now when I began screaming.”

His voice was soft and husky when he spoke. “Nights at sea will sometimes disturb your sleep with horrible dreams. I hope that you will rest more peacefully for the rest of the night, Miss Elizabeth. Good night.” With that he left her cabin and closed the cabin door gently.

Elizabeth was at a loss for the depth of her response to James’ kiss. She should have felt embarrassed to be found in her night dress and to be comforted as a parent would comfort a child with a bad dream. Her response was certainly not the response of a child to a parent. It had felt so warm and comforting in his arms and she had never wanted him to stop kissing her. What would Aunt Felicity think of this turn of events? Who would know that her first kiss would be like this? Try as she might, she could not remove from her mind and body the sensation of that kiss. Had Captain O’Rourke felt something as well, or was he again just being considerate and protective? More importantly, how was she to face him again in the morning after that kiss?

For his part, he was just as amazed by the depth of his feelings. When she had responded as she did, he felt more fully his feelings for her and the warmth of emotions that were worlds beyond his usual sallies with women on shore leave. These feelings worried him and he vowed that he would try to keep his distance until he could sort them out properly. Still the sight of her in that soft clinging gown was a hard memory to forget as he tossed and turned in his cabin that night. The soft scent of rose clung to him also, as it clung to every encounter with Elizabeth. She was a mere slip of a girl and he an experienced man of the world; and yet . . . there was something different about Elizabeth. His feelings for her were not casual, of that he could be sure. The source of them and the depth of them were something that would haunt his night and the nights to come.

CHAPTER FIVE

The next morning, James arose from a sleepless night, dressed and went on deck to relieve his frustration by sharp orders to the crew. Because all was organized and well orchestrated as usual, he had very few complaints to issue. Woe be to the crew member who did not respond quickly enough that morning. His usually sharp eye caught all as he tried to move the events of last night to the back of his mind. When Samuel came on deck, he advised him that Miss Major's door would need to be repaired while she was out today. He did not explain why and left the older man to his own devices as he moved to the rail. He was looking for a return of the two toughs from last night, but when the dock area was surveyed, they were not in view. James returned to Samuel and told him that he was going into town to see what he could learn about Benjamin Whitfield and his connection to the two rough looking customers who followed Samuel, James and Elizabeth last night. He instructed Samuel to not allow Elizabeth to leave the ship until his return.

Samuel went below to determine if Miss Majors was yet awake. He could hear no sound from within the cabin, so determined that she must be still sleeping. He had no indication of why the cabin door had been broken into, but assumed that Elizabeth was alright. He knew by now that James growing feelings for Elizabeth would have meant that he was only trying to protect her from whatever had occurred last evening to require the breaking of the door.

James went directly to his business associates in St. George looking for answers to his questions. Mr. Fitzgerald, a long time business associate, was able to see him immediately. "I will get right to the reason for my inquiry," James stated. "I need to know everything that you can tell me about Benjamin Whitfield and any known associates. He was a passenger of the Alliance from Wilmington, North Carolina to here and has been following me and another passenger since our arrival in St. George. Last night, two toughs were seen in his company and they in turn followed Samuel Pearson's carriage and my carriage back to the Alliance. I don't like it Fitzgerald and I need to know what is behind it."

William Fitzgerald was as straight forward as James and did not beat about the bush. "Whitfield is a shadowy character here in St. George and has connections in London. Nothing has been able to be attached to him directly, but he certainly moves in a shadowy world. He has business ties with a solicitor in London named Charles Cross."

James asked "Is Charles Cross related in any way to Hilary Cross?"

William replied that Charles Cross is the son of Hilary Cross who moved the business to his son due to illness and advanced age. "The son is nothing like the father, however. Rather shady deals have been connected to the son with nothing ever proved to date."

"I have a passenger named Elizabeth Majors on board. Her father did business with Hilary Cross before the American Civil War and she is on her way to London to conclude her father's estate. It sounds as if she may be unknowingly in the middle of plans by the son that may involve her inheritance. I intend to get to the bottom of it when we reach London," James replied heatedly.

William smiled knowingly. "It sounds as though this Miss Majors is more than just a passenger, James. Are you telling me that the famous Captain O'Rourke has finally lost his heart?"

James smiled for the first time since the prior evening. "You know me too well, old friend. Yes I believe that Miss Majors is a very special lady indeed. If you were to meet her, you would understand why."

"Good luck to you and to Miss Majors," William stated. "I know that you will keep her safe until you can sort out what is behind the stalking of you both."

"Have no fear, William; I will keep her safe and we will have this matter sorted in short order," James stated firmly.

On that speech, James left the offices of William Fitzgerald to return to the Alliance. He had already decided their course of action. Once the resupplying was completed, the Alliance would be leaving St. George under cover of darkness and head toward London one day ahead of schedule. The quicker that he could get Elizabeth to London and sort out the issues ahead, the better it would be for both of them. In London he would have a virtual army of men who could protect her. He knew also after last night that he would be protecting her well beyond this voyage. It was his intention to court Elizabeth during the voyage to London. He had made that decision during the sleepless night when he knew that Elizabeth was on the other side of his cabin wall. He wanted her beside him in his cabin and in his life. He just had to make sure that Elizabeth felt the same. He would take his time, but he had made up his mind and would not be deterred.

When Elizabeth awoke at last on that morning, she laid still for a moment trying to remember if the kiss that she had shared with James was one of her many dreams from the night before. One look at the broken lock on the cabin door told her that it had not been a dream. Unlike the terrible dreams that preceded it, the memory of James holding her in his arms and soothing her with his kisses was very real and a memory that she would not soon forget. Was it possible, she asked herself, that James had developed feelings for her as she had for him? What exactly did she feel for him, she wondered? Did she care for him or was it just an amazing thankfulness for his kindness and consideration? If she were honest, she had to admit that no man like Captain O'Rourke would spend so much time and consideration on a lady just because she was his passenger. Surely last night was an indication of developing feelings for her, or were kisses like the one that they shared just an everyday thing for a man of the world like James O'Rourke? Perhaps the key to her many questions would be in the manner in which he reacted when they were next alone together. Feeling that was the right course, she got up and got dressed to see if another trip to St. George would be possible. Perhaps if the Captain was too busy, Mr. Pearson would be able to take her to St. George and give her the chance that she needed to sort out her feelings away from the ship and away from James and the memory of last night.

When she came above decks, she saw that the crew was in unison in resupplying the ship for the two week voyage to London. Shore leave had been cancelled in advance of an early departure this evening. She was unsure why the plans had been changed, but hoped that she was not the cause of their expedited departure. She could not see James anywhere in the midst of the organized chaos above decks, but did spy Mr. Pearson at the rail.

"Good afternoon, Miss Majors!" Mr. Pearson stated on her approach. "We will be departing for London in just a few short hours."

"Is there a reason for the early departure?" Elizabeth asked.

"Captain O'Rourke has a second sense for weather changes and wants to get ahead of the worst of the storm season. He should be back from his errands in short order and will want to talk to you about the change in plans. In the mean time, why don't you go down to the officer's dining room and let Cook prepare a lunch for you. I am sure that he will have something ready for a late meal."

Elizabeth dutifully went below to the officer's dining room still mulling over the change in plans that Mr. Pearson was alluding to. While she was there, Samuel directed that the steward repair the lock on Elizabeth's cabin door. He knew that James would be taking no chances with her security going forward. Samuel had scoured the waterfront during his breaks from oversight of the resupplying but had found no sight of the toughs from last night. Typical, he thought; rough characters such as that type only came out at night to prey upon their victims.

Elizabeth found the Cook cleaning up from the luncheon meal and only too happy to prepare a late lunch for Elizabeth. While having her first meal of the day, she thought again about the real reason for the early departure and hoped that she had nothing to do with the change in plans and the expedited work load on the part of the crew. The Cook reassured her that the Captain had a second sense about the weather and probably could feel a storm coming on. If that was the case, he would want to get out to the open sea as soon as possible.

Elizabeth finished her meal and then returned to her cabin. She noted that the door lock had been repaired in her absence, with no questions asked. She hoped that the crew did not find it odd that the door had been broken down last night. She found that where the Captain was concerned, his wish was their command without question. She was probably the only person aboard who could question the Captain's direct orders, as she had done on more than one occasion.

James had returned to his cabin and was lying across his bed when he heard her return. He knew that their next meeting could be awkward, but determined that he would behave as naturally as possible in the hope that she would not feel embarrassed by the feelings that had passed between them last night. Certainly he was not embarrassed, but truly amazed to have such strong attraction and feelings of protectiveness all at the same time. He was treating her like a younger sister, but had feelings that were anything but brotherly for her as he lay on his bed. He could not wait to hold her in his arms again and to expand his embraces of her to much more than a paternal kiss. Was he testing his defenses to see if he had actual feelings for her? At this point he was unsure; he just knew that he wanted to be with her again.

Within the hour the ship had concluded its resupplying and James went above decks to supervise the departure from St. George. Elizabeth came up shortly thereafter to take one last glimpse at the beautiful island. She hoped that she would again have the chance to see more of the Bermuda Island on her return to Wilmington once the London business was concluded.

Unbeknownst to Elizabeth, but within view of James and Samuel Pearson, Benjamin Whitfield and the two toughs from last night were again seen on the dockside. The early departure had appeared to take them by surprise. Whitfield was seen hailing the next passing carriage and James and Samuel were left wondering what Whitfield's next move would be.

As the sun began to set on their movement into open waters, Elizabeth sought out Mr. Pearson by the rail. "Did all go according to plan?" Elizabeth asked.

"All is ready and we are taking off ahead of schedule to London. If all goes according to plan, we should have you in London in two weeks time," Samuel stated. James moved towards the rail seeing Samuel in conversation with Elizabeth.

"We will not be having our usual first night dinner this evening, Miss Majors, but I am hopeful that you will join me for dinner tonight," James stated in a meaningful way.

"I would be happy to do so, Captain O'Rourke. Please let me know what time you would wish me to be ready," Elizabeth asked smiling.

"The steward will call for you at 8:00 p.m. sharp," James replied. He was instantly taken back to their first night on this ship, the first night dinner and all that had transpired since that time in such a short interval.

"I will be ready, Captain," Elizabeth responded. James watched her walk away and for all to see, the affection in his eyes for Elizabeth was abundantly clear. A great deal had changed in a few short days but he knew in his heart that his path was clear. He would court Elizabeth during the next two weeks and let fate decide the next course for them both.

Elizabeth changed again for the evening dinner. She wore a rose pink dress with short sleeves, a tight waist and a sweetheart neckline. It was more daring than the turquoise dress in that more skin was exposed, but since it would only be James, she was no longer shy about dressing to her best advantage. She wanted to have James admire her and was not shy about wanting his attention and affection.

The steward knocked on Elizabeth's door at 8:00 p.m. sharp and escorted her to the Captain's cabin. When the cabin door opened, arrayed on the table were delicacies not unlike those of their first night aboard ship; but now there was no Benjamin Whitfield to spoil the evening for either James or Elizabeth. She could enjoy her dinner and her time with James without interruption by other passengers. James breath caught as he saw Elizabeth at the door. His first thought was how beautiful that she looked. His second thought was how he would keep his hands off her during the dinner. He would keep her within his line of sight but on the opposite side of the table in order to maintain his composure. That decision was quickly cast aside when Elizabeth came to his side and thanked him for the lovely invitation and dinner. She was shy Elizabeth again, relying on her good manners and southern charm to overcome the awkwardness of the night before. James decided to puncture that façade as quickly as possible. He seated Elizabeth on the end of the table and not the opposite side and quickly filled her glass with the first wine.

"To a safe passage to London and to the beginning of a new life for you," James toasted Elizabeth.

"Thank you, Captain O'Rourke and safe passage to you as well," Elizabeth replied smiling.

"I think after last night, you can call me James from now on. You mustn't be embarrassed about last night. I have felt a change in our relationship and I believe that you feel that a change has occurred as well."

"You must call me Elizabeth, then," Elizabeth said blushing at the remembrance of last night. "I too have felt a change in our relationship, but did not know if I was alone in that thought."

"You were most certainly not alone and you will not be alone in the future if you wish it," James said huskily. At that moment, the steward returned with the first course of the meal and the moment was temporarily put aside. The steward wisely left the door open as he moved from the cabin with course after course. Wisely, thought James as he did not wish to scare Elizabeth or to move too rapidly with his plans for courtship. He wanted her to have a comfort with him and to understand his respect for her feelings and that she was not just another passing fancy.

At the conclusion of the meal, James asked Elizabeth if she would wish to go above decks while he smoked his after dinner cigar. She gladly said she would and stopped to grab her shawl. While she obtained her shawl, James noted the door repair and noticed another lock that had been placed on her door from the inside. He had to admit that his crew was looking out for Elizabeth's welfare as well as James'. He wondered if others had spotted the ruffians last night on the dockside and the reappearance of Benjamin Whitfield. That thought was pushed aside as Elizabeth rejoined him in the corridor. At least he knew he could keep her safe on the open seas where no gangs would be bothering Elizabeth or James.

They went on deck together and Elizabeth took his arm as they moved to the rail. The sky was clear with a multitude of stars above them. "Mr. Pearson stated that we may have departed St. George early because of storm season being upon us," Elizabeth stated in an effort to break the silence between them.

"That's right, Elizabeth. This is the worst time of year for the big storms and the sooner we can set off for London the better it will be. The Alliance has weathered many a storm, so I don't want you to worry about the open seas that we have ahead of us."

"I wouldn't worry about anything when you are in charge, James," Elizabeth replied. James looked at her then and saw the light in her eyes. He was immensely touched by her faith in him and by the affection that he saw there. Throwing away the last of his cigar, he reached out to take her in his arms as he had done at the Carlyle. He reached down for a brief, chaste kiss, but felt the yearning again returning. Elizabeth placed her arms around his neck and returned his kiss, modestly at first and then with more feeling. He knew that their feelings were reciprocated without words. Again he tried to confront his growing passion as Elizabeth responded to James' kiss deepening it with each movement. James heard footsteps coming from below and broke the kiss and the spell. Elizabeth pulled away and the two stood wordless, watching the waves and fighting the waves within. After a brief time, James stated that he would take her below as the night air was beginning to chill her. She thought it was not the night air, but his touch that created the chills that she felt whenever she was near him.

At her cabin, James kissed Elizabeth on the forehead in a chaste kiss good night. Elizabeth again placed her arms around his neck and then reached up to kiss him good night. The kiss began as a modest kiss again and expanded with each movement of Elizabeth toward James. His hands came to hold her face on both sides. Her eyes when they parted had the same misty look that she had had the night before. James was glad for the new lock on Elizabeth's door as he wished her good night and pleasant dreams. As he returned to his cabin, he knew that his would be haunted again by those shining eyes. Sleep would be hard to come by and the dreams if they were to come would be of a chestnut hair slip of a girl who had somehow found a way to touch his heart.

The next morning arose hot and sunny. On board ship there was no respite from the sun, so Elizabeth with her fair skin was compelled to stay below in her cabin. The ship was making excellent time and with each passing hour, James thought of the challenges ahead that they would face in London. He had convinced himself that the best way to keep Elizabeth safe was to assist in her dealings with Charles Cross. He wanted to make sure that Charles Cross and his associates were clear that they were not dealing only with a twenty-two year old novice, but with a man of the world who was only too happy to protect Elizabeth and her interests. He had two weeks to convince Elizabeth of the sensible nature of his plan. When he thought of those words however, the past two nights passed before his eyes and he knew that Elizabeth shared the same feelings that had so conflicted James.

Elizabeth devoted herself to updating her diary and putting to paper the amazing developments of the past two nights. She knew that James had strong feelings for her and she only hoped that those strong feelings also meant real affection and that she was not a passing fancy that would end upon their arrival in London.

The day passed quickly with updates to her diary and a long nap to catch up on the sleep lost over the past two nights. By the end of the day, Elizabeth felt stronger then she had in days and went above decks to learn about the evening plans. She was surprised by the worried looks on the faces of the crew as she ascended to the deck. James came to her immediately as he saw her come above decks. His ever watchful eye had been waiting for her for some hours.

"Elizabeth, I don't want to alarm you; but it looks as though we might be in for some of the bad weather that I told you about last night," James stated. Elizabeth looked at him in a puzzled manner as the sky was so bright without a cloud to be seen.

"I don't understand, James. The sky is so bright and there are no dark clouds anywhere on the horizon," Elizabeth replied.

"I know that it is hard to understand, but you must trust me that bad weather is on the way. I have seen it in the barometer and know the signs. I want to prepare you for what may occur and we will talk shortly over dinner. I don't want you to be frightened, but we must prepare," James responded.

"I won't be afraid, James; not so long as you are at the helm," Elizabeth said shyly.

"Why don't you go below and the steward will rap for you at 8:00 p.m.?" James stated. He watched her go below and as always felt that chest tightening with the desire to protect her at all costs. He needed to tell her this evening that for her safety and to maintain his focus, he needed her to stay below throughout the storm. If he were worried about her, he could not protect the ship and all aboard in the storm that was yet to come.

At 8:00 the steward rapped on Elizabeth's door and as always, she was ready for the knock. He escorted her to James' cabin where the dinner was already set on the table. This time he closed the door to leave the two alone. The Captain had some serious things that he needed to say to Elizabeth and did not need to be interrupted.

Elizabeth sat down at her customary place and looked worriedly at James's face. "What is it that you need to tell me James?" Elizabeth asked.

James did not immediately sit down but stood at the bulkhead looking out over the sea. "In the next few days, we will be heading into a hurricane. I have seen the signs many times and expect it to begin tomorrow. At first, the sky will be as blue as today with the sun so bright it will hurt your eyes," James continued. "Then the sky will start to darken and the winds will begin." Elizabeth listened intently but had lived through hurricanes before. She thought to tell James this when he made his first pause.

"The winds will worsen and at the worst portion of the storm; a quiet will overtake the ship. You will think that the storm is over and will want to come above decks. I beg you to stay below until the crew tells you that the storm has passed completely. The eye of the storm is the quiet portion, but the back half of the storm is sometimes worse than the first. That is why it is so important that you stay below with the doctor in the officer's cabin area. I don't want you to be alone during the storm, but I cannot be with you as my task is to be above decks while the storm is at its worst," James stated.

"Won't that be very dangerous for you, James?" Elizabeth asked quietly.

"I have survived many a storm and know the best way to keep us safe. You must trust me that I will be fine." He did not wish to explain to her about the tether lines that would keep him from going overboard. He wanted to keep the worst of the experience from her so that she would worry less.

"James, I have lived in Wilmington my whole life. I have been through bad storms before. We always went to the summer kitchen at the bottom of the house to ride out the storm," Elizabeth stated.

"I know that you have lived through storms on land, Elizabeth; but this is an entirely different experience. The ship will groan and rise and fall on waves larger than you have ever seen. We will get to the other side, but I must have full concentration on the storm and not worry about your safety. Can you do as I ask, Elizabeth?" James asked worriedly.

"Of course, James; I will do whatever you need me to do so that I do not add to your worries," Elizabeth replied.

"We have come a long way in a very short time, Miss Majors. There was a time not too long ago that you would have bristled at taking orders from me," James said smiling.

"Now I am taking orders from James and not from Captain O'Rourke," Elizabeth responded with the same smile.

"Then come over and give James a kiss and not Captain O'Rourke," James said. Elizabeth moved over to the bulkhead and put her head on his shoulder. He knew that they would come through this trial stronger and closer. James kissed Elizabeth on the forehead as before in a paternal manner. When he looked into her eyes and saw the same passion as before, he kissed her on her full lips until they were red and swollen. As always, he pulled back before losing control and said huskily, "I think we had better start our dinner before it gets cold." James moved away from Elizabeth but held onto her hand as he guided her to her seat.

Dinner was spent quietly taking in the magnitude of what lay ahead of them. When at last dinner was completed and the dishes taken away by the steward, James looked intently at Elizabeth again. "When this storm is over, Elizabeth Majors; there are things that I want to say to you; things that you may think it too early for me to say. I want you to know how much you mean to me and what a difference you have made in my life. I will say no more until this storm is over." Elizabeth longed to hear the words that she hoped James would say to her. She had known about her attraction to James even when she was angry at him and frustrated by his paternal behavior. She knew now that very paternal behavior was masking his growing feelings for her; feelings that he feared as they had come upon them both so quickly.

James took Elizabeth's hand and brought her to her feet. "Let's go above deck while I have my cigar. It may be the last time that you have fresh air for some time."

They went above decks and stood together, Elizabeth's hand on James' arm. She looked at the quiet waters beyond them and was so amazed to imagine that a storm was imminent. She quietly prayed for the safety of James and for the safety of the entire crew in the storm to come.

CHAPTER SIX

As James predicted, the storm began to close in on the ship the next day. The storm clouds moved in with a vengeance and the barometric pressure dropped significantly. The wind hot and humid as the *breath from the mouth of hell* began to overtake the ship, as well as the churning waves that are characteristic of a hurricane. Elizabeth dressed in the coolest and thinnest gown that she possessed and placed her heavy hair in a snood. She intended to ask Dr. Wilkinson if she could be of assistance to him in his surgery during the storm. If she was expected to stay below decks for the duration; she would have to stay busy or she would surely lose her mind. Her worry about James and his safety was uppermost in her thoughts. She would need to stay focused during the duration or her nerves would definitely get the best of her. It had been that way during the war whenever she worried about the fate of her father. She could not think about that now, but only how she could help James and the crew during the storm.

After she had prepared a small bag, she went above decks to see James before heading to the passenger portion of the ship. Mr. Pearson would return to his customary cabin during the storm, although he did advise Elizabeth that he did not expect to spend any time there. James and he were in for the fight of their lives for the next several days to keep the ship, its crew and passenger safe. They had weathered many a storm before and knew what would be needed to help the ship through the worst of it.

James saw Elizabeth come above decks and went to her instantly to carry her small bag. “You know what you promised me last night, Elizabeth,” James said gravely.

“I do James and I have packed enough for a few days stay in the passenger portion of the ship until the storm has passed. I do wish you would let me help you in some small way,” Elizabeth replied worriedly.

"You can help me by staying below decks and staying safe. I can't focus on the work ahead if I am worried about you and your safety," James said more fiercely than he had wished.

"I know that you are only concerned about me and my safety. I understand and I promise to stay below decks whatever may occur." James took her hand and escorted her to the most spacious passenger cabin so that she could settle in before the worst of the storm hit. Once he had returned to the deck to supervise preparations for the storm, Elizabeth went to Dr. Wilkinson's cabin and knocked on the door. "May I be of any assistance to you during the storm, Dr. Wilkinson? I have some experience nursing relatives and would dearly love to keep busy while the storm rages."

Dr. Wilkinson took pity on Elizabeth and told her that he could find plenty to keep her occupied in his surgery. He closed his cabin door and led her to his surgery. He asked that she begin by rolling bandages for the expected injuries to the crew. As he explained, flying debris could result in injury to the crew members. He tried to keep his comments brief and with limited detail as he did not want her to worry about the Captain who would take the brunt of the storm. He understood the bond that had grown between them and knew that the less that Elizabeth knew about what lie ahead, the better for them all.

"The best thing that you can do after finishing with the bandages is to take a rest yourself. We may become very busy in the next few days so we should rest as much as possible before the worst of the storm hits. You also need to keep your stomach as full as possible with crackers or bread to fight the seasickness that may accompany the worst of the rocking caused by the intense waves. It is not unusual for passengers and crew to take ill during the worst of the storm," he stated.

After completing her task, Elizabeth returned to her temporary cabin to lie across the bed. She found it hard to sleep as she worried about the storm and most of all about James' safety.

Elizabeth awoke to the sound of groans coming from the ship. She realized from the tossing that was occurring that the storm had started in earnest. Dressing quickly, she returned to the surgery to lend her assistance. All was quiet for the time being, but Dr. Wilkinson expected injuries as the day wore on. He was proven correct when crew members started coming to the surgery with severe cuts and abrasions from the debris that loosened from the storm and from the battering that crew members took as they moved through their customary tasks above decks. Dr. Wilkinson explained that the crew members would take shorter stays above decks due to the pounding of the waves and wind. Elizabeth's first thought was for James and whether he would also take shorter stays above deck, but she said nothing at this juncture. She focused on the patients coming into the surgery and assured their comfort while in her care.

The hours wore on and the intensity of the storm continued to grow. Each crew member who came to the surgery was soaked to the skin. She could only imagine how wet and tired James must be as he struggled with the mounting waves and wind. She summoned the courage to ask one of the crew members if all was well above decks. "You will be worried about the Captain, then," Mr. Collins stated. "The Captain has weathered many a storm in these waters. He has fought the devil himself more than once. You mustn't worry about the Captain. He will get us through this storm as he has many before." Mr. Collins could see the worry on Elizabeth's face and thought to calm her fears.

"Does he have plenty of food and drink to sustain him through the storm?" Elizabeth asked. Mr. Collins shared a look with Dr. Wilkinson at that moment and thought better of his answer. He knew that the Captain would take no rest or nourishment while the storm raged. Only during the eye of the storm would he assess the damage to the ship and then take some nourishment to fight the back side of the storm which would follow. “Aye, Mistress Majors; the Captain is well taken care of. You mustn’t fret about him or any of us. We are used to such things and learn to deal with whatever God sends our way.” Elizabeth smiled then as she cleaned the wound from the injuries that Mr. Collins had received.

Many patients followed throughout the first day of the storm. The crew members would come to the surgery as they took breaks from their shifts and be bandaged up to return above decks. After leaving the surgery those who were still mobile would move onto the crew mess for soup, a brief rest and then a return above decks. Elizabeth noted however that the Captain never came to either the surgery or to the mess for nourishment. She hoped that his steward was taking care of him, but remembered her promise to not attempt to go above decks until the storm had abated. Dr. Wilkinson asked several times that she go and rest, but as the crew members continued to come to the surgery, she continued to assist.

On the morning of the second day of the storm, a major crash was heard above decks. Elizabeth scanned the faces of the crew members assembled to determine if this was an expected sound or something that should create worry for them all. “Don’t worry, Mistress Majors; that is just one of the small masts, a mizenmast or foremast hitting the deck. The mainmast is strong and will get us through this storm.” All of the crew had been told to answer her questions, but to allay Elizabeth’s fears and to not worsen the anxiety that she must be feeling both for herself and for the Captain.

By mid day on the second day of the storm, a terrible quiet descended on the ship. The winds began to stop just as quickly as they had started and the rain that had battered the ship ceased. Elizabeth thought at that moment they must be passing through the eye of the storm. All of the crew members who were mobile hurriedly returned to their posts so that the damage to the ship could be assessed and any necessary temporary repairs completed in anticipation of the back end of the storm.

"Is there anything that I can do to assist Dr. Wilkinson?" She already knew the answer but wanted to make sure that she could not be of some assistance to anyone on the ship, especially James.

"No, Miss Majors; your assistance has been invaluable to me, but it is best that you stay below decks. The eye of the storm will pass very quickly and the back end of the storm can be just as fierce as the front end, sometimes worse so. I would not want you to be caught above decks when the back end of the storm approaches." Dr. Wilkinson suggested that she return to her cabin to rest until the crew returned to the surgery. She did so, but knew that she could not sleep as long as James continued in danger. She lay down on the bed and said another silent prayer for James and for the crew who risked their lives to bring the ship safely through the storm.

In what seemed like a very short time, the ship began again to groan as the winds resumed and the pounding rain returned to devil the ship. Elizabeth returned to the surgery awaiting the next influx of wounded crew members. She asked the doctor if there had been any news of Captain O'Rourke. "The Captain is an experienced mariner, Miss Majors. He will get us through this storm and with any luck; we will have a record time to London with the wind behind us." The doctor could see that Elizabeth was not convinced, but at least they had continued to keep her spirits up during the worst of the storm.

For what seemed like an eternity, the storm continued to batter the ship. Crew members returned to the surgery on break to have minor abrasions tended. One crew member had broken a leg from a fall experienced in a trough of a wave as those above decks were hammered by the motion of the waves. By keeping her hands busy, Elizabeth was able to endure her concern for James and for the exhaustion that she knew he must be experiencing.

As the storm began to abate hours later, Dr. Wilkinson thought it safe enough for Elizabeth to return to her original cabin. He could see the toll the storm had taken on her and knew that she was in need of rest and nourishment. Elizabeth went to her temporary cabin and gathered her small bag. She had not had the opportunity to change her clothes for two days and had barely touched any of the items that she had packed. She had assurance at that moment however, that she had helped James' crew in their hours of need and felt in doing so, that she had assisted James in some small way as well. As they began to go above decks, Elizabeth spotted a giant wave crashing across the decks of the ship. It was only then that she saw James tethered to the wheel of the ship. It occurred to her then that the only way he could keep his footing and maintain control of the vessel was to be tethered to the ship in this manner. She understood also how so many injuries had occurred when she saw the debris that littered the deck of the always immaculate ship. The wave passed over James and he appeared to lose his footing at that moment. Elizabeth called out to James when she saw the wave and his fall and fainted on the spot. Her last sight of James had been of him tossed to the ship deck. Dr. Wilkinson saw Elizabeth swoon and picked her up to take her to her cabin. James seeing her faint gathered himself from the deck floor and quickly labored to the doctor's side. Mr. Pearson assumed his place as the worst of the wave subsided.

"I believe that Miss Majors has merely fainted, Captain. I am sure that it is a result of fatigue. She has barely eaten or rested for two solid days." The rain continued to pour down on all of them but for the first time in two days, the sky was beginning to lighten which was an indication that the storm was subsiding. James tenderly took Elizabeth from Dr. Wilkinson's arms and carried her down the passage to his cabin. He kicked open the cabin door and proceeded to place Elizabeth in the center of his own bed. Mr. Jones the Captain's steward was following behind with blankets and towels to dry Elizabeth whom he had seen faint and was now soaked to the skin. He handed the towels and blankets to the Captain and noticed for the first time that the Captain's hands were shaking. Dr. Wilkinson came from behind and noticed the same. "Let me take care of Miss Majors, Captain. I believe she just needs some rest and she will be on her feet in no time." He motioned to Mr. Jones to get his bag and some laudanum for Miss Majors. Captain O'Rourke would not budge, however and remained at the doctor's side. "Perhaps I should get Miss Majors changed into some dry clothes Captain. Would you have a night shirt that I could change her into?"

At this suggestion, James charged into action and pulled a night shirt from his cabin dresser. "I will step outside while you attend to Miss Majors," James replied. "I will be outside in the passage if you should need me."

Dr. Wilkinson had never seen the Captain shaken by anything and realized at that moment the depth of James' feelings for Miss Majors. The doctor quickly toweled her hair and face and changed her into the night shirt offered by Captain O'Rourke. Mr. Jones knocked on the cabin door at that instant and brought the doctor's bag. Dr. Wilkinson administered a dosage of laudanum to Elizabeth in the hopes that he could make her sleep. He believed that her exhaustion was the only real injury and that it could best be relieved by several hours of intense sleep.

At that moment, James returned to his cabin to check on Elizabeth. "I have given her some laudanum, Captain. I hope that I can get her to sleep off the effects of the past two days. She has rarely stopped her work in my surgery and I believe is completed exhausted. She will be much better after she gets some rest. By the look of you, Captain; you would also do with some sleep as well." James had toweled off the worst of the wet, but continued to stand in soaking clothes as he looked at Elizabeth's peaceful face.

"I will change and return in just a moment, doctor. I will need to know if there are any instructions for me or for Mr. Jones as you return to the surgery. I know that you will have patients waiting for you, but I appreciate your taking the time to check on Miss Majors." James went to Elizabeth's former cabin to change out of the soaking clothes and had returned to his own cabin moments later.

"She will rest now, Captain. It is the best thing for her and for you as well. As soon as she awakes, we will get some food into her and she will be fine," Dr. Wilkinson added. He left the cabin then and as he closed the door, saw James kneel beside Elizabeth's bed.

James knelt beside Elizabeth and checked her face for any sign of pain or illness. He noticed the dark stains beneath her eyes and knew that she had been without sleep for several days just as he had been at the helm of the ship. Her hair was spread across the pillows and gave her the look of a mermaid as she rested. At that moment the worry about Elizabeth and the affect of the past two days overtook James and he sat down on a chair beside the bed holding Elizabeth's hand as she slept. Mr. Jones returned to the cabin with some soup for James, but in seeing the two exhausted and sleeping covered the Captain with a blanket and crept out of the cabin and shut the door.

James slept in this position beside the bed for about two hours. He had trained himself long ago to take two hour naps so that he could go above decks and check on the status of the ship. As he awoke, he remembered that Elizabeth was in the room and beside him on the bed. He immediately checked on her and finding her fast asleep, prepared to go above decks to survey the damage from the storm. Mr. Pearson was at the helm and the waves had subsided. "How is Miss Majors, Captain?" Mr. Pearson asked.

"She is still sleeping," James replied.

"Aye, I expect she will sleep for some time. Dr. Wilkinson has told me that she barely rested for two days helping him in the surgery. She is a wonder, Captain O'Rourke. Could you imagine a lady such as herself making sure that all and sundry are taken care of before she takes care of herself? She told Dr. Wilkinson that she needed to keep her hands busy so as to not worry about the storm. I think she was most worried about you, however. I saw how she fainted when she saw the wave crash over the deck."

"You are right, Samuel; she is a wonder. We are all very lucky to have her onboard; I am the luckiest of all. I intend on asking Miss Majors to marry me when she awakes, that is if she will have me. She is one of the most extraordinary women that I have ever met and I do not intend on letting her get away!"

Samuel looked at his Captain with amazement. "Let me be the first to congratulate you, Captain. You could not have chosen better. She may be a little thing, but she has more pluck than many a man that I have met. I believe Captain you have met your match!"

"Aye, Samuel; I agree with you. I believe I had met my match when first I laid eyes on her. With each passing day I see that more and more. Please keep this news to yourself until the lady in question accepts me."

"I think there is no worry about that, Captain. That lass was meant for you there is no doubt. We must celebrate when the happy news is confirmed. The crew will definitely drink to your health and to that of your lady! Why don't you get some more rest, Captain? You will want to be at your best when Mistress Majors awakes."

In the Captain's cabin, Elizabeth slept on. James tried without success to rest in her cabin, but he could only smell the rose scent that reminded him so much of Elizabeth and could not find sleep. He returned to his cabin and stretched out on the window seat so that he could be near her in the event that she awoke and needed something or called out for him.

For a solid day Elizabeth slept. James would check on her to make sure that she was well, but like the Sleeping Beauty of the story, Elizabeth slept on. James busied himself with his charts to determine how far the storm had taken the Alliance from their course; but his attention kept returning to Elizabeth in the center of the large bed. If she didn't wake soon he thought he would send for Dr. Wilkinson to check on her again.

Shortly thereafter, he heard a movement in the bed and looked across at Elizabeth who was smiling at him. James bounded to her side and sat on the chair beside the bed. "How did I get into your bed, James?" Elizabeth asked smiling.

"I carried you to this bed, Miss Majors after you defied my orders to stay below until the storm was over," James said mockingly.

"Don't be cross, James. I thought the storm was over and was coming on deck to return to my cabin. When I saw the giant wave come across the deck and saw you fall, I was so terrified that I think I fainted."

"Why would you be afraid for me and not afraid for yourself?" James asked tenderly.

"Because I would not want anything to happen to you James, not ever," Elizabeth answered.

"And why would that be, Elizabeth?" James continued.

"Don't make me say it, James; you are supposed to say it first," Elizabeth replied.

"And what would that be exactly, Elizabeth; that I love you Elizabeth Majors? In spite of myself, I love you!"

"That is exactly it, James; I love you, James. I couldn't think it possible to love someone after knowing them for such a short time, but I love you James!" Elizabeth exclaimed.

James thought his heart would burst at that moment. Everything that they had been through over the past two days paled at that moment and only Elizabeth and he remained in the world. He gently lifted her into his arms and kissed her tenderly. “I am going to go get the doctor to check on you and will be right back. Don’t go to asleep again, Sleeping Beauty. I have many things to say to you on my return.”

Mr. Jones was summoned to return with the doctor and Elizabeth sat up in the bed. “How did I get into this night shirt?” Elizabeth asked.

James smiled his wicked mocking smile and replied “How do you think you got into that night shirt?”

“I would hope Dr. Wilkinson, as he was with me when I fainted,” Elizabeth replied.

“You would be correct, Mistress Majors; but only because I was overruled at the time,” James said laughing.

At that moment Mr. Jones returned with Dr. Wilkinson. James and Mr. Jones stepped out while Dr. Wilkinson examined Elizabeth. James ordered a meal for them both from Mr. Jones and asked him to gather some of Elizabeth’s things so that she could change into her own clothes as soon as the doctor had concluded that she was well enough.

Dr. Wilkinson came out of the cabin and smiled at James. “Our patient is doing very well indeed. I think she needs some food and additional rest and will be doing just fine.” James thanked the doctor and went along the passage to his cabin.

“I have ordered us some food and wondered if you would like to change into your own things before we have dinner? Mr. Jones is gathering some things for you as we speak. You are not to over tire yourself, Miss Majors and that is another order!” James said laughing.

“Aye, aye Captain; I will make myself ship shape and Bristol fashion while you are away!” Elizabeth replied.

James was so pleased to hear her laughter again that he ignored the obvious taunt. She must be feeling better indeed, James thought as he went along the corridor. He was in need of a good bath and a shave before he scared Elizabeth to death with his whiskers.

When James returned an hour later to his cabin, Elizabeth was dressed and her hair was demurely platted to one side. James first thought upon seeing her was his usual mantra; self control, James; self control. Elizabeth lifted her arms to him and James hurried to her side, sweeping her to his arms and to the table. His mantra was soon forgotten as he kissed Elizabeth first gently then deeply and fully as she responded to his embrace. When her lips parted and his kiss became more passionate, the control, self control mantra slowly melted away.

Mr. Jones took this moment to knock with their dinner. James quickly returned Elizabeth in her customary seat and shouted *come* as the steward arrived with their dinner.

"The dinner will not be up to our usual standards as Cook is still recovering the galley from the storm. This is good nourishing soup, however; and will soon put some roses back in your cheeks."

"Thank you, Mr. Jones," Elizabeth said shyly.

"Thank you, Jones; that will be all," James replied drolly.

Jones closed the cabin door and James looked at Elizabeth laughing. "You know you have the entire crew under your spell. They are all in love with you, but I can hardly blame them."

Elizabeth smiled at James. "There is only one person that I love on this ship and you have no competition and no equal." James squeezed her hand and filled her glass with wine.

"Be careful, my beauty; I may be plying you with wine in order to have my way with you," James said mockingly.

"You are a complete gentleman, James. I know that I am safe with you," Elizabeth replied.

Such an innocent, James thought. Self control James; self control, he reminded himself.

When the dinner had been cleared and James sat with his brandy he set a box in front of Elizabeth. The box contained his mother's engagement ring; a single sapphire framed by a diamond on each side. The ring was part of a set purchased by his father as a wedding gift for his mother. James intended to give one piece of the set to Elizabeth each day until their wedding so that she could wear the entire set on her wedding day.

Elizabeth slowly opened the box and saw the exquisite ring inside. She gently began to cry at the gesture and the beauty of the ring.

"It was my mother's ring. She would have been very pleased to see you have it," James stated. James was on his knees before her and placed the ring on her ring finger.

"James, I am so happy. I love you so much and only want to make you as happy as you have made me," Elizabeth replied smiling through her tears.

James embraced Elizabeth and gently lifted her from her chair and placed her in the center of the large bed. "You must sleep now, Elizabeth. We will talk more in the morning."

"James, let me watch over you tonight as you have watched over us all."

"Elizabeth, were I a dead man, I could not stay in this room with you and retain my self control."

Elizabeth laughed at that comment. "I love you, James O'Rourke."

"I love you, Elizabeth Majors. Now go to sleep before I change my mind!"

James closed the cabin door and went to sleep in Elizabeth's cabin. The usual telltale smell of roses was now comforting, as it would always remind him of Elizabeth. How many days until London was his final thought as he drifted to sleep.

The next morning, James dressed hurriedly and went above decks to survey the repairs underway from the aftermath of the storm. With a swift wind behind them, the Alliance was making good time despite one of the missing masts lost in the storm. Repairs would be needed when they reached Dublin, but in full sail, they were moving swiftly.

Mr. Pearson smiled as he saw James approach. “We are making good time, Captain despite the storm. If this wind continues, we should make London in five days. When Miss Elizabeth regains her strength, the crew would like to hold a Thanksgiving feast. They know it will be more subdued then usual with Miss Elizabeth aboard; but they wish to thank you and Miss Elizabeth for her kindness to the crew.” James was very moved by the gesture and assured Samuel that he would pass along the crew’s plans to Elizabeth.

James went below to check the surgery and to check on any crew members that may require further care by the doctor. Dr. Wilkinson concurred with Samuel Pearson’s plans on the part of the crew. “The crew is very grateful to Miss Elizabeth for her kindness. As always, Captain; your skill has brought us through another deadly storm and the crew wishes to thank you for your efforts as well.”

When James had completed his check of the crew and repairs, he went below to tell Elizabeth the news. He knocked on his cabin door and found her at his desk updating her diary. “Samuel and the doctor have just told me that the crew would like to have a feast of Thanksgiving for surviving the storm. It seems that they also would like to express their appreciation to you and your kindness during the storm.”

“James I only did what anyone would have done in the same circumstances. I can’t stand by and not help when others are in need, particularly when your hands were full in keeping us safe. I was only too happy to help anyone in need,” Elizabeth replied.

“Beauty, bravery and humility; you have all of the attributes that anyone could admire. I am a very lucky man and can share you only because I am so very proud of you and your thoughtfulness. I will let Samuel know that you will be happy to participate. It will be a good time for us to make our announcement to the crew as well. I know they will want to share their good wishes with you. Promise me you will not overdo today. You will be a bride in just a few days, Miss Majors!"

"Are we to get married in London then, James?" Elizabeth stated surprised by his announcement.

"Absolutely; you don't think I would give you time to change your mind do you?" James answered mockingly.

"There is no fear of that, my darling. I will be so honored to become your wife," Elizabeth replied.

"I will collect you at 6:00 p.m. sharp for the Thanksgiving feast," James responded.

"I will be ready, Captain!" Elizabeth responded.

James informed Cook that he was supportive of the idea of a Thanksgiving feast and all made plans for the evening's festivities. The crew joined into the spirit by bringing tables and benches to the decks so that the crew could be assembled together. James knocked for Elizabeth promptly at 6:00 p.m. as he had promised. She wore a blue dress to match her new engagement ring. James was struck as always at how casually she took on any challenge and how lovely she looked. How lucky he was to have won the hand of the fair Elizabeth. He would do whatever was needed to keep her safe and to make her happy for the rest of his life.

The crew was assembled on deck with tables spread for all and benches at each. James took Elizabeth to the place of honor to accept the thanks of the crew. Mr. Pearson stepped forward and expressed his thanks on behalf of the entire crew. "Captain, on behalf of the crew and myself, I am expressing our thanks for your skill in bringing this ship and our crew through the latest storm." The crew shouted hearty cheers to Captain O'Rourke. Mr. Pearson then continued on. "Also on behalf of the crew, we wish to thank Miss Elizabeth for her help to Dr. Wilkinson and her kindness to all and sundry." The crew shouted a second round of cheers.

James thanked all assembled and let the crew in on his news. "Miss Majors and I are engaged to be married. She has agreed to be my wife." The crew launched into another round of cheers. Dr. Wilkinson stepped forward then to lead the assembled in prayer before the meal began.

"I will read from Psalm 107," Dr. Wilkinson stated.

"Those who go down to the sea in ships, Who do business on great waters, They see the works of the Lord, And His wonders in the deep, For he commands and raises the stormy wind, Which lifts up the waves of the sea. They mount up to the heavens, They go down again to the depths; Their soul melts because of trouble. They reel to and fro, and stagger like a drunken man, And are at their wits' end. Then they cry out to the Lord in their trouble, And he brings them out of their distresses. He calms the storm, So that its waves are still. He guides them to their desired haven. Oh, that men would give thanks to the Lord for His goodness."

Elizabeth had heard that passage many times through the years, having grown up in a city by the sea; but never had the words had greater meaning than at this moment. She thought about James' skill and that God was with him through each moment and with all mariners as they go down to the sea in ships. The tears were in her eyes as she smiled at James at the conclusion of Dr. Wilkinson's prayer.

All assembled settled into a festive meal with fiddle music to follow. James walked to the rail with Elizabeth holding her hand in the moonlight. "In just a few short days, you will make me the happiest man on earth Elizabeth."

"It is so hard for me to remember that only a few short weeks ago I was alone in the world," Elizabeth responded. "Today I feel a part of a family here and a world that we will make together."

"You are important to all here and to those that you haven't yet met that comprise the larger world of the O'Rourke fleet. You will be a part of that larger family as well. Someday, God willing, we will start our own family and you will be the center of that family also. Let's leave them to their revels, Elizabeth. There are things that I would say to you alone," James said earnestly.

James and Elizabeth went below to spend time together as had become their custom before turning in. Waiting on James' chart table was another box which matched the one from the night before. James handed the box to Elizabeth and stood at the bulkhead waiting for her to open the box. "This box is like the one from last night," Elizabeth said. She opened the box to find a pair of sapphire earrings that matched Elizabeth's engagement ring.

They were the second piece of the wedding set given by James' father to his mother. "They are beautiful, James. Thank you so much," Elizabeth said smiling.

"Put them on Elizabeth; I want to see you with them on." Elizabeth put on the earrings and moved to the bulkhead window seat. "You will make a beautiful bride, Elizabeth," James replied smiling.

"James, I am so happy and want to do everything possible to make you happy as well," Elizabeth responded.

James pulled Elizabeth down to the window seat beside him. "I think we are both very lucky and can spend the rest of our lives thanking God for our good fortune in finding one another." James kissed Elizabeth then and held her as if he never wanted to let her go.

*****

The next few days passed in the type of peace that James and Elizabeth both craved. They both sought the joy that their impending wedding would bring and the happiness of returning to Ireland to begin their new life together. Each evening they spent time together and James presented another piece of the wedding jewelry parure purchased by James' father for his mother. The fact that both Elizabeth and

James' mother shared the same September birthday month was just one more bond between them. Although James had not yet shared his concerns about Cross and Whitfield to Elizabeth, he was placing his plan in action to secure Elizabeth's safety once they arrived in London. While Elizabeth rested and updated her travel diary, James met with Samuel to discuss their security plan once they reached the capital.

"On our arrival in London, I will make the necessary plans for our wedding day and will meet with my friend Inspector Flynn of Scotland Yard. If there is any truth to my suspicion about Cross and Whitfield, Flynn will know. I would like you to select your four best men; two to ride with you and Elizabeth in the carriage and two more to ride in a chase carriage. I don't trust Cross nor Whitfield and I will not let either of them harm Elizabeth in any way," James stated firmly.

"Aye, Captain; you know how this crew feel about you and about Miss Elizabeth. We will have double guards on the trip to Cross' office and double guards on the ship for each watch as long as we are in London."

"It is my belief that we can protect Elizabeth easier on board the Alliance then in a London hotel. We will know precisely who is coming for us if they try to board the Alliance and we will be ready for them. I want this matter resolved as quickly as possible. Elizabeth has been through so much in her young life. I don't want her to worry or to suffer any longer for any reason," James replied.

"Aye, Captain; we will keep her safe," Samuel assured James.

"There is another more personal favor that I have for you. I would like you and Mrs. Pearson to stand for Elizabeth and me at our wedding. She will have no female family or friends who can stand for her and no one to walk her down the aisle. I know it may not be the wedding of her dreams, but I would like her to have a special day all the same."

"It will be my honor, Captain and I know that Mrs. Pearson will be happy to assist Miss Elizabeth."

That evening James reviewed the next day's plans with Elizabeth. "Samuel will be taking you to Charles Cross' office in the morning, Elizabeth. I have some business to conduct as soon as we arrive. I will also be making the plans for our wedding, Elizabeth. I can't wait to make you my bride. In just one more day, my darling girl; we will start our new life together."

"James, is there anything that you need me to do in preparation for our wedding?" Elizabeth asked.

"No, I have contacts for the church and have asked Samuel and Mrs. Pearson to stand up for us at the wedding if that is agreeable to you."

"I can't wait for our new life to begin. Tell me about my new home in Ireland," Elizabeth replied her eyes shining.

James went to the wall and took down a print of Broadlands his family home. "You will love Broadlands, Elizabeth. It is located on the coast, just like Wilmington but of course, much cooler. We will look for some winter clothes for you in London while we are visiting. Of course, we may need to look for a larger size since you will probably have a baby on the way by winter," James said with a wink.

"James, do you really think so?" Elizabeth asked blushing.

"Well I certainly hope so and I will do everything in my power to assure that we start our family sooner rather than later," James said laughing.

James had led Elizabeth to their favorite window seat at the bulkhead. "In one night's time, I will show you the depth of my love for you. I want you to understand that there is no higher expression of love between a man and a woman then the love we will express as man and wife. I don't want you to be embarrassed in anyway. If you have questions or don't understand something, always be open to ask me anything and keep in mind that we will keep no secrets from each other," James stated tenderly.

James pulled Elizabeth to him then and gently kissed her forehead, eyes and mouth. He reached up and took the pins from Elizabeth's hair until it fell about her shoulders. "My beautiful mermaid," James said huskily.

"James," Elizabeth said smiling, "aren't mermaids usually portrayed as well, undressed?"

"So they are, darling girl; so they are." James laughed then a full and happy laugh and pulled Elizabeth into his side. One more night and I can show you the true depth of my feelings, James thought with a sigh.

CHAPTER SEVEN

The day of their wedding arrived bright and cool with the first hint of autumn in the air. As Elizabeth moved about the cabin, Mr. Jones the steward knocked with water for bathing and a note from James.

My darling girl,

Happy Wedding Day. I will send word about the time of our wedding to Samuel. He has sent a note to Charles Cross asking for a meeting for you regarding your father's estate. All is in hand. I will send word to Samuel so that you will know when to meet me in church. Until later my love, I am your James.
6:00 a.m. 10/1/1865

Elizabeth read and reread the note as she prepared for the day. James had taken care of everything and when she returned to the Alliance later in the day, she would be a married lady.

A second note arrived via Samuel Pearson and was also brought to her by Mr. Jones.

My darling girl,

I have made arrangements at Chelsea Old Church – All Saints which is just a short ride from our current location. The wedding will be held at 5:00 p.m. this afternoon. Samuel knows the church and will deliver you there. Mrs. Pearson will be there to help you dress. I will have a trousseau ready for you. Don't forget to bring the jewelry set.

Love, James.

Trousseau, Elizabeth thought; he has thought of everything.

The third note of the morning came from Mr. Pearson regarding her appointment with Mr. Cross. They were to meet Mr. Cross at 10:00 at his offices. Samuel would come to collect her at 9:00. She checked the clock and knew she had only a short time to prepare for her first meeting.

Samuel knocked at 9:00 and off they went to the meeting with Charles Cross. She had travelled from Wilmington to Bermuda to London for just this meeting. Elizabeth asked Samuel if they would return to the Alliance before the wedding. "Aye, Miss Elizabeth; you will have time for luncheon and a brief rest before the wedding." Off they went with the planned escort of crew members which Elizabeth had not seen, in tow.

James had started his day as per his note at 6:00 a.m. The ship had landed at 5:00 a.m. and preparations had begun for the day. His first visit was to the church of his uncle to make arrangements for today's wedding. He knew that his Uncle Father Colin O'Rourke would smooth over any difficulties to see his favorite nephew married. Colin was so shocked by the news that he called in all of the church staff to begin preparations immediately. "If only your mother and father could be here to see this blessed day, James. I know they will be here in spirit. I cannot wait to meet the girl who finally brought you to marriage. She must be quite the lady indeed."

"You wait until you meet her Uncle Colin. I knew as soon as I met her that I had met my match and Samuel will tell you the same," James replied smiling.

"You run along and take care of all of your other errands. We will have the church and wedding feast taken care of here," Father O'Rourke proclaimed.

Once arranged, James next stop was to obtain a special license for purposes of the service and to find a wedding outfit for Elizabeth and trousseau for the wedding night. He knew this was a bit unconventional, but he had certainly studied her form enough over the past weeks to judge her size and he could not take the risk of Elizabeth riding unescorted around London attempting to find her wedding finery. To arrange Samuel as her escort with the four crew member bodyguard detail was difficult enough without arousing suspicion on Elizabeth's part; much less arranging a day of shopping as well.

His last visit would be to Scotland Yard and his friend Inspector Flynn. He intended to get to the bottom of the Charles Cross and Benjamin Whitfield connection. He was certain that his instincts were correct and until he was convinced otherwise, he would protect Elizabeth with all of the tools at his disposal until he could get her home safely to Broadlands. Winter shopping could always be done at home in Ireland if the danger to Elizabeth was as real as he suspected.

The wedding plans were completed, the special license secured and the feast arranged. Elizabeth's trousseau had been selected and sent onto Chelsea Old Church for her preparations this afternoon. The only task remaining was his visit to Inspector Flynn. He had left this to last as he knew it would occupy a good deal of time and he did not relish this intrusion on what should be the happiest day of his life. However his promise to protect Elizabeth at all costs was the driving force behind this visit.

He had known Inspector Flynn since they had both attended boarding school together. He knew that he could both trust him with the information that he was to share and with the responsibility of keeping Elizabeth safe. When he arrived at Scotland Yard, he was immediately taken into Inspector Flynn's office. "So to what do I owe the pleasure James O'Rourke? It must take some amazing story to bring you here!"

"Well Hugh, you are right about that. I am to be married today at Chelsea Old Church and I would love for you to come if you can find the time. The wedding will be at 5:00 this afternoon," James replied.

"I will be there old friend, if only to meet the woman who made you change your mind. There must be a thousand hearts across the world grieving the loss today!" Hugh replied laughing.

"When you meet her you will understand. She is from America and a real corker as father would have said. She was one of my passengers from Wilmington and one thing led to another and well here we are, ready to be wed."

"So except for a wedding invitation for today, to what do I owe the pleasure of this visit?" Hugh asked.

"My bride to be came to London to settle her father's estate. You know I don't care about the money as I have plenty of my own. What I do care about are some shady characters involved with her father's estate. Have you ever heard of a Benjamin Whitfield or Charles Cross?" James asked.

"Have I heard of them?" Hugh replied. "They are the subject of several pending investigations and two potential murders. Nothing has been connected directly to them, but we know that they are involved. Both of the parties murdered had estates that were to be settled by Charles Cross' father Hilary. He was reputed to be an upstanding gentleman, but the same cannot be said of the son. It appears that Charles Cross may be mixing some embezzlement with the settlement of estates. Benjamin Whitfield is probably the one who orders the dirty work as I do not expect that Charles Cross would get his hands dirty."

"Benjamin Whitfield was a passenger from Wilmington to Bermuda also. At first I thought he was just trying to pay court to Elizabeth, which I was having none of, but as we arrived in Bermuda; I began to suspect that his motives were not just romantic in nature. He began to show up at locations in which Elizabeth and I were to be found and there were teams of professional thugs that began to follow us when we were about in Bermuda. I even took the precaution of leaving a day early in Bermuda to make sure that we got away from a bad situation. I suspected that there might be a connection between Whitfield and Cross knowing that Elizabeth would be travelling alone to resolve her father's estate. I knew that my instincts were correct, but I had no idea how right they were. Our wedding today is no mere fancy. I want to be able to protect her as best as I can and know that I can do so on board ship much better than in a local hotel. She is meeting with Cross as we speak, but has Samuel and four crew members acting as bodyguards along for the ride. After today, she will never meet again with Cross without me present," James stated heatedly.

"I can place a detail of men around Cross' office and we can tail Whitfield and Cross and any connections that may take place. I agree that you can protect Elizabeth better on board the ship as you will know if anyone tries to board. I am sure that your plan to leave early in Bermuda was a good one. Did you suffer any delay in arriving in London?"

"We hit a major storm outside Bermuda which delayed our arrival. I don't know if Whitfield would have followed directly after our departure or if he had been delayed by the storm as well. Regardless, I wanted to put this matter in your hands so that we could plan for her protection and get her out of London as quickly as possible," James replied.

"Do not fear, old friend. You get back to your wedding planning this afternoon. I will take care of extra security and we will see if we can catch Cross and Whitfield in the course of behavior that will put them away for good," Hugh stated.

James left Flynn's office more convinced than ever of the effectiveness of his planning, but more worried than ever about Elizabeth's safety. He would get a note back to Samuel to have a triple guard on Elizabeth as they proceeded to the church this afternoon and a triple guard on board the ship tonight just in case Whitfield and his goons showed up. His only concern now was for happiness for the rest of the day and to get Elizabeth as far away from London as he could, as quickly as he could without causing too much distress to her.

While James completed his tasks for the day, Elizabeth set off with Samuel for Charles Cross' office. Elizabeth was so pleased that she could see Mr. Cross today, their first day in London and happy that the purpose of her trip could be addressed so quickly. She hoped that the business end of the day would not take too much time so that she could focus on the happy end of the day; her wedding to James and the beginning of their new life together.

Samuel had made sure that the guard of crew members that accompanied the carriage was not seen when they departed the Alliance and that the follow-up crew took their place directly behind the carriage. They were to serve as look out on the outside of the building while Samuel, Elizabeth and the other two crew members were on the inside. All had been given strict instructions to not be obvious to Elizabeth.

They arrived at Charles Cross' office at 10 minutes until 10:00. Samuel paid the coachmen and they went inside for the interview. Upon arriving at the offices of Hilary and Charles Cross, Samuel waited in the outer waiting room while Elizabeth met with Mr. Cross. The two crew members assigned to the inside of the building waited in the outside hallway of the offices. All tried their best to serve as lookout without being too obvious to those coming and going. The clerk showed Elizabeth into Charles Cross' inner office upon arrival.

"Miss Majors, what a pleasure to meet you at last in person," Charles Cross stated. He was turning on the charm for Elizabeth. He had not expected such a lovely lady and thought it would do no harm to be as gallant as possible to her.

"Thank you so much for seeing me on such short notice, Mr. Cross. As you know, my father had worked with your father in the past and I believe there should be a file with all of his directives as well as correspondences that I have sent prior to my visit from Wilmington," Elizabeth stated.

"There is indeed a file and I have been going through it since I received your first letter from Wilmington. My goodness; I did not expect that you would come all of this way and on your own but only that we should conduct our business via the mails. I certainly am glad to welcome you to London, however; and hope that we can do all that is possible to complete our transactions within two to three months. The course of probate of course does not run quickly, but we will do all in our power to move the wheels of justice along," Cross replied.

"I had hoped that the correspondence that I had sent at the time of my father's death would be sufficient to complete our work. I have sent you a copy of my father's death certificate and the probate work from New Hanover County in North Carolina. I know that the course of war delayed many things, but the process ran quite smoothly on our side of the Atlantic. What do we need to do to assure that my father's estate can be closed here in London?" Elizabeth inquired.

"Miss Majors, I certainly would not want you to worry your pretty head over such matters. All is in hand and we will certainly see what we can do to assist in the process. Would it be helpful for you to receive a small draft on your father's account to pay for your expenses while you are here in London? I am sure there are many sites that you would wish to visit while you are here. If you will let me take the liberty, I can arrange tours of historic sites of interest that will keep you occupied while this process works its way through the courts. I am sure that you will enjoy the shopping here in London also. I can arrange for shopping at some of our finest establishments while you are visiting and we can schedule a monthly meeting to confirm the success of our venture. How does that sound to you?" Cross asked.

Elizabeth was doing her best to not become angry at Cross' patronizing manner. "I appreciate the offer, Mr.

Cross; but would like to expedite this process so that I may settle my father's final directives. Can you give me a schedule of when and how that can be expected?"

"I will be happy to do so, Miss Majors. Why don't we plan on meeting again on Monday and I will have that schedule prepared for you and also a draft from your father's bank that will finance your little shopping excursions. If you will excuse me, I do have another client who will be coming in and I must be off to court on another matter. It has been so lovely to meet you in person and I trust we will meet again on Monday with more news of your affairs."

"Until Monday then, Mr. Cross. Shall we say 10:00 again?"

"That will be fine, Miss Majors. Thank you again for coming all of this way to resolve these matters." Charles Cross then saw Elizabeth out to the outer waiting room and returned to his office.

Unseen by Elizabeth and Samuel, Benjamin Whitfield had entered an adjoining office while Elizabeth had met with Charles Cross. He was seen by the lookout crew downstairs and by the upstairs crew as well. They did not believe that he had recognized them, however and had this information to report to Mr. Pearson when they returned to the Alliance. They had also spied a gang of rough looking men who had gathered on the opposite side of the street from the Cross offices. They were anxious to see if the carriage carrying Mr. Pearson and Elizabeth would be followed once the meeting had concluded.

When Elizabeth and Samuel entered the carriage downstairs, he hastened to ask Elizabeth how the meeting had gone. "The man was impossible, Mr. Pearson. All he wanted to talk about was my shopping while here in London. If I didn't know better, I would swear that he had no interest in resolving my father's estate and was just talking gibberish to get me out of the office. I am more determined than ever to not be put off. I did not come all of this way to sightsee and shop, although it would be pleasant to do so with James should our schedule permit. Do you think that Mr. Cross will take me more seriously if James were to accompany me to my next meeting? Mr. Cross has made an appointment for me for this coming Monday at 10:00."

"I think it would be well for you to fill in the Captain on all that took place. He will know what to do next, Miss. Our Captain has a head for business and will know what's what in this matter, don't you worry," Samuel Pearson replied.

"Thank you so much for coming with me today, Mr. Pearson. There is so much to take in about London and all of these business matters. It has been a great comfort to have you with me today. Thank you also for agreeing to stand up for James and me along with your wife this afternoon. I am so anxious to meet her," Elizabeth stated.

"It is our pleasure, Miss Elizabeth and our honor. I have known the Captain all of his life and his father before him. I have never known a better man in my life. I am just glad that he has found someone to share his life with. I told him he had met his match with you and so he has. We will get you back to the ship so that you can take a short rest before we get you to the church to get ready. This will be a long day indeed but a happy one. Don't you let that Mr. Cross bother you in any way! The Captain will soon sort out that matter and you will be off on your honeymoon. The autumn is beautiful at Broadlands and you have the holidays to look forward to. Much happiness is in store for you Miss Elizabeth and no two people have deserved it more in my opinion," Samuel stated smiling.

"Thank you again, Mr. Pearson. It is so exciting isn't it? To think that I will be married to James before the end of the day; it is like a dream come true," Elizabeth replied.

As they arrived back at the Alliance, Samuel gave the sign to the two crew members standing guard to stay out of the way until Elizabeth had gone back on board and was safely below decks. They would then convene in his cabin and go over what they had seen and heard.

Elizabeth went on board ship and to James' cabin so that she could freshen up before the wedding. Samuel would come for her at 3:00 p.m. so that they could get to the church and give her plenty of time to get ready for the wedding.

Once Elizabeth had gone below decks, the crew members met in Samuel's cabin as per their pre-arrangement. "We saw that Whitfield character coming into an office right next to Cross," said Timmons, one of the bodyguard detail. "We saw two toughs across the street from Cross' office while you and Miss Elizabeth were inside. They grabbed a passing coach and followed you to the Alliance. They know where she is for sure and wouldn't have followed unless there was foul play afoot. I don't like it, Mr. Pearson. None of us like it and we have agreed to stand guard today at the wedding and this evening. We don't want anything to upset Miss Elizabeth on her wedding day." All of the bodyguard detail nodded approval.

"You did well, lads. The Captain will be pleased to see that his plan worked, although I am sure he would rather that we didn't have to plan at all. Whitfield and Cross are up to something that is for sure. Miss Elizabeth is not to know. The Captain will sort it out when he hears about it in the morning. For now, all we need to do is keep Miss Elizabeth safe until the wedding. The Captain will take care of all thereafter."

In her cabin, Elizabeth was trying to eat a light lunch and take a short rest before the big excitement began. She had laid out her hankie and would take the sapphire jewelry parure as James had asked her to do. She knew that she needed to rest, but was finding it hard for sleep to come. She had asked Mr. Jones to wake her in plenty of time so that she would be ready for Mr. Pearson's knock at 3:00. She had certainly learned the value of promptness with so many nautical men in her life! Samuel had told her that James would also dress at the church so that she would see him only when she was coming down the aisle. It was all like a dream but all coming true!

At 3:00, Samuel Pearson, prompt as ever, knocked on Elizabeth's cabin. She opened the door ready to proceed to the church. Samuel thought she looked like a beautiful bride already and she was not even in her wedding finery. "Are you ready, Miss Elizabeth?"

"I am indeed, Mr. Pearson; it will not be long now."

The carriage was waiting at the dockside. The Chelsea Old Church was right up the road from their berth. They could have walked in the best of times, but given the Captain's orders, a carriage ride would be the only form of transportation for Miss Elizabeth.

When they arrived at the church, Mr. Pearson took Elizabeth to the bride's chambers so that they could prepare for the wedding without James seeing her until the wedding itself. Mrs. Pearson was waiting to take over the honors. Mr. Pearson introduced Elizabeth to his wife and then took off for the groom's chambers to find James and brief him on the day's events.

"Why Captain O'Rourke has thought of everything, Miss Elizabeth. Here is a dress that he has picked out for you, a veil and even flowers. You have worked a miracle on our Captain O'Rourke. He was always the kindest of men, but we never thought he would settle down; not until he met you. Here I am prattling on because I am that excited to see you and he wed. What a great day for the Captain and for all that know him!" Mrs. Pearson stated.

"Thank you so much for agreeing to stand up for me, Mrs. Pearson. I do not know anyone in London except for the Alliance family and I certainly think of them as such. Everyone has been so kind to me while I have been with them. It is an experience that I will never forget," Elizabeth replied with shining eyes.

"Once you are dressed, Father O'Rourke wants to come in and get to know you also. It is just grand that a member of the family will be marrying you both. The wedding feast will be in the church hall also so you don't have a thing to worry about, just enjoy the day," Mrs. Pearson replied.

While Elizabeth was dressing, Samuel briefed James on the meeting of the day. "You were right, Captain. I know your instincts from old and you were right about everything. Charles Cross gave Miss Elizabeth the run around and she was none too happy about it. All he wanted to talk to her about was site seeing and shopping when she had come all of this way to get matters sorted out. While we were inside the offices, our lads saw Whitfield come into the building. His office was right next to Charles Cross so there is something up between the two of them. Two toughs were seen by our outside crew across the street from Cross' office. When Miss Elizabeth and I got into the carriage, they caught the next one and followed up to the Alliance's berth. They know where she is, so something must be planned. I have tripled the guard like you asked and men will be here at the church as well. We will keep her safe alright."

"Thank you, Samuel. You have done well as always. I have met with my friend Inspector Flynn of Scotland Yard and he tells me that Whitfield and Cross have several outstanding investigations going on related to mysterious deaths of clients that can never be traced to them, but for which they have amassed small fortunes as the clients who died were without kin. That sounds exactly like Elizabeth's situation. Since they never expected her to cross the Atlantic to resolve her father's estate, she is in even more danger. Luckily they think that she is here on her own and defenseless. We will stay one step ahead of them until I can get her out of here and home to Ireland. I will let Inspector Flynn sort out the rest of the matter. All I care about is her safety," James replied fiercely.

While they met in the groom's chamber, Father O'Rourke knocked on the door of the bride's chamber. "Come in

Father," Mrs. Pearson called out. "Our bride is decent but not yet ready for her groom."

"I had to take the opportunity to meet the young woman who conquered our James. We never thought we would live to see the day, but we are very glad that it has arrived. How are you my dear?" Father O'Rourke inquired.

"Thank you Father for taking your time to make my wedding day such a happy event," Elizabeth replied. "I can't believe how much work you have all done in such a short time!" said Elizabeth.

"Not a bit of it; that is what families do. To see James happily married has been the dream of all of us; but we did not believe we would ever see it. Here we are and we are happy to help. Is there anything that you need to ask me before we begin?"

"I don't believe so, Father. Thank you again for all of your wonderful assistance and for agreeing to marry us on such short notice," Elizabeth replied.

"I will see you in the sanctuary then, Elizabeth. Lovely to meet you and you will make a beautiful bride," Father O'Rourke stated.

After Father O'Rourke left, Mrs. Pearson put the finishing touches on Elizabeth's wedding finery with the music in the sanctuary just beginning to start. "Are you nervous at all, Miss Elizabeth?" Mrs. Pearson asked.

"I think I am more excited than anything else," Elizabeth replied.

"Just remember how much the Captain loves you and everything will be fine," Mrs. Pearson responded.

At that moment, Samuel Pearson knocked on the door to bring the bride to the front of the church through the side garden. The wedding would begin promptly at 5:00 pm as all things in the Captain's world were promptly done. He smiled first at Elizabeth and then over her head to his wife. "Sure if she isn't as beautiful a bride as you were, my dear," Samuel stated.

"Oh, Samuel Pearson; I appreciate the compliment, but no one could hold a candle to Miss Elizabeth. She is as pretty as a picture! Why she looks like a china doll!" Mrs. Pearson replied.

Elizabeth took one last glance in the mirror before leaving the bride's chamber. The dress fit her as though it had been made for her. The neckline was sweetheart in detail, just like the turquoise dress that she so loved. The sapphire jewelry set was her something blue for the day. She had the sapphire engagement ring, earrings, necklace, bracelet and the tiara which held the beautiful shear veil that James had selected for her. Down the back of the gown, tiny pearl buttons went the entire length of her dress. Tiny seed pearls dressed the front of the gown with tiny white slippers also encrusted with seed pearls to complete the dress. She carried a bouquet of red roses and there was yet another note from James along with the flowers.

In the symbolism of love, red roses are used to say I love you and are also the symbol of unconditional love. They also stand for courage and respect. Red roses are used to express deep feelings of love to a very special person. These roses stand for all of that and more, Elizabeth. I love you and can't wait for you to be my wife.

James

The final note of the day touched her more than any of the prior ones. When she read that note, she started to cry. Mrs. Pearson watching her said, "You mustn't cry and go down the aisle with a red nose, Miss Elizabeth! Like I told you he is the best man I know and you are both wished much happiness by us all."

"Ready, Miss Elizabeth?" Mr. Pearson asked.

"Ready, Mr. Pearson," Elizabeth answered.

Mr. Pearson brought Elizabeth to the front of the church through the side garden. In that way she would not be seen by any of the other guests or by James before her walk down the aisle. The doors were closed when they arrived at the front entrance to again sustain the mystery. As the strains of Trumpet Voluntary were heard, the doors were opened by members of the crew. They all were finely dressed and clean shaven for the event. In deference to the fact that Elizabeth had no family or friends in London, members of the crew had located on both sides of the aisle so that Elizabeth would feel that the entire crew was part of her family. Just as she had felt when reading the red rose note from James, Elizabeth could feel the tears welling behind her eyes. Just keep calm and carry on, she told herself. Don't go down the aisle with a red nose, she thought!

At the end of the aisle waiting for her and Mr. Pearson was James and Father O'Rourke. How fitting that she was to be married by the groom's uncle? It was truly a family affair. As she looked at James at the end of the aisle, all she could think was how handsome he looked in his morning suit and how much she loved him. As they reached the rail, Father O'Rourke asked all to sit and began the service. Samuel Pearson answered when Father asked who gives this woman in marriage. Elizabeth thought then of her own father who should have been here today and thanked James again for thinking of everything that would give her comfort on this special day. She held tightly to James' hand as Samuel moved her hand from his own to James' waiting hand.

The solemn vows had such special meaning when one was hearing them with the love of your life beside you. Elizabeth had attended so many weddings, especially during the war when young couples wished to seal their love prior to the groom's departure to war and though those words had always touched her heart, never more so than when she was saying them to James.

At the conclusion of the vows, Father O'Rourke stated with joy that James could kiss his bride. He lifted her veil and kissed her gently on the lips. Their smiles said it all. For that moment, they were alone in the church and no one else was present for either of them.

The happy couple departed down the aisle and used the same side garden to arrive at the church hall for the wedding feast. Once there, Elizabeth saw the lovely arrangements and the head table where she and James would sit. All she could think of at that moment was being alone with James and thanking him for the beautiful service and all that he had done to make their day a special one.

"Are you happy, darling girl?" James asked as they sat down at the head table.

"I am so very happy, James. I can't wait to be alone with you so that I can thank you properly for all that you have done to make this beautiful day for me," Elizabeth replied.

"We have plenty of time for that, Elizabeth. I can't wait to be alone with you also. But for now, we can enjoy the wedding feast and the dancing and all of the happiness of the day. I love you, Elizabeth O'Rourke!" James responded smiling.

At that moment, Father O'Rourke came to the head table and gave the blessing for all assembled before the beginning of the feast. He blessed the young couple with long lives, much happiness and many children. All assembled laughed at the last item and James smiled warmly to the blushing Elizabeth.

The wedding feast was a hearty one and all enjoyed the delicious food and company of friends and family. Samuel Pearson rose to speak at the end of the meal. "Captain and Mrs. O'Rourke; it has been my honor to participate in this wedding in a number of roles. No man has ever known a better Captain and speaking for us all, we are proud that our Captain has found a lady who is worthy of him. I ask that we raise our glasses to the Captain and his lady." All assembled said, "To the Captain and his lady."

The next speech was from Father O'Rourke. "I know that it may not be traditional for the priest to give a speech, but in this case, I am speaking not only as the officiate, but as the uncle of the groom. I have known James all of his life. He has not only been a nephew to me, but more like a son since the passing of his mother and father. I have told him for many years that his true happiness in life would be with a wife and family. Like many young men, he has had to see the world, but unlike many young men; seeing the world brought him back a treasure to last a lifetime. That treasure is our Elizabeth who I welcome to the family as I bless their union today; to James and Elizabeth."

The next speech was from Hugh Flynn. "I have been a friend of James since boarding school days. We have been through many a scrape together, which we will not discuss in front of Elizabeth and Father O'Rourke. It is my great honor to be here today to see James properly settled. I look forward to getting to know Elizabeth in the future and to share with her the many stories of our youth; to James and Elizabeth." James slapped Hugh on the back as he took his seat.

At the conclusion of the speeches, the fiddlers began the music for the evening. James rose and pulled Elizabeth to her feet. They began the first dance which was a waltz. Elizabeth could not help but remember the first time they had danced at the Carlyle Hotel in Bermuda. She had thought then that that night was the happiest night of her life. Little did she know that that night in Bermuda was just the first night that led to this day and all of the happy days that were yet to follow.

Hugh came to their table then and regaled Elizabeth with a tale or two of their happy youth. He told her that he had many more stories, some of which would not be appropriate for a wedding. Elizabeth loved the camaraderie and the true feeling of family in the room. It was something that she had missed for so long. The room felt like coming home, although it was so far from her own home town of Wilmington, North Carolina.

James returned with Elizabeth to the dance floor. As he whirled her across the dance floor, he too was carried back to their first dance at the Carlyle Hotel. His thoughts also returned briefly to the menace that was unknown to Elizabeth on that night and was still unknown to her today. He would make a point of thanking Hugh for his support as well as the Alliance team in assuring Elizabeth's safety.

After several more dances and the cutting of the cake, James motioned to Samuel that he and Elizabeth would be returning to the ship. Samuel nodded to the crew that would continue as the bodyguards for James and Elizabeth. Without her being aware, they continued the drill of protection which they would continue for as long as Elizabeth was in London. Elizabeth went from table to table thanking each member of the crew who had attended and asked them to continue to enjoy themselves for the evening. When she reached Father O'Rourke, she kissed him on the cheek for arranging this beautiful day. He stated that he would see them again prior to their departure for Ireland.

James and Elizabeth went through the side garden to the front of the church. There a carriage was waiting to carry them back to the Alliance for their wedding night. When they returned to the Alliance, James nodded to the triple guard that had been put in place to repel all nature of attacks to the ship. The newly wedded couple returned to James' cabin as man and wife.

As soon as the door was closed behind them, James gathered Elizabeth in his arms for what he called a proper kiss. Elizabeth smiled and warmly returned his kiss. "Let me help you with the veil and with your dress, Elizabeth," James stated. He first gathered the veil from her hair and the sapphire tiara. He handed the veil to Elizabeth so that she could fold it gently. She would wrap it tomorrow in the tissue paper in which it had left the shop. As there were no single women in attendance at the wedding, Elizabeth placed her bouquet in a vase and told James that she would dry the flowers for placement in her diary.

James then began the slow process of unbuttoning the many small pearl buttons that cascaded far beyond the waist of the wedding gown. The pearl buttons were small and he wondered how well he would manage in undoing them. He certainly did not wish to tear the beautiful gown which he knew that Elizabeth would preserve for their future daughter should they be blessed with a daughter. "This may take a while, Elizabeth," James said laughing. "I have never seen so many buttons. I didn't realize the back of the dress when I was choosing the front. I am not sure that I would have selected this one had I known," he said laughing.

"It is so beautiful, James. I can't believe how well you could make out my size when you selected it."

"I was studying your form for several weeks, Mrs. O'Rourke and had a good sense of what would fit you," James said laughing.

"You did an excellent job, Captain O'Rourke. I must compliment you on your shrewd observational skills." Elizabeth was trying to keep the conversation light to cover her growing nerves at the night ahead and the new intimacy between James and herself as he helped her undress.

As James reached the end of the pearl buttons, he motioned to Elizabeth to step out of the gown so that he could help lift the heavy fabric. Elizabeth stood in a skirt of tulle petticoats which had given shape and volume to the beautiful gown. At this juncture, James offered to step out to change in Mr. Pearson's former cabin so that Elizabeth could have some privacy. "On the chair you will find a trousseau gown that I have selected for you for this evening, Elizabeth. I hope that you like it."

Elizabeth had seen the beautiful silk gown and robe on their return to the cabin. She could not believe how kind James had been and how he had thought of everything in advance of this day. She changed out of her petticoats and corset, quickly bathed and placed the silk gown and robe on. She kept on the beautiful pearl slippers as a reminder of her special day.

James took his time in bathing and changing in order to give Elizabeth ample time to change. He did not want to hurry the night and wanted to do everything to make her comfortable and relaxed for what lie ahead. He placed on a nightshirt which was not his usual sleeping attire to make her more comfortable with the intimacy that was to follow. The night shirt he covered with a robe that went to the floor. After a decent interval, James knocked on the cabin door as he had done so many times in the past few weeks.

When he opened the door, his breath held in his chest; before him was his mermaid come to life, as Elizabeth had let down her chestnut hair which rested over her shoulders and back. The silk gown and robe matched her ivory skin and made for a breath taking sight. James walked to her and clasped his hands in the chestnut hair. "You look so beautiful, Elizabeth. Every time that I think you could not be more beautiful, I am proven wrong." James kissed Elizabeth then fully and intensely.

On the table, Mr. Jones had left a bottle of champagne chilling and two glasses. When James released Elizabeth from the embrace, he popped the cork and poured two glasses of champagne. His hope was to relax Elizabeth and take away her nerves at the wedding night to come.

James set down at the familiar window seat with the two champagne glasses and Elizabeth followed and sat down next to him. "To my lovely bride; cheers, my love." Elizabeth drank the offered champagne and felt the warm liquid reach her stomach. James quickly filled the glass a second time as soon as Elizabeth had finished her first glass.

"If I didn't know better, Captain O'Rourke, I would think that you were trying to get me intoxicated!" Elizabeth said laughing.

"Is it working?" James answered laughing as well.

Elizabeth and James laughed at that moment and James took the champagne glass from her hands. He looked her seriously in the eye for a moment and then began to kiss her forehead, eyes and finally her lips. He gathered her hair again in his hands and deepened the kiss as was his custom. At that moment, he pulled Elizabeth to him so that she was resting on his lap. He traced a path with his fingertips down her beautiful white neck and followed those traces with kisses that ended at her breasts. Each time he returned to her mouth and then began traces with his fingertips followed by kisses. After several moments, James lifted Elizabeth in his arms and placed her in the center of the massive bed. If it killed him, he had made up his mind that he would go slowly and would be gentle with the luscious woman in front of him.

James looked at Elizabeth in the center of the huge bed, so innocent, so beautiful. He made a silent prayer that he could keep his vow to take his time and to not unnecessarily frighten or hurt Elizabeth.

He shed his robe beside the bed and sat on the side of the bed next to Elizabeth. Elizabeth lifted her arms to James who came to her without hesitation. He repeated his embrace from before kissing her forehead, her eyes and then her mouth. Each time he kissed her mouth he deepened the kiss more intensely. With his fingers first he traced her neck down to her breasts. With one hand he untied the sash to her robe and with the other cupped her luscious breasts. Elizabeth pulled back then into the bed unsure of the new sensations. James followed and began kissing her again, using the kiss as a means of relaxing Elizabeth to the new sensation to follow. After several moments, Elizabeth's soft moan told him that he could continue. His hands travelled further over her flat stomach and to her most intimate area. James gathered Elizabeth's gown with one movement removed it and then his own night shirt. He stretched out beside Elizabeth allowing her to become accustomed to the intimacy of his nearness. Elizabeth began again to retreat into the bed. James weight prevented her escape. James continued his embrace of her neck, breasts and stomach. Ever so gently he traced one finger along her thigh to her inner thigh. Elizabeth's eyes opened widely at this new intimacy. "James, I don't know what I am supposed to do," Elizabeth said panicking.

"Shush love, you will like it I promise. You don't need to do a thing, love. Just feel the sensation and the love that I have for you." Elizabeth clearly needed more convincing. He knew from their courtship that she liked it when he kissed her. He did so again deeply, allowing his tongue to mate with hers for the first time. She moaned when he did so giving him the indication that he could proceed further.

"Elizabeth, love; I need you to know that you may experience some pain the first time that we make love. I am trying to prepare you and not scare you, my darling girl. The pain will only last for a short time I promise. I love you Elizabeth and would not hurt you for the world."

"James, I love you and know that you would never do anything to purposely hurt me," Elizabeth whispered huskily. The look of worry on her face he tried to forget as he kissed her deeply and intensely waiting as before for her body to relax and for her arms to again circle his neck.

James felt like a complete cad at that moment knowing that she was truly unprepared for what would next follow. James resumed his intimate assault moving from her thigh to entering her slowly with his fingers. Again Elizabeth's eyes opened and she tried to retreat further into the bed. James remained unmoved and continued to caress both her mouth and her most intimate areas. When at last Elizabeth began to moan and move against his probing hands, James moved to enter Elizabeth and to prepare himself for her reaction. Elizabeth shuddered at first and began to softly cry. "Please, James; you must stop," Elizabeth said crying.

"It will be better in just a few moments," James whispered. "Shush love, you will like it I promise. I promise,

Elizabeth; the pain will stop in just a moment." James felt like a murderer at that moment and yet had never felt so good at the same time. This is what it feels like, he thought to himself; to take a wife to bed and not just a woman. This is what it feels like to care more about the other person than yourself.

James tried desperately to remain perfectly still so that Elizabeth could become accustomed to the sensation. Gradually beads of perspiration formed on his forehead as he resisted the temptation to move within her. Slowly Elizabeth opened her eyes and placed her arms again around James' neck. She could see his struggle and sought to comfort him; although not knowing what or how to do so. It was the signal that he needed that she was recovering from the pain and wanted him as much as he wanted her.

James began to slowly move within Elizabeth and all thoughts of caution and hesitation gradually began to disappear. There were no words then, only feelings. Elizabeth instinctively moved against him which erased all remaining hesitation from his love making. The feelings became more intense as the two deepened their response one to the other. When James could feel his climax approaching, he called Elizabeth's name so that she would open her eyes and look into his face at that moment. "Elizabeth, I love you," James whispered huskily.

"James, I love you so much," Elizabeth said with tear stained eyes. At that moment, James reached his climax and both shuddered for a moment at the intensity of their feelings. James kissed Elizabeth once more and pulled her into his side as he rolled to his back. After a few moments to recover, James looked at Elizabeth and asked if he had hurt her.

"Only at first, James as you said. It was the most wonderful experience of my life. I had no idea that love could be so wonderful! I know I have no basis of comparison, but James it was magical."

"I had no idea that I could ever feel for anyone what I feel for you. I can truly say that I had no idea that love could be so wonderful until I met you. The next time, you will not experience the pain that you experienced this time. I promise." He kissed her forehead again and held her as if he would never let her go.

Throughout the night, James felt Elizabeth's hands on his shoulder or his arm or his chest as if she had to convince herself that he was real and not an illusion. James was all too aware of Elizabeth's presence in the bed, but promised himself that he would have self control at least until the next night so as to not hurt her further. He laid in bed listening to her quiet breathing taking in the events of the past few weeks that had led him to a riverside church in London and to his wedding night. Somehow it had all seemed pre-destined that he would meet a slip of a girl looking for passage to London on the very day that his ship would be in a berth in Wilmington, North Carolina. He remembered that one day in the future they would need to sell Elizabeth's house in North Carolina and more pressingly deal with Cross and the matter of Elizabeth's inheritance. For now, however, these were all matters for another time. He moved further into the bed, stretched his back and pulled Elizabeth closer into his side. For now, all that mattered was his new wife and keeping her safe and happy. All the other matters would wait.

CHAPTER EIGHT

The next morning was Sunday and Elizabeth woke in the large bed that she had shared with James the night before feeling as though she was in a fairy tale. She looked around the cabin and saw her beautiful wedding gown from last night and the veil, both selected for her by James. She looked at his profile now as he slept and could not believe that this handsome man was her husband. What had she ever done to deserve such happiness?

When she thought back to the day before, it was all a blur of activity; music, vows, wedding finery and the wedding feast culminating in the wedding night. That part was the most amazing part, as she could not imagine that such activities actually took place between a man and a woman. Thankfully James seemed to be very experienced in that department, so she would need him to be patient with her to make sure that she didn't inadvertently do something wrong. First and foremost she just wanted to make him happy. When he had told her that making love would hurt, she couldn't believe it at first, but then saw the wisdom of his warning. She thought she would die for a moment, but that moment passed and what followed was so blissful that she could still not believe it had happened. She felt quite naughty lying in bed without her nightgown feeling the masculine feel of James. It was the differences in their bodies; his so strong that it appeared to be carved from marble instead of flesh; hers all curves and softness. To her it appeared for all the world that the saying opposites attract would certainly apply to them.

As she was staring at James' profile, she saw him look down at her. He smiled then his warm, loving smile and she cuddled closer into his shoulder. She is like a kitten, he thought at that moment. If I touch her cheek she leans into the touch; so loving and gentle is she.

Elizabeth began rubbing James' muscled chest. Although she appeared to be absentmindedly touching him, the affect was all too real for James. "Elizabeth," James whispered huskily, "you do know that what you are doing is arousing to me, don't you?"

"I am just thinking of the differences in our two bodies. Whereas you are so muscular it is as if you are carved from marble, I am all softness and curves."

"I know, Elizabeth, how I know. If you don't stop rubbing my chest I may be forced to show you the affect of that action and you are much too tender for me to do so."

Elizabeth looked up at James with her beautiful brown eyes. "James, I don't think that I am so very tender. Please love me as you did last night."

James did not need a further invitation. He had only been feigning sleep for the past hour and was trying desperately to not become aroused just by laying next to his beautiful wife. He again cautiously moved towards Elizabeth not wanting to hurt her further. He kissed her deeply causing her lips to swell and redden. When he touched her this time, she knew what to expect. He felt the chills run down her arm and legs with each caress. The lovemaking was slow as it had been the night before. James was not sure that she was truly ready for such intimacy so soon after their wedding night. Not until he was sure that she was ready for his intimacy did he move further to enter her. When he did so, the reaction was just as dramatic as the night before. Elizabeth shuddered with the response, not in pain this time, but in pleasure. James found it nearly impossible to stay motionless this time and both responded with a passion that James had not found in his previous encounters with women. He was struck anew by the love that he felt for Elizabeth; a love that was almost frightening in its need to protect her in all things. When he felt his climax approach, he again called Elizabeth's name so that she would look him squarely in the eye as his moment of climax was reached. He grabbed a handful of her mermaid hair and again pulled her into his side as he rolled over into the huge bed. He realized that he was glad that today was Sunday and that no work would be done on the Alliance. He did not think that he would be worth much today other than attending church and napping with his beautiful new wife.

When next they awoke, James got up to wash and dress and left Elizabeth in the huge bed. Although he knew that in the heat of passion Elizabeth had lost her shyness, he also knew that it would be harder for her in the light of day. Once he had left the room for the adjoining cabin, Elizabeth found her missing nightgown and robe and began brushing her hair. She heard James call for water from Mr. Jones and assumed that some would soon be arriving at her door. She hoped when they were washed and dressed that some breakfast would soon be heading her way as well. She found that she was starving and also hoping that James would agree to some sightseeing after church.

As if on cue, she heard Mr. Jones at their cabin door with the wash water and he softly knocked to let her know that it was ready. James was next door loudly splashing and singing which made her giggle as she prepared. She wondered how she was going to act normally around James after last night and this morning. How, she thought, would she look him in the eye after what had occurred? I guess it will all become a natural part of my life in due time. Today I shall have to keep from blushing every time I remember my wedding night. I definitely think I need to go to church, Elizabeth thought.

As if reading her mind, James called from the adjoining cabin. “My love, would you like to go see Father O’Rourke again and attend church?” James called to her. “We could thank him for the wedding and the wedding feast if you would like to do so.”

“I was just thinking the same, James. I believe you have read my mind,” Elizabeth called back.

James smiled to himself and thought it was not possible that he could be so happy and planning the most simple of outings; to go to church on a Sunday. No one would have believed this as little as two months ago and yet here we are and it has come to past just as his uncle had told him it would for many years on each stop in London after a long voyage. James could feel an *I told you so* coming from his uncle and welcomed the experience.

Elizabeth finished dressing and thought that she would no longer have to worry about missing any of her buttons now that she had someone to check each time she went out and about. She would ask James once they reached the carriage if they could go site seeing after the church service.

James knocked on the cabin door shortly thereafter and Elizabeth turned to ask him if she had gotten all of the buttons fastened on the back of her gown. He was caught anew at her beauty and how easily she carried it. To the rest of the world she was just a regular person as far as her behavior was concerned; as far as he was concerned, she was the entire world.

"What did you do before you had me to fasten your buttons, Mrs. O'Rourke?" James teased.

"I covered my back with a shawl mostly, hoping that no one would notice," Elizabeth responded.

"Leave it to you to always have an answer, Mrs. O'Rourke!" James replied.

"Ah but that is only to you, Captain O'Rourke!" Elizabeth replied. "To everyone else I am just a shy southern belle!" Elizabeth responded smiling.

"So you are; so you are. How is it that I don't intimidate you then?" James asked.

"Because you are so sweet, James," Elizabeth answered back.

"Don't let the crew hear you say that! You will ruin me for sure!" At that, James provided Elizabeth with his arm and they went above deck to proceed to church. Father O'Rourke will not recover from seeing me two days in a row, James thought. Domesticated at last!

James gave the nod to the crew members on deck and the gangplank was let down for their departure. He had taken no chances last night and would continue to be vigilant as long as they were in London.

A carriage stopped in front of the berth and they were off to church. James had told Mr. Pearson that he would handle security today, as his only plan was to go to services. If they changed their mind to take in some sightseeing, James would return to the ship to make sure that the necessary guard was along for the ride.

The carriage arrived at the church as the bell was tolling for the start of service. James and Elizabeth went inside and took their place in the pew. Elizabeth immediately was carried back to the day before and the wedding day that would always remain in her memory.

At the conclusion of the service, James caught Father O'Rourke's eye and they went to the inner chapel to meet with him. Colin O'Rourke asked them to dine with him in the rectory adjacent and their lunch was spent with him.

"So, Elizabeth; how do you like married life?" Father O'Rourke asked with his eyes shining mischievously.

"I like it very well indeed, Father. James is the perfect husband," Elizabeth replied smiling.

"Is he now?" Father O'Rourke laughed. "Well you have had not quite twenty-four hours in which to judge, so we will see what your response will be in one year."

"I suspect it will be the same, Father," Elizabeth answered smiling at James and his uncle.

"Spoken like a true southern belle, James. You had to go a long way, but I think you have found your treasure. Make sure that you do nothing to lose it," Father O'Rourke said looking intently at James.

"I agree uncle and vow that I will do all that is needed to protect my treasure," James replied.

"Along those lines, I have a wedding gift for you both. Please take these St. Christopher medals for both of you. He is the patron saint of travelers and of mariners, so I think it is appropriate for you both. Until you are home at Broadlands you continue to travel, Elizabeth and James, you will always be a mariner."

"I am not so sure about that, uncle. I may have found something that would make me wish to stay on dry land," James said looking at Elizabeth and brushing away a stray hair.

"I give you both God's blessing until we meet again," Father O'Rourke said.

"I hope that you will come visit us for the holidays, Father," Elizabeth stated.

"I would like that very much, Elizabeth," Father O'Rourke replied.

"By that time, we are sure to have a new family member on the way," James said smiling. Elizabeth blushed as always, but was happy too in the knowledge that they may soon start a family.

"So what is planned for the remainder of the day?" Father O'Rourke asked?

"I would love to see a bit of London while we are here if it would not interfere with any plans," Elizabeth responded.

James had anticipated this request and happily agreed. He would wish to return to the ship briefly to assemble the team that would follow Elizabeth and James, as Elizabeth and Samuel had been supported the day prior. James would take no chances until they could leave London.

The first stop in the sightseeing tour was Buckingham Palace; a must for all out of town visitors. This was followed by a tour of St. Paul's Cathedral and Westminster Abbey. At the conclusion of these sites, Elizabeth asked for only one more; the Tower of London and the Crown Jewels. At the conclusion of the last site, James asked Elizabeth if she had seen sufficient sites for one day. "Oh yes, James; thank you so much for the wonderful tour."

"Are you ready to return to the ship, darling girl?" James asked.

"Oh yes James, please. Knowing that I have a meeting again in the morning with the horrid Charles Cross, we had better call it a day."

"Tell me about your meeting yesterday," James asked anxiously.

"So much has happened, James that I forgot to tell you the details of my meeting with that odious man. He was no help whatsoever when I met with him yesterday. He asked that I meet with him again on Monday morning at 10:00. The thing is James that I don't think that meeting will be worthwhile either. I had corresponded from Wilmington before I met with him yesterday and yet nothing has been done in the matter of settling the estate," Elizabeth replied.

James could see that Elizabeth was becoming agitated again just relaying this information from her meeting. "You are not to worry, my darling girl. This is your honeymoon and you shouldn't have any worries. I will accompany you to the meeting and we will soon have it all sorted." James placed his arm around Elizabeth and pulled her closer to him in the carriage. "It will soon be sorted and we will be on our way home," he said fiercely.

CHAPTER NINE

When James and Elizabeth returned to the ship, James made his excuses and headed for Samuel Pearson's cabin. Samuel was in and the two traded information on the visit to Charles Cross' office and the security that would be needed on the return visit on Monday. "I do not intend to waste any time with Charles Cross, Samuel. I intend to demand a schedule of when all matters will be resolved for Elizabeth's estate issues and have done with it. The sooner we can be free of this city; the better I will like it," James stated heatedly.

"Aye, Captain; there is something not right between Cross and Whitfield. What respectful London solicitors have a gang of ruffians at their disposal to terrorize clients? It makes no sense unless some game of intimidation is underway. The crew is of one mind; that we will not let anything happen to Miss Elizabeth, Captain and the men have taken turns to cover double shifts to make sure that all is safe on the Alliance," Samuel replied.

"It is most appreciated, Samuel. I know the men are anxious to get home as much as I am and I intend to make short work of Charles Cross on Monday. If I need to leave this in the hands of Scotland Yard, so be it. My principal concern is that we not upset Elizabeth more. She has been through enough and I just want her to be happy and safe in Ireland," James responded.

"We will be ready, Captain when you are ready to depart in the morning," Samuel replied.

Having resolved the plan for the morning's meeting, James went below to find his bride and remind her that they were still on their honeymoon. James had asked Cook and Mr. Jones to have a special dinner for them this evening and more of the champagne they had enjoyed on their wedding night.

When he arrived at their cabin, he heard Elizabeth humming. "So Mrs. O'Rourke, are you ready for your dinner?"

"I am James. I am famished. It must have been all of the touring today," Elizabeth replied smiling.

"I will let Cook and Mr. Jones know that we are ready for our dinner. We may need to make it an early night so that we are ready for tomorrow's meeting." James gave her a devilish smile after giving the last speech.

"Are you sure that is the only reason that you want to have an early night?" Elizabeth asked smiling.

"I may have a few other things in mind, Mrs. O'Rourke. After all, we are on our honeymoon; are we not?" James asked mischievously.

"Are we having champagne again?" Elizabeth asked grinning.

"We are indeed, darling girl as I recall you quite enjoyed it last night," James replied.

"So what delicacies are we having for dinner this evening?" Elizabeth responded.

"I was thinking maybe oysters," James said mockingly. You know about oysters, Elizabeth?"

"I am from Wilmington, James. I am familiar with oysters," Elizabeth replied smiling.

"Are you familiar with the affects of oysters? They are considered an aphrodisiac in many cultures, you know," James continued laughing. As he did so he came up from behind and placed his arms around Elizabeth's narrow waist.

"So are these fried oysters or raw?" Elizabeth continued on unfazed by the comments or James' touch.

"Whichever way the Captain's wife desires," James answered kissing Elizabeth's neck.

"I love you, James O'Rourke!" Elizabeth said, turning in his arms and planting a kiss on his lips.

"I love you, Elizabeth O'Rourke! Did your family ever call you anything other than Elizabeth?" James asked.

"I am from the south, James; everyone has a nickname or a shortened name in the south. My father called me Lilliebeth when I was growing up," Elizabeth said smiling. "Your turn, James; tell me your nickname when you were growing up."

"I was Jamie growing up or Jamie boy to my father. I was always James to my mother just like I am James to you."

"Tell me about her, James," Elizabeth said sitting in their favorite window seat.

"She was beautiful like you and the center of my father's life and my life. When she passed, the light of my life died, until the day I fell in love with you." James had come to sit beside Elizabeth in their favorite evening spot.

"James, we both have had such loss in our lives. I think in so many ways, we have found each other to fill that hole in both of our lives. Would you agree, my love?"

"Yes, I think that is a bond for you and me. My father and I took to the sea because there was too much of a void in our home. I think that I have stayed at sea because returning home to an empty house has been too painful to remain for any length of time. Broadlands was a stopping off place and no more for me for years. I want to make it a true home again. I want it to ring with our laughter and with the laughter of our children."

"That is what I want also, James; more than anything in the world," Elizabeth said smiling up at him.

"Now, where is Jones with those oysters," James said smiling.

The next day rose cool and crisp. Autumn was definitely on its way. James thought to himself on rising from the bed that they would need to stop off at a ladies apparel store today, as Elizabeth must have some clothes for the coming winter. It would be the first real winter that Elizabeth had experienced so it would be important for her to be prepared with all of the needed gear. He looked back at Elizabeth quietly sleeping in the huge bed and thought again of their good fortune in finding each other. He could not wait to start a family and create a real home with his beautiful mermaid.

Elizabeth woke upon hearing James washing and singing in the adjoining cabin. She dreaded the upcoming visit to Cross' office, but also knew that she would have James with her and that everything was so much better when he was by her side.

She hurriedly washed and dressed so that she would be ready when she received the customary knock from James. He was so kind in dressing in the adjoining cabin. Even though their intimacy grew with each passing day, she was not yet prepared for that level of intimacy and James instinctively knew that as he did so many things without her saying a word. She had never been so blissfully happy and seeing Charles Cross today was not going to change that.

James knocked on the door a few minutes later as she was trying to do up the back of her gown. He laughed and came to her aid as usual with the pesky buttons on the gown. "Mrs. O'Rourke, I believe the weather change is telling me that we need to shop for some winter gear for you today while we have the chance. You are going to experience your first real winter this year and I need to make sure that you are prepared properly," James said in his customary commanding manner.

"Do I have anything to say about this, Captain O'Rourke?" Elizabeth said mockingly.

"Not in the least, Mrs. O'Rourke. Now grab your purse and hat and we will be off," James said laughing.

James and Samuel had arranged the guard that would accompany James and Elizabeth throughout the day. Elizabeth was still unaware of the extra precaution and it was exactly as James wanted it to be. He would take care of security and Elizabeth would be none the wiser for it.

James and Elizabeth set off for the shops prior to their meeting with Charles Cross. James viewed it as an excellent way of taking care of their chores prior to the meeting and he hoped would place them both in a positive mood for their meeting with Cross.

"I think that you need to have at least five winter gowns, a cloak, hat, gloves, scarf; all of the necessary winter items. We can always shop in Dublin for any other items at Christmas that you may need or want."

"James, I am sure that I would not need so many things at once," Elizabeth replied.

"Nonsense; you have not had to dress for real winter weather and I can't have you getting sick. Besides, I like to spoil you in case you haven't noticed, Mrs. O'Rourke!" James said laughing.

Elizabeth felt as though she was in a dream when they entered the ladies shop. James pronounced the list of items that would be needed and the shop staff began to scurry around the store bringing items for *the gentleman* to view and *the lady* to approve. In addition to the five gowns, cloak, hat, gloves and scarf that James had outlined, Elizabeth selected a muff for church and a dress for special occasions. "That dress will see a lot of use, as I intend to bring Broadlands back to life when we get home. We need to have music and dancing again at the holidays as we used to when mother and father were alive."

James eyes were shining when he spoke of his plans for the future and Elizabeth could not help but be swept up in the excitement of her new life. When all of the shopping had been concluded, James gave the address of the berth for the Alliance so that everything could be delivered and ready for their return to the ship. Only the odious visit with Cross remained on the required list for the day, then they could return to sightseeing, resting, or whatever else suited their fancy.

James and Elizabeth arrived at Charles Cross' office ten minutes ahead of schedule. "We might as well get this over with Elizabeth. I don't want you to worry as I will be happy to deal with Cross in whatever way is needed," James stated sternly.

When they arrived at Charles Cross' door, the clerk showed them into his office. When Charles Cross saw James, he looked mildly annoyed. James held out his hand and introduced himself to Cross. "I am surprised to see that Miss Majors has an escort to this meeting today. You understand solicitor/client privilege, I may only speak with my client in matters pertaining to her father's estate," Cross said in an annoyed tone.

"You may speak of any matters pertaining to my father's estate in front of my husband, Mr. Cross. James and I were married on Saturday. I am Mrs. O'Rourke now," Elizabeth said hastily.

"My congratulations to you both," Cross replied without joy. "I had no idea that Miss Majors was engaged. Well, let us get down to business then, shall we. As I explained to your wife on Saturday morning, Captain O'Rourke; the matter of an estate settlement is quite delicate and all the more so given the fact that Mrs. O'Rourke's father's estate is between two countries and the fiduciary laws of two countries. It may take some months to address all of the finer points of the estate and as much as a year before all matters can be resolved with all finality. These matters cannot be rushed if they are to be done properly."

"I happen to know that my wife sent correspondence on the matter of her father's estate at the time of his death and has corresponded on numerous occasions since that time. I would like to know the status of the estate given the information that has been provided thus far," James said brusquely.

"Again, Captain O'Rourke; these are not matters that can be rushed. Should you wish to return next week, I can give you a better feel for the schedule that we will follow in the resolution of the estate," Cross replied.

"I am very sorry, Mr. Cross; but Mrs. O'Rourke and I intend to return to our home this week. As I am sure you understand, Mrs. O'Rourke and I are on our honeymoon and wish to have this matter sorted prior to our departure. I would like to know if we may return tomorrow to sign the necessary papers and move this estate along to resolution," James answered.

"I would not possibly be able to respond that quickly, Captain O'Rourke. Perhaps there is a solicitor that I may correspond with that could keep you informed of our progress?" Cross said acidly.

"I will expect a full report in the morning, Mr. Cross and a schedule of resolution of the matter. Should that not occur, we will be moving the matter to another solicitor in London. My solicitors in Dublin will be certain to sort out this matter rather quickly I believe. They will be in contact with you in the event that we do not have a schedule of resolution in the morning," James replied angrily.

"As I believe I said, Captain O'Rourke, tomorrow is much too soon for a resolution of such a complicated matter. I will be happy to provide you with a schedule of resolution at your home address should you be so kind to leave it with my clerk," Cross replied coldly.

"I shall be providing your clerk with the name and address of my Dublin solicitor, Mr. Cross. If I do not have a resolution of the matter in the morning, my Dublin solicitor will be handling the matter going forward. Good day to you sir," James replied and reaching the door for Elizabeth, left the office in short order. James left the information as promised with Cross' clerk and left the building in a huff.

"He is a cold fish and that is without a doubt. What does he take us for that we can continue to be put off for resolution of a matter that should have been sorted before our arrival? Don't worry, my love; my solicitor will have this sorted in short order," James stated helping Elizabeth into the carriage.

Benjamin Whitfield entered Charles Cross' office shortly after the departure of Elizabeth and James. "I knew that O'Rourke had his eye on Elizabeth Majors. She is a beauty without a doubt. I had hoped to spend some time with Miss Majors aboard the Alliance or whilst in Bermuda, but O'Rourke was always there meddling and keeping everyone away from the prize of the ship. Now what are we going to do Charles? If his solicitor starts to snoop around, they are bound to find out that Elizabeth's estate has been reduced while in our hands," Whitfield stated pitifully.

"Pull yourself together, Whitfield. It will not come to that. I too had designs on Miss Elizabeth Majors from the first time that I saw her picture from her father. O'Rourke has gone and ruined it for the both of us. I am afraid that Captain and Mrs. O'Rourke will have to meet with an unfortunate accident, Whitfield just as the others have done," Cross replied angrily.

"Charles, we don't dare try this again. The authorities are bound to become suspicious if there is yet another accident involving one of our clients. This is especially the case with someone as well connected as O'Rourke," Whitfield replied.

"Then we will have to make sure that nothing connects the unfortunate accident to us. Now where is the Alliance berthed?" Cross asked.

"We have had a tail on them since their arrival. We know exactly where the Alliance is berthed, but O'Rourke has been too smart for us and has posted extra guards whilst in London. Our men have not been able to get near the ship or near Elizabeth."

"Then we will have to draw them out, won't we. Where did they get married? They must know someone in London to have arranged for a marriage so quickly. Find out who married them and maybe we can gain some leverage in that matter. Don't make me think of everything, Whitfield. What am I paying you for?" Cross replied angrily.

"I will see what I can find out," Whitfield replied lamely. "Surely someone in the area of the Alliance must know something useful about O'Rourke. I will see what I can come up with. It won't be easy however. O'Rourke is not like the others; he's smart and he has Elizabeth protected like the crown jewels. I can't say I blame him there, Cross. Do we have to do away with Elizabeth? I would like to have a go at her again if we can dispense with O'Rourke. After all, she has no family. Who would miss her if we can take care of O'Rourke?" Whitfield asked.

"It is too risky. I know that you had your heart set on that one, but we need to dispense with them both. We can't leave any witnesses behind to ask questions about the two of them and their fortune. Besides, now that they are married; Elizabeth's estate would fall to O'Rourke anyway. Both of them need to be out of the way. See to it and quickly before they leave London!" Cross snapped.

Whitfield slithered from the office to find the usual gang of rough characters that took care of the unsavory part of their business. Surely someone would know something useful about O'Rourke and his business matters; something that would lure them both off of the ship and to their end without questions being asked.

As Elizabeth and James returned to the ship, James was just beginning to recover his usual good spirits. "Cross is worthless, Elizabeth. I am sure that his father was an admirable man and your father had great trust in him. The son is another matter altogether. I made up my mind before we left his office that we are leaving London no later than Wednesday. I will have one last interview with Cross tomorrow and then we will leave it to the solicitors to resolve."

"I am so sorry that it has ended in this manner James. I am sure that my father had no idea what kind of man Charles Cross would have become or he would have never left his estate in his hands. I hate that it has become such a bone of contention and that you should have one more issue to deal with James," Elizabeth stated worriedly.

"Your worries are my worries, remember? Besides, this is a matter for solicitors to battle over. I promise we will have it sorted in short order. We just need to have two legal minds going at one another and all will come out well in the end. You are not to worry, Mrs. O'Rourke. You are on your honeymoon and will soon be leaving for your new home. That is all that I want you to concentrate on and me of course. You can concentrate on me whenever you like," James said laughing.

"I do concentrate on you, Captain O'Rourke. You are my first thought in the morning and my last thought at night," Elizabeth responded.

"I like the sound of that, Mrs. O'Rourke. Why don't you go below for a rest before luncheon? I need to get the crew started on preparations for a Wednesday departure."

Elizabeth went to their cabin and saw the parcels from this morning's shopping trip. He is the most considerate man, Elizabeth thought. I have yet to get him a wedding gift, so I will need to determine what he might like or need and take care of that on Tuesday before we leave. She busied herself with sorting the shopping parcels and unpacking the items that she would need for the next few days given the change in the weather that they were experiencing. Autumn was definitely upon them and the weather may turn cooler still as they headed to Broadlands, Elizabeth thought. She may need these items sooner than later.

Later when James returned to the cabin, he found Elizabeth sorting the morning's parcels so that she would have what would be needed for the next few days of travel. "James, I have yet to get you a wedding present. What would you like or need that I could buy for you before we leave for home?" Elizabeth asked.

"I neither need nor want anything, Elizabeth. Your love is all that I could ever need," James said grinning.

"There must be something that you would like?" Elizabeth continued.

"There may be a few things, my love, but they are not found in any shop," James said mischievously. "I *want* my beautiful wife in my life forever. I *need* my beautiful wife in my bed. Those are the only things that I want and need, Elizabeth," James said kissing her deeply. "Now, where is our lunch? That altercation with Cross has given me a powerful appetite."

After luncheon, Elizabeth took a walk on deck to get some fresh air. The crew was in a frenzy of work, preparing for the departure of the Alliance on Wednesday. James was firm in his decision that the crew would not be kept longer from their families at home in Ireland and neither would he keep Elizabeth away from Broadlands another day longer than needed. He couldn't wait for her to see it and would no longer delay their departure.

As she moved to the rail, Elizabeth saw a young man in a cap running up to the gangplank. "This note is for Mrs. O'Rourke," she heard him say. The note was passed to one of the crew members who in turn passed it to Elizabeth. She went below decks to their cabin to read the note. She couldn't imagine who it could be from as she only knew two people in London.

The note was from Father O'Rourke and he was inviting her to the church for tea and to meet him before the Alliance was scheduled to leave London. Elizabeth left the note on the table and took off to meet Father O'Rourke. This would be the perfect opportunity, she thought; to discover an item that James would like for a wedding gift and it could remain a surprise that way. Her inquiry of him earlier in the day had not produced a suggestion that Elizabeth could use, at least not one in a shop as James had so pointedly noted.

Elizabeth was able to slip away unnoticed in the frenzy of preparation currently underway above decks. She reasoned that she would be gone for such a short time that she would not be missed by anyone on board. Besides, she could gain insight from Father O'Rourke as to a surprise gift for James. She hurried along the river bank to the Chelsea Old Church anxious to see Father O'Rourke again.

When she arrived at the church, she pushed open the heavy entrance doors to gain access to the church. The church was very quiet; there was not a sound of music or conversation within. "Hello," Elizabeth called, "Father O'Rourke? Are you there? Uncle Colin; it's Elizabeth." There was no response and no sound coming from the church.

"You won't find him here, Miss Elizabeth," a voice called out from behind her. "He is detained at the moment and won't be available to you." The voice from behind her as she discovered, belonged to none other than Benjamin Whitfield.

"Mr. Whitfield, what are you doing here?" Elizabeth asked.

"I am waiting for you of course, Miss Elizabeth," Whitfield answered.

Elizabeth began to have a chilling feeling that all was not well here in the church. "It was I who sent you the note. How like you to come as soon as one of the O'Rourke men curls a finger."

"Mr. Whitfield, I was here to see Father O'Rourke. If he is not available, I will be returning to the Alliance and to my husband."

"Oh no, Miss Elizabeth; excuse me, Mrs. O'Rourke; you are not going anywhere. I brought you here for a reason."

"Mr. Whitfield, I don't believe we have anything further to discuss. My husband and I are leaving London and we will have no further business of any sort here."

"It was meant to be so simple, Miss Elizabeth. I was to follow you from Wilmington to London to find out all that I could about you. But every way I turned, that damn Captain O'Rourke was in the way. I couldn't even have a conversation with you without O'Rourke interrupting and keeping you from me."

Elizabeth could tell from Whitfield's manner that the man was unhinged. All she could think of was getting to Father O'Rourke or getting back to the Alliance. As if he could read her mind, Whitfield stated "You are not going anywhere, Miss Elizabeth unless it is with me." Elizabeth continued to withdraw within the church moving cautiously away from Whitfield with the intent of getting to Father O'Rourke to gauge his condition or obtain his help. "I don't believe you are listening to me, Miss Elizabeth. I told you that you are not going anywhere. If Cross had his way, I would be killing you today, or having you killed. But I have other plans for you, Miss Elizabeth. I could never do away with anyone as beautiful as you." Whitfield had been moving closer to Elizabeth as he spoke as she moved further into the darkness and the safety of the enveloping church.

"Cross had it all planned out, Elizabeth. You would have never discovered that he was embezzling from your father's estate as you were an ocean away. But you had to get it into your head to come here and have a face to face with Charles Cross. Now he will never let you go because he will know that you are a threat to him; you and James O'Rourke of course. I would have liked to deal with Captain O'Rourke first, but perhaps this ruse will draw him out in the event that he comes looking for you."

Elizabeth had a horrible vision then of James coming to find her and walking into the trap that Whitfield had set for them both.

"I see that you have already considered my plan for the day. If I lure you here and your husband comes to find you; I have both of you in my planned attack. Rest assured that I am not here alone, Elizabeth. I have a gang of rough men working with me. They are holding your husband's uncle as we speak and will be here in just a moment to dispense with you, provided of course that we cannot reach an understanding," Whitfield continued.

Keep him talking, Elizabeth thought. If he continues to talk you have more of a chance that James will come with the crew from the ship to address the situation.

"Mr. Whitfield, I am not sure what you and Mr. Cross had in mind, but I am sure that you never had any intention of truly harming anyone. Perhaps scaring us, but not actually harming us. Were you to carry out this plan, you would be the responsible party and no one else. Mr. Cross would simply walk away and leave you holding the blame."

"I had thought of that, Elizabeth but all I really am concerned about is that husband of yours. I never had any intention of harming you in anyway, quite the contrary. Were it not for Captain O'Rourke, you would be on my arm now Elizabeth and not his. Once your husband is out of the way, you and I will have the opportunity to get to know one another and you will find that I am a very considerate person and more than willing to take care of you, Elizabeth."

As Whitfield continued to talk, Elizabeth had to resist all impulses to run, as she knew for a fact that he had gone mad. He was talking as if the two of them were a couple, when in fact they had never been more than casual acquaintances as passengers on the same ship.

As Elizabeth led Whitfield further into the church, she noticed the main door to the church starting to open a slight crack. She was not sure who was entering the church, but was hoping that anyone would come that she could send to get help. As the door widened, she saw James and several members of the crew behind him. She dare not say anything in the hope that James could overtake Whitfield without him being aware of his presence.

"I kept telling Cross that it was folly to do away with you, Elizabeth," Whitfield continued. "You are far too lovely to destroy. I know that you will come around the more you think of it. I can give you a London Town House, carriages, fine clothes; anything that your heart would desire. I am well connected Elizabeth and not without means. Anything that you may wish would be my desire to provide. You have only to ask."

James continued to move stealthily towards Whitfield who in turn moved closer to Elizabeth in the nave of the church. At that moment the ancient floor creaked beneath the feet of James and the members of the crew that followed him. Whitfield turned and saw that they were not alone.

"O'Rourke," Whitfield called out, "so glad that you could join us. I have been hoping that I would have the chance to meet you and settle our differences man to man."

"It's over, Whitfield," James shouted, "let Elizabeth go. This is between you and I Whitfield; leave her out of it."

"Oh no, O'Rourke, I will take care of you and Elizabeth is my reward. I told Cross that I wanted her from the beginning and now I will claim my reward."

James saw the Scotland Yard officers from the corner of his eye coming from the inner chapel. That meant that Father O'Rourke had been freed and that Inspector Flynn and his men were moving to surround Whitfield. Hopefully any hired ruffians outside had been gathered up and were being dispatched to the Yard as they spoke.

"This was Cross' idea you know," Whitfield continued. "This is the third client that he has dealt with in this same manner. He thought that Elizabeth would be the easiest mark, as she was a woman. Who would have thought that she would be the most difficult of all? Don't come any closer, O'Rourke; I know what your game is and it is not on!" Whitfield shouted. He pulled from his coat a gun and when Elizabeth saw the gun; her first fear was that James was in his direct path. The Scotland Yard officers started down the nave towards Whitfield from the opposite direction.

"It is indeed over, Whitfield; over for you that is," James replied heatedly.

At that moment, Elizabeth screamed to pull the attention away from James. The gun went off in Elizabeth's direction, just as the Scotland Yard crew bore down on Whitfield. James rushed to Elizabeth's side. All that he could see was blood flooding her dress on the left side of her body. He knelt down beside her and saw her eyes flutter. "Elizabeth, darling girl, it's James. I am going to try to see how badly you have been hurt." As he spoke, he saw the blood stain begin to expand and was trying to maintain his composure as he worried about the extent of her injuries.

"James," Elizabeth whispered, "please take me home." James wasted no time in gathering Elizabeth in his arms and carrying her from the church. Scotland Yard had subdued Whitfield in the church and had heard most of his rants and raves which had implicated himself and Cross. James had only one concern at that moment and that was getting Elizabeth back to the ship. In the waiting carriage, James placed Elizabeth on his lap and continued to probe to find the source of the bleeding. In doing so, he found Elizabeth's St. Christopher medal had been pierced by one of Whitfield's bullets and had lodged in her corset and another bullet had appeared to have injured her left arm. James prayed that the wound looked far worse than it actually was, but the worry by James was every bit as real. Until he could get her to the ship and properly checked by Dr. Wilkinson, he could not be sure that there was no additional injury.

When they arrived at the Alliance berth, James ran up the gangplank calling for Dr. Wilkinson as he ran. He took Elizabeth to their cabin for further examination by Dr. Wilkinson who rapidly followed behind.

"Captain if I may; let me do a thorough examination to make sure that there is no injury that you may have missed. I will come and get you as soon as I have finished. If you have a night shirt handy, I will help her change into that as well and we will get these blood soaked clothes off of her."

At the words blood soaked, James came to attention from his haze of worry. "Thank you, doctor I will wait outside." James knew that he must have looked like a mad man at that point having raced like a lunatic from the ship to the Chelsea Old Church after reading the note in their cabin. If Elizabeth had awakened at that moment and seen his face, she would have thought her injuries far more life threatening. He needed to calm himself both for her sake and for his own. The fear of what could have happened was far worse than the reality that had happened.

Only in the flurry of activity related to the departure preparations could Elizabeth have slipped away without being seen by any of the crew. Knowing the handwriting was not Colin's, James could only assume that the note was written to lure Elizabeth away. When he and the security members of the crew arrived at the church, they could tell that something was amiss. No music or voices could be heard from within. There was no activity in the outer gardens or anywhere adjacent to the church. As James entered the church, he could see that Elizabeth was trying to keep Whitfield talking so that she could figure out what next to do. When she saw James come through the door, she continued to lure Whitfield deeper into the church so that James and the crew members had more room to maneuver and take Whitfield down. She had no idea that James had also alerted Scotland Yard and that they had been following Whitfield for several days along with his hired men. No one had seen the gun until Whitfield had pulled it and it was too late.

Elizabeth had screamed as soon as she saw the gun, as she feared that Whitfield was aiming for James. Whitfield was so inexperienced with a gun that he shot Elizabeth by mistake when her scream startled him. After the shots were fired, the Scotland Yard men were able to take down Whitfield. In the confusion James had raced to Elizabeth's side to determine the extent of her injuries. Fortunately the bleeding was far worse than the wound, but James could not have known that when he arrived beside Elizabeth. All Elizabeth had said was *take me home James, please*. Those words haunted James as he paced the hallway outside of the cabin.

Dr. Wilkinson came outside of the cabin after what seemed like an eternity and found James pacing madly. “Captain, Mrs. O’Rourke is doing very well. The wound was superficial, but bled quite profusely so I have dressed the wound and we will change that dressing daily until she recovers. I have given her a dose of laudanum both for the pain and to let her rest from the experience. I think it best that she sleep so that she can recover both mentally and physically from this attack. If agreeable Captain, I would like to share this diagnosis with the crew. They think a great deal of Mrs. O’Rourke and I saw some very worried faces when you carried her on board.”

“By all means, Dr. Wilkinson; I will stay with Elizabeth until she awakens. I don’t want her to be alone,” James replied.

“We will send you some dinner, Captain and you may want to change. If she wakes and sees your clothes, she may be more worried that you were injured in the incident with Benjamin Whitfield or that her injuries are more serious than they truly are.”

The doctor was right, so James went to the adjoining cabin to wash and change. When he saw his shirt in the mirror, his only thought was that the blood he saw in the mirror belonged to Elizabeth. He had been correct to mistrust Cross and Whitfield, but even he had no idea the extent of their complicity and their evil doing. He knew that he would need to follow-up with Scotland Yard in the morning and provide a statement on the incident. He also needed to check on his Uncle Colin; but after seeing Elizabeth fall, there had been only one thought in his mind; get her to safety.

When James returned to their cabin, Elizabeth was asleep in one of his night shirts looking like his mermaid again with her hair spread across the pillows. She looked so peaceful after such an ordeal that all James wanted to do was protect her and apologize for the experiences that she had just endured.

Jones rapped quietly on the cabin door and came in with dinner for James. It was his hope that Miss Elizabeth was awake and able to eat, but he could see that she was resting. He said nothing as he laid out the food as the Captain appeared to be in no mood for conversation. He could report to the crew that Mrs. O'Rourke was resting quietly and that was good news.

After James had eaten and drank a bit, he went over to the bed and pulled up a chair. He felt Elizabeth's forehead and hands and she felt a normal temperature. His hand embraced her cheek and her silky hair. He could not wait to see her eyes open and to see her beautiful smile. James finally stretched out on the bed next to Elizabeth and felt her warmth through the night shirt. He started to re-live the day's events and could not believe that they had actually occurred. Thank the Lord and St. Christopher, Elizabeth's wound was a graze only. He would do whatever it took to help her recover from this experience. His only thoughts now were of home and Elizabeth.

CHAPTER TEN

In the morning after a sleepless night on his part, James leaned over to check on Elizabeth. He had been fearful all night of accidently hurting her or rolling over in a way that would add further pain to her injury. Elizabeth looked up at James and smiled. It was all that he needed to greet the day. "I will be right back. I am going to get Dr. Wilkinson to check on you," James said smiling.

Dr. Wilkinson bounded through the door a few minutes later. He checked on Elizabeth as James again paced in the hallway. James called for Jones to bring hot water for Elizabeth once the doctor had concluded his examination. Dr. Wilkinson came into the hall a few minutes later to say that Elizabeth was doing well and asking to see the Captain.

"My darling girl," James called out laughing. He went to the bed and embraced Elizabeth happily. Elizabeth grimaced as her arm was crushed in the embrace. "I am so sorry my love. I forgot the injury. What can I do to help you? Did you want me to help you bathe?"

"No darling," Elizabeth said blushing. "I will be fine. May I borrow another night shirt? It will be easier to get over my arm and the bandage."

James ran to the next door cabin and returned with a fresh night shirt. "I will check on you in a few minutes to make sure that you are alright," James said smiling.

Elizabeth got up to move to the table to bathe. She felt cramped from the long stay in bed, but otherwise good considering the events of the past day. She quickly bathed and changed into the fresh night shirt. The doctor had cleaned the wound and changed the bandage and they had tied a ribbon over the bandage in a bow. The doctor felt that the last touch was in keeping with the spirit of his patient and a good sign that Elizabeth was dealing with the injury and the manner in which it was received.

When James returned to their cabin, Elizabeth was brushing her long hair, tangled from the long sleep. "Let me do that for you, Elizabeth. I know it must be difficult with the injury. How are you really doing, my love?" James asked anxiously.

"I can't believe this has happened, James. How could people who are supposed to be responsible and esteemed in their community connect themselves with such monstrous ruffians? Have you been able to see, Father O'Rourke? Is he alright?" Elizabeth asked worriedly.

"He is fine, darling girl and only you would ask about him first. He will be coming today, as will Inspector Flynn of Scotland Yard. Uncle Colin will be giving his statement to Hugh and of course he wants to see you and how you are doing. You will also be asked to give a statement to Hugh, love. I know it will be difficult, but everything has to be official when this matter comes before the magistrates and then the courts. I don't think that Cross or Whitfield will be bothering anyone again. Hugh says that everything will be sorted here in London on that front. You were the third victim of those two. The other two victims are not alive to tell the tale."

Elizabeth began to cry when she heard the last explanation. James came to her instantly and began to carefully embrace her, protecting her arm and injury in the process. "My darling girl, you know that you are safe now. I know that I was meant to be with you and protect you from the beginning. Had I shared what I knew and suspected about those two, you would have never left the ship on your own and this would have never happened," James said.

"James, you were just trying to protect me and keep me from being frightened of those monsters. I have been so blessed, James that I feel that I am being ungrateful by complaining at all. It just has been so overwhelming that it is all like a very bad dream. Do you remember my dream on the ship in Bermuda? It is almost as if it came to life," Elizabeth replied anxiously.

"I remember your nightmare very well, Elizabeth. It was the first night that I accepted my attraction to you. As horrible as this whole experience has been, remember that we have survived it and it will only make our love stronger." James started to hug Elizabeth again and she cringed slightly at the impact to the wound on her arm and chest. "My darling girl, I am so sorry, I will need to think of another way to continue our honeymoon without impacting your injury each time," he said worriedly. "Let me just hold you," James said huskily.

James held her as if he never wanted to let go. He stroked her hair and rocked her gently. Elizabeth started to cry from the sheer relief of being with James again and the release of the memories of that terrible day.

There was a knock on the door and James went himself to answer it. It was Mr. Jones the steward to advise the Captain and Mrs. O'Rourke that Inspector Flynn and Father O'Rourke had arrived and were asking to see them.

"Thank you Jones. Please show them down," James replied.

"Are you ready for this, love? I am so sorry to put you through all of this again, but we must have everything officially done so that those two do not escape justice," James stated worriedly.

"I will be ready, James. Please help me into my robe and then I will be ready to face whatever needs to be done," Elizabeth replied.

Shortly thereafter, Father O'Rourke and Hugh Flynn knocked on the cabin door. They found James sitting at his chart table and Elizabeth in her robe still in bed at James insistence.

"Come in both of you. I have insisted that Mrs. O'Rourke remain in bed to accept her guests. That is at my insistence so you know. If she had her way, she would be up and dressed and wanting to show her famed southern hospitality to the both of you and I would have none of it," James said heatedly.

"So I see you have kept your sense of humor then, James. I am relieved to see it," Father O'Rourke replied. "Elizabeth; how on earth can anyone look so lovely after what you have been through?" Father O'Rourke exclaimed.

"I have had wonderful care, Uncle Colin. Please sit down and tell us how you are doing," Elizabeth replied.

"I am tougher than I look. I have dealt with rough men my entire career here in London. I will admit that these ruffians had more ruthless things in mind than stealing from the collection boxes, but it takes more than a couple of thugs to keep Colin O'Rourke down," Father O'Rourke stated.

"It looks like you have a good shiner, Uncle Colin from the whole adventure. Have you had that looked at by a doctor? I can bring Dr. Wilkinson over to have him take a look while Hugh here takes each of our statements," James stated.

"That would be worthwhile, Jamie. I don't want them to get the best of me," Father O'Rourke replied.

"Let me order some breakfast for Elizabeth and some refreshments for us all and we can each give Hugh here our statements and have this matter sorted. I am sure that you know that Elizabeth and I are still on our honeymoon. The quicker we can get this behind us, the better it will be for everyone concerned. I intend on pulling out for Dublin in the morning; assuming that we can do that and that Hugh will have everything that he needs to hang those two bastards. Excuse me, Elizabeth; but that is how I feel," James said heatedly. Elizabeth just smiled at James and made no comment.

"Right, let's start with Uncle Colin so that he can be seen by the doctor. James, is there someplace close that I can meet with Uncle Colin and take down his statement?" Hugh asked.

"Come this way, Hugh. I have the cabin down the passageway set up for you." When Uncle Colin and Hugh were both in the hallway, James informed them that the pieces of evidence from the incident had all been carefully maintained in the nearby cabin as well. He did not want Elizabeth to see the blood stained dress, the St. Christopher medal or the blood stained shirt and jacket that he had worn the day before. He assumed that Hugh might need these items as well as the forged note for purposes of trial. "I will collect each of these items, James. You would be amazed at the impact of physical evidence in a trial of this sort. The testimony of all of you will have a tremendous impact of course, but the physical evidence is sometimes the most compelling to a jury. I understand your concern about Elizabeth. If she saw how close she came . . . well, we don't need to discuss it now. Let's get Uncle Colin's statement and proceed one by one," Hugh replied.

Hugh had brought a second inspector with him to take down the statements as they were provided. He asked thoughtful questions to provide a step by step chronology of the facts that would be helpful both for his investigation and for the jury when the matter came to trial. Once Father O'Rourke had provided his statement and been examined by the doctor, he came to sit with Elizabeth to keep her mind off of the issues before them.

"So James has told you about Broadlands, has he? Oh you will love it Elizabeth. It is right on the coast, as you know; so it will be like Wilmington, but colder of course. You will see your first snow which will not be amiss come Christmas," Father O'Rourke stated.

"I am so glad that you mentioned Christmas, Uncle Colin. James and I intend on doing a real old fashioned family Christmas and we so hope that you will join us. I know it is a very busy time of year for the clergy, but I was thinking maybe after Christmas itself on Boxing Day or the day after and then stay until New Year. What do you think?" Elizabeth asked smiling.

"That would be a joy and what you need to do Elizabeth; think of the future and the happiness that you two will have together. Don't give another thought after today of those two ruffians Cross and Whitfield. They will get what is coming to them and you will have your life to lead with Jamie. He has been looking for you since he was eighteen years old and weren't you on a dock in Wilmington, North Carolina waiting for him? It was meant to be," Uncle Colin stated.

James completed his statement with Hugh and then came in to check on Elizabeth. "Are you ready for Hugh, darling girl? I have asked him and his man to come to the cabin to take your statement so that you don't have to move. The doctor has given orders that you get rest after this part is over. Are you ready for him then, love?" James asked worriedly.

"Yes, James; I am ready. Thank you," Elizabeth replied bravely.

Hugh Flynn came into the cabin with his associate Sgt. Emerson. They had boxed the physical evidence and left it in the cabin used for the interviews until they had completed the last one with Elizabeth. At James' request, they were not going to show the physical evidence to Elizabeth at this time as they feared that the sight of it would bring back the horror of the previous day. They regretted requiring her to provide the detailed statement but it would be required as part of the standard procedures.

"Elizabeth, I am going to ask you a series of questions and you try to provide me with the answer to the best of your recollection, okay?" Hugh stated. He took her slowly through the chronology of the events, beginning with the trip to Bermuda and any interaction that she may have had with Whitfield during the trip and moving on to London and the exchanges there, ending with the fateful day in Chelsea Old Church where she nearly lost her life. He also took her through each encounter with Charles Cross, starting with her correspondences with him and ending with the meetings in London during her stay. No detail was too small. By collecting this information while the memories were still fresh from the events of the day, Hugh would have the information he needed to place before the magistrates and to place before the judge and attorneys during the inevitable trial.

"Thank you very much, Elizabeth. I know that was very hard for you and we very much appreciate you providing your testimony. This will be prepared in statement form and provided to the magistrates and will be available for the trial of Benjamin Whitfield and Charles Cross. I shall provide you with a copy when it is formally compiled so that you may review it prior to the trial. I think I had better go get James for you now and let you rest. Thank you again, Elizabeth. You did a brilliant job," Hugh replied.

Hugh and Sgt. Emerson left the cabin in search of James. Hugh knew from the look on Elizabeth's face that she badly needed rest and that she needed her husband's comfort more than anything else.

When James came to their cabin, he immediately went to Elizabeth's side. "How are you, darling girl?" James asked.

"I don't know which part is worse, James; living this whole nightmare or reliving it. It is all so unbelievable as to be surreal. I can't get my mind around the fact that this has happened to us, James; it just doesn't seem real," Elizabeth stated.

"I know, love. I feel the same way. Hugh said that the information from all of us has been very helpful. They will go before the magistrates so that Charles Cross can be picked up. Whitfield is already in the lock up thanks to Scotland Yard's quick action." James held Elizabeth then trying to lessen the tension of the morning and to provide the comfort that he knew only he could provide. He rubbed her back and shoulders and kept whispering words of comfort.

Gradually Elizabeth calmed and looked up imploringly into James' eyes. "James, please love me like you did on our wedding night. I need to feel your strength and to block out all of this ugliness and hatred."

"I don't want to hurt your injury and Dr. Wilkinson says you should rest love," James replied tenderly.

"I know, James, but I have rested and I just need you to hold me and love me," Elizabeth answered.

James carefully lifted Elizabeth onto the huge bed and draped her across his lap, kissing her forehead, her eyes and her mouth and stroking her back as he did so. He paused with each new caress to make sure that Elizabeth was not hurting and wanted him to stop. Each time she would look up at him and say *please, James.*

James gently lifted her so that she was straddling his lap. He gently cupped and caressed each breast then returned to her lips, kissing them deeply until they were red and swollen. His own self control was sorely tested as he found that he needed Elizabeth as much or more than she needed him. He needed to touch and worship his wife who he had come so close to losing. The thought of that potential loss made his love making all the more intense for him. He seemed to breathe in Elizabeth's rose scented skin and wanted to touch and caress every inch of her body. With care he gently lifted her night shirt and repeated the same embrace to every inch of her skin, suckling each breast as he made love to Elizabeth. Elizabeth moaned and held onto James' back as if she would never let go. After feeling the need arise in them both, James gently entered Elizabeth, calling her name as he did so. The lovemaking, gentle at first; had become more and more intense for them both. The rush of feelings was overwhelming to them both. The lovemaking carried with it the fear of loss and the joy of survival rolled into one. Their climax when they reached it was magical for them both. They did not move, but held onto each other motionless for some time thereafter.

When next they awoke, James looked down at Elizabeth's beautiful face and thanked God for her safety. She looked up at him smiling and stretched out like a cat after a long rest. "How are you feeling, my love?" James asked worriedly.

"Much better, James; and you?" Elizabeth asked.

"Wonderful knowing that you are improving and that we are soon heading home. Ready for something to eat?" James asked.

"I am rather enjoying lying here with my husband for the moment," Elizabeth said shyly.

"Mrs. O'Rourke, you will be the ruination of me. How shall I explain to the crew that I am lying in a bed with my wife when there is work to be done?" James said teasing.

"We shall say that you are taking very good care of me indeed and that we are continuing our interrupted honeymoon. How is that for an answer?" Elizabeth answered smiling.

"An excellent answer indeed and one that I shall relish telling, almost as much as telling the crew that I am sweet, to use your words!" James said smiling.

"Well, you are sweet whether you want to admit it or not!" Elizabeth replied.

"Mrs. O'Rourke has spoken, so she has and so shall it be!" James was content to lie in the huge bed with Elizabeth, holding her as if he could not believe his good fortune in finding her and then by God's grace, having her survive the attempted murder.

*****

The next morning, James took control of the wheelhouse himself as the Alliance pulled out of its berth headed for Dublin. He would leave nothing to chance until London was behind them and they were again in the open sea. Elizabeth had slept through the night. James would not allow anyone to wake her. She had been through too much and he was very happy that the statements were behind them and that both Whitfield and Cross would be held for questioning and charging. If both Elizabeth and he needed to return for a trial in the future, that would come later. For now, James needed to take Elizabeth home as she had asked.

Once they were clear of the Thames and back in the English Channel, James went below to check on Elizabeth. She was still sleeping and James decided to let her rest. He knew she would need to process what had occurred to her for days and weeks in the future. He was most relieved that she could sleep and do so without laudanum and uninterrupted by nightmares.

The Alliance landed in Dublin the next morning. Elizabeth went above decks to say goodbye to the crew members who would be disembarking to meet their families. They all wished her well and were grateful that she and the Captain had been spared worse injury at the hands of Cross and Whitfield. She felt that she was part of a special kindred spirit that had watched over her without her knowing during their stay in Bermuda and in London. She felt a member of a large family as James had predicted and it was a wonderful feeling.

James had sent word ahead that the carriage from Broadlands would be needed today and that not only James would be picked up, but the new Mrs. O'Rourke as well. Elizabeth had packed all of the items from her original cabin as well as the parcels purchased in London and they were all placed in the carriage. The Alliance would be in port for the repairs caused by the hurricane on the way to London. In all, it had been a very eventful voyage for a variety of reasons and James was anxious to return home to introduce Elizabeth to the staff and to inform Father O'Rourke that all was well upon their arrival.

As they drove through the countryside outside of Dublin, the bay was visible as well as the beautiful green countryside. "It is just like it has been described in the story books that I have read; so beautiful and green. I love it already!" Elizabeth exclaimed.

"I am so glad, Elizabeth. I can't wait to show you your new home," James said smiling.

A half hour or so outside of Dublin, the carriage pulled into the gates of an estate that was directly above the water, overlooking the Irish Sea. "It is beautiful, James. I can't believe this is my new home." They had just turned into the estate of Broadlands, James' family home. It was on a bluff overlooking the ocean, the perfect home for a mariner and for a family of mariners.

Waiting at the entrance was Seamus Kennedy and his wife Bridget. They had looked after the property for as long as James could remember. He was honored to introduce his wife to Seamus and Bridget and to the other servants gathered to meet their new mistress. "Seamus, Bridget, I would like you to meet Mrs. O'Rourke. Elizabeth, this is Seamus Kennedy and his wife Bridget."

"I am so happy to meet you and to be here at last," Elizabeth said.

"Welcome to Broadlands, Mrs. O'Rourke; welcome to your new home," Seamus exclaimed.

James escorted Elizabeth inside and took her for a brief tour of the house. When they arrived at his master suite, James told Elizabeth that she would have to excuse the masculine nature of the house. "It has reflected its occupants for too long. When you see something that you would wish to change, you just let me know and we will get it done. I want you to feel that this is truly your home and that it reflects you and your personality," James stated.

"I can't imagine changing a thing, James. Everything is steeped in history and your family's heritage," Elizabeth replied.

"We will take a walk later and I will show you the gardens and the pathway down to the water. We will visit the village tomorrow and I can show you the family church. There is so much to take in I know, but I am anxious for you to see everything," James said smiling.

Elizabeth's luggage and parcels had been brought up to the suite and she began unpacking and making herself at home. There was so much joy at finally being home after the long voyage and the drama that had occurred in London. Once she had settled, she thought to write to her neighbor in Wilmington to let the pastor and his wife know what had occurred since her absence and that she would not be home again for several months. As she sat to write the letter, it was hard for her to imagine the changes that had occurred in such a short time. As she looked around her she realized that she was well and truly home and that her life in Broadlands would just be the start of the happy life of her dreams.

After an hour or so, James came to find her in the master suite to take her on a tour of the gardens and the path to the sea. "My mother and father both loved the sea so much that father had a path prepared with benches along the way so that they could walk to the water each night. It was my own private beach growing up and has many happy memories for me," James recalled as they walked through the gardens and the path to the sea edge.

"I love it already, James. It is so beautiful; there is no wonder that you love it so much, my love," Elizabeth said breathlessly.

"It has been a shell of a house for so long now. I want to bring it back to life again. We should have a ball to introduce you to the county and so that you may meet those friends of my parents. There will be many stories circulating about the southern belle who stole my heart and survived an encounter with the scourge of the south; that is our south which is London," James said smiling.

"Will everyone know so quickly?" Elizabeth asked.

"Rest assured once the crew has dispersed, the stories about you and your near miss at the hands of Benjamin Whitfield will be the stuff of legend. Everyone in the county will want to meet the lady who stole James O'Rourke's heart," James stated.

"Are you such a legend in the county, then?" Elizabeth asked laughing.

"Let's just say that many a mother has thrown her daughter's cap in my direction, but without success. There was another fate awaiting me on the other side of the Atlantic; a mere slip of a thing that captured my heart within moments of meeting her, just like a lightning bolt!" James said laughing.

"A lightning bolt reminds me of the hurricane. Have the repairs to the Alliance been scheduled?" Elizabeth asked.

"She is in dry dock now and the repairs will continue for some time. Don't worry; neither the Alliance nor her Captain will be returning to the sea for quite some time. Her Captain has other things on his mind at the present time!" James said smiling. He reached down to kiss Elizabeth and pull her gently to his side. They walked on in silence with both James and Elizabeth thinking of the tricks of fate that had brought them together and welded their alliance in such a short period of time. When at last they reached the private beach, Elizabeth was astounded.

"It is so beautiful, James; our own private beach. We will have to have picnics here James!" Elizabeth exclaimed.

"Picnics and midnight swims," James said kissing Elizabeth's forehead. "You do know how to swim don't you?"

"I have been bathing before, but not actually swimming. Isn't the water awfully cold?" Elizabeth asked.

"Maybe cold to you now because you are used to such warm water in Wilmington. But you will find it very refreshing next summer. I will teach you how to swim and the babies when they come. That will come later of course but for now; I need to get you back to the house, Mrs. O'Rourke. Bridget will be putting on her best meal this evening to show her skills to her new mistress. I know you will want to dress for dinner," James stated.

They walked hand in hand up the path back to the main house. "I will be up in a few minutes, Elizabeth. Take your time in getting ready. I will check your buttons for you," he said laughing. Elizabeth turned to smile at him as she headed up the main staircase. James stood for a moment watching her climb the steps amazed at his own good fortune.

Back in the main suite, Elizabeth bathed and changed for dinner. She thought that she would wear the navy blue dress as it would match her jewelry parure. She would certainly not wear the tiara, but the remaining set would match beautifully with the blue gown.

As James did not return to the main suite, she assumed that he was dressing in a nearby room. He was so considerate in that way. Although she was still a young bride, she had not yet gotten accustomed to dressing or undressing in front of James. She assumed that someday like their love making it would become an everyday occurrence, but it had not yet reached that point in their relationship.

At 7:00 p.m. sharp, a rap came to the door. Elizabeth called come in and James came from behind the door looking very dapper and handsome as always. "I have come to check those buttons, Mrs. O'Rourke. It would not do to have you at your first Broadlands dinner with buttons undone. That is for later you know!" James said mockingly.

"I believe I have reached them all, Captain, but you are welcome to check to make sure that all is ship shape and Bristol fashion!" Elizabeth said laughing.

"It certainly is that and much more. Have I told you how beautiful you are yet today, Mrs. O'Rourke?"

"You have not and I may just get my feelings hurt that you haven't," Elizabeth said laughing. James kissed her hand and they headed downstairs for dinner.

"We are dining in the breakfast room, because it is smaller than the dining room and I don't want you across the room from me when we are eating dinner," James said. "It is a more intimate room and since we are accustomed to that, I thought you might like a more private room for our meals, if you have no objections," James asked.

"This is perfect, James; just like our meals on the Alliance. You are the most thoughtful man," Elizabeth replied smiling.

"Anything to keep my bride happy!" James said laughing.

Bridget came in at that time with the first course of the meal. "I have made all of the Captain's favorites this evening, Mistress as is our custom. If you can provide me with the menus going forward, I will be happy to add some of your favorites as well," Bridget said smiling.

"Thank you so much, Mrs. Kennedy. I am sure that everything that you make is wonderful," Elizabeth replied. Bridget exchanged glances at James who beamed back at him.

James explained the origin of each of the dishes provided for dinner and whether or not they were family favorites or ones that he had acquired on his travels. "I want you to understand that you are to provide your thoughts and ideas about the running of the house, Elizabeth. I don't want you to think that we have to run the house as it has been run in the past just because it has always been done that way. Any ideas that you have, you be sure to share with Bridget. I know that she will appreciate a female hand in the running of the house," he stated.

"James, I did have one thought about the master suite. Do you remember how much we enjoyed the window seat on the Alliance?" Elizabeth asked.

"I enjoyed it for a number of reasons, my love, but go on," James said teasingly.

"I was thinking that it might be nice to add a window seat to the master suite so that we could sit and look over the water when we have time together," Elizabeth said shyly.

"I think that is a grand idea. I was also thinking about using the adjoining room as my dressing room so that you don't hurry about trying to change before I get to our room," James said laughing. "I know you from old, Elizabeth O'Rourke. While I am thinking about it, have some more of this wine, my love."

"Are you plying me with liquor so that you can have your way with me, Captain O'Rourke?" Elizabeth said in mock horror.

"That was the general plan!" James replied laughing.

Bridget heard the two talking and laughing and said to Seamus that it was like old times again. "She is so like the Mistress, Seamus. The Master can't take his eyes off of her and she has brought him back to life again."

"Aye, I have noticed the same. I wish them all the happiness in the world. I have already heard some of the stories from the lads on the Alliance. Our new mistress has not had a happy life. I think it was one of the things that drew the Master to her; they have had the same sad life up until now. Then there was the threat on her life back in London," Seamus stated.

"Threat, what threat?" Bridget asked. Mr. Kennedy proceeded to tell his wife the whole story of what had occurred in London and how both Elizabeth and James were lucky to have escaped with their lives.

"Who would have ever thought it? She looks like a person without a care in the world and yet she has had her share of tragedy. I think you are right, Seamus; they can both share the losses in their lives and build a life together," Bridget replied.

At the conclusion of dinner, James told Elizabeth that he would have an evening cigar and come up directly. Elizabeth excused herself and went up to the master suite to change for the night. James sat reflecting on the past several months and the changes that had occurred in his life. He had never remembered being this happy since he was a child and both parents were alive. What a difference one person had made in his life.

James returned to the adjoining room to change for the night and to count his many blessings. In the morning, he would start a building crew on the ideas that Elizabeth had shared with him. He wanted her to think of Broadlands as her home and not just his home. Someday soon, he hoped they would start a family and she would truly look at Broadlands as her home though so far from her childhood memories.

James came into the master suite later and found Elizabeth sitting up in bed dressed in her white lace robe. "If that is not a sight to gladden a man's heart; a beautiful bride sitting in a man's bed waiting for him," James said smiling.

"James, I have one question?" Elizabeth responded.

"What would that be, love?" James said stretching across the bed, his head on her lap.

"Are all of your beds huge? I have never seen such large beds as this one and the one on the Alliance!" Elizabeth asked smiling.

"A man needs plenty of room to maneuver," James said huskily.

"Oh James; you are incorrigible!" Elizabeth said laughing.

"Not at all, my love, not at all; I need only a little encouragement of a night; like a smile from my beautiful bride!" James replied.

"I have noticed that your Irish brogue along with your Irish charm have become much thicker since your return home. I love them both," Elizabeth responded kissing James.

That was all the encouragement that he needed. He pulled her down beside him and began kissing her in earnest. The room was lit by candles as he had requested and his bride looked like an angel to him. He was thinking thoughts that were far from angelic, however. He quickly untied her robe and pulled it past her shoulders. In doing so, he saw the lace ribbon tied over the place of Elizabeth's gunshot wound. "Does it still hurt terribly, love?" James asked anxiously.

"It does, James; but I just cover it with the bandage and the ribbon because I didn't want you to see the scar," Elizabeth responded shyly.

"Stuff and nonsense love; do you not think that I have more scars than enough on my body from all of the years at sea? What do scars mean but that you have lived your life and come through to tell the tale?" James replied.

"I know, James but this scar just reminds us both of an unhappy memory and an ugly man and his ugly plans for us both," Elizabeth responded.

"I know, love; but he wasn't successful and we both lived to tell the tale. When we are blessed with a baby or two or three, there will be scars from that as well. You won't hide those scars from me I hope?" James asked.

"That is different, James; those are scars born of love for the babies that will come to us, God willing," Elizabeth replied smiling.

"This scar was born of love also, as I recall. You screamed so that Whitfield would take his attention from me and nearly got yourself killed in the process. I would say that was a scar born of love also," James said.

At that, James removed Elizabeth's nightgown as she lay beside him. "Let me look at you my beautiful girl and let's hear nothing more about hiding scars. Do you think I wouldn't love you if you weren't beautiful? Nothing you could do would end my love for you." James gently kissed the location of the gun wound and began to ravish Elizabeth with his lips and his hands. Elizabeth responded in a shy manner at first, but then as freely as she had done since their wedding night. He pulled her onto his chest and held her there letting her become accustomed to his hardness. "Doesn't that feel good, Elizabeth?" James asked.

"No James; it feels wonderful!" Elizabeth responded. With that response, Elizabeth began kissing James neck and chest, taking the initiative in their love making for the first time.

"Oh, darling girl; you don't know what you do to me!" James responded huskily. He rolled her onto her back and began his cherishing of her body beginning with her neck and proceeding to her chest, navel and abdomen. Elizabeth was struck again by the intensity of her response to James. It was as if she had found her second half. In the height of their passion for each other, Elizabeth lost all shyness and responded to James lovemaking in a way she did not believe imaginable.

For James' part, each time he made love to Elizabeth he felt a greater intensity than the time before. She was the missing part of his life; the part that brought him to life. He realized before meeting her that he was doing nothing more than running from life, constantly on the move, constantly working to fill the emptiness of his life. Being with Elizabeth was like removing the veil from his eyes and reawakening his soul to life. When he faced the possibility of losing her at the hands of Whitfield, he realized that he would do anything to keep her safe and make her happy. Bringing her joy only intensified his own.

When they had reached their climax, James rolled to his side carrying Elizabeth to him. He could feel her tears on his chest and turned to her to make sure that he had not hurt her. "Elizabeth love, did I hurt you? Why are you crying?" James asked worriedly.

"When we make love, James it is so intense that I just become emotional. It is like nothing that I have ever experienced. Thank you James for bringing so much joy to my life," Elizabeth responded through her tears.

James leaned in to kiss Elizabeth and said huskily "I thank God for you each day."

CHAPTER ELEVEN

Elizabeth woke the next morning in the center of the huge bed. She looked for James, but thought as usual he must be up and doing as was his custom. There was a note on the bedside table along with her night gown and robe neatly folded.

Darling girl,

I have gone down to Dublin to hire a building crew to start work on our projects. I should be back by luncheon and then we can go down to the village and visit the local church.

Love, James

Elizabeth loved James' notes and saved all of them in her jewelry box. He was the most considerate man and always made her feel so loved.

Elizabeth bathed and dressed quickly and went downstairs to the morning room. Bridget was there gathering up dishes from James' breakfast. "I could have brought you a tray, Mistress if you would prefer," Bridget said.

"I wouldn't want to put you to any trouble, Mrs. Kennedy. I will be happy to have breakfast here. It is a lovely room with wonderful sunlight," Elizabeth replied.

"What would you like for breakfast, Mistress? I have oatmeal on the stove or maybe a fry up? Do you like eggs and Irish bacon or sausage if you prefer?" Bridget asked.

"Eggs and Irish bacon sounds lovely, thank you," Elizabeth replied.

After breakfast, Elizabeth continued to write her letters home. Reverend and Mrs. Haynes would need to be advised that she would not be returning as quickly as expected. They would be surprised by her wedding and move to Ireland. She would ask that her letters and all other mail be forwarded to Broadlands for her response.

Her next letter was to her friend Lavinia Cole. She asked if she would send some recipes from home that she could share at Broadlands. She also told her of her new married status and asked her to advise their mutual friends.

When she had finished her letters, she placed them in the hall for posting and went upstairs to collect her shawl. The garden and path to the beach would be her destination. She advised Mrs. Kennedy where she would be in the event that James returned while she was away.

Elizabeth had always loved long walks and had taken them in Wilmington whenever she had a chance. During the war when horses were impossible to find, walks were the only way to complete errands and to visit with friends and family. The garden path to the private beach was Elizabeth's favorite part of Broadlands already. She knew that she was going to spend a great deal of time there. She may even learn to swim if James found the time.

The benches that James' father had placed along the path were wonderful places to take in the beauty of the surrounding area and the peace of the Irish Sea. She assumed it would not always be so peaceful, but enjoyed its beauty on this gorgeous autumn day. She closed her eyes and enjoyed the peace of the setting after several months of turmoil.

She heard a sound in the path after an hour or so and turned to find James coming to meet her with a wicker basket on his arm. "I believe that you mentioned a picnic darling girl. Bridget has been so kind to pack one for us and since we have a fine autumn day with some remaining warmth, I thought it a good place to have lunch. What do you say to that idea?" James said warmly.

"What a wonderful idea, darling. You are the most considerate man," Elizabeth said kissing his cheek.

"And sweet; don't forget sweet," James said mockingly.

"So you are, so you are; even if your crew would not always agree with that assessment," Elizabeth responded.

James spread out a plaid blanket on the beach and helped Elizabeth down to sit on the ground while he spread out the feast before them. "I believe that you have a mission to make me gain weight, James. You are always feeding me the most delicious food," Elizabeth stated.

"Oh you will gain weight soon enough, darling girl," James said huskily, "and not just from the wonderful food."

Elizabeth smiled at him shyly and arranged the dishes on the blanket ignoring his last comment.

They sat enjoying their picnic for a good hour or more. The space was so beautiful that Elizabeth could understand why it was James' favorite location and that of his parents before him. James stretched out on the blanket with his head on her lap as he had done the night before.

"So, when is the ball that I will hold for you to occur?" James asked.

"In America we have the Thanksgiving day celebration in November as a celebration of the harvest. Is there something similar here?" Elizabeth asked.

"We have days of Thanksgiving usually celebrating some victory or other of the empire. Tell me more about this Thanksgiving," James asked.

"We hold it in November and the main focus is the harvest and the thanks for the harvest. During the war years, there was nothing much to celebrate, but before the war it was a quite common occurrence," Elizabeth replied.

"I think we should celebrate Thanksgiving in November as is your custom by giving the ball that I want to hold for you to introduce you to the community. As your story will be legend by then, the whole county will want to meet you," James said smiling.

"What story and what legend?" Elizabeth asked confused.

"The story of how you captured the heart of Captain James O'Rourke and then saved his life from an assassin's bullet of course. That coupled with the fact that you come from America should mean that the house will not be big enough to house all those who will want to come and meet you," James said laughing.

"Are you serious, James? How would they even know about me?" Elizabeth asked astonished.

"When the crew dispersed, trust me the stories began. Bridget and Seamus have already heard them, so I am sure that you are legendary throughout the county by now and maybe into neighboring ones as well," James said smiling.

"That is awful, James. They will not be coming to meet me, but to come to peer at some sort of circus freak!" Elizabeth said starting to become anxious.

"Elizabeth, I was joking. Of course they will want to meet the most beautiful woman in the county, but you have to admit, it is not every day that they meet an American in fact most of them have never met an American. Add to that the mystery of the intrigue in London and there is bound to be curiosity. It is only natural, my love. Don't worry; everyone will love you just as the crew loves you and everyone else that meets you. Now, stop frowning and tell me how we will go about letting the county know that they are invited," James asked.

"Well if I was at home, I would leave my card at the various households and then I would return for a visit and invite them personally. Since I am not at home and don't have my cards made yet, I guess we could go to the houses and invite them individually. I am not sure how many people we are talking about," Elizabeth replied.

"How about we announce it in church on Sunday? That would just about cover everyone. I don't think that our friends and neighbors will stand much on ceremony when it comes to cards and the rest. Besides we would be visiting from now until November if we took that approach," James responded.

"Did you say that we were going into the village this afternoon and the church? We could start then with the local priest and maybe make a notice for the parish hall," Elizabeth replied.

"Capital idea as always. I need to get you out of the house anyway while the builders are working upstairs. Do you need anything from our room or can we go as we are to the village?" James asked.

"I should get my hat, James and then I will be ready," Elizabeth replied.

"Excellent. Let's get started so that we can be back in time for supper," James said smiling.

James ordered the carriage for their tour of the surrounding area. They visited the village and the parish church. He took her to the graves of his father and mother. Elizabeth asked if it would be permissible to plant roses at their grave site so there could be roses all summer. James touched her cheek at her thoughtfulness and said "I think they would like that and would love that their new daughter would have such a lovely thought with them in mind," James said smiling. "Let's see if Father O'Donnell is in."

James and Elizabeth went into the parish church where they found Father O'Donnell. "Father, I would like you to meet my wife, Elizabeth," James said proudly.

"What a pleasure to meet Mrs. O'Rourke," Father O'Donnell replied. "I have been hearing a great deal about you; the entire village is abuzz. The crew members have told me stories of your voyage and the incident in London. I hope you are recovering well from your injury."

"She is indeed, Father," James responded. "We are here to invite you to a ball at Broadlands to welcome Elizabeth to the community and so they can see a real life American in the flesh," James said laughing.

Father O'Donnell laughed at that remark. "I am sure that most of the community thinks of Miss Elizabeth as a cross between a southern bell and a frontier lady. Most of our parishioners and people of the village have never met an American before you see," Father O'Donnell replied.

"The ball will be the weekend of the start of advent; in America, that is Thanksgiving weekend. So we will celebrate Elizabeth's introduction to the community with an American holiday," James said smiling.

"I am sure the community will embrace your marriage and the way that you will be bringing Broadlands back to life. Bless you, Elizabeth O'Rourke. I will be sure to mention the ball in the announcements on Sunday," Father O'Donnell replied.

James took Elizabeth through the village and introduced her to neighbors anxious to meet the famous American who had stolen the heart of their Captain O'Rourke.

"So you were serious when you said the whole village had heard of me," Elizabeth said as they drove home.

"I was quite serious, darling girl. Tonight at the pub all who did not meet you will be hearing of the charms of the famous American, Elizabeth Majors O'Rourke. And I am the lucky man who married her. They will probably ask me to step out of the way so that they can see the famous American," James said laughing.

"I think I am already embarrassed, but I will be so glad to meet the community. Once they meet me, hopefully I won't be such a novelty," Elizabeth said smiling.

"I wouldn't count on that, darling girl; you will always be a novelty to the good folks around here. Not all women can say that they come from across an ocean to meet their intended and save him from certain murder all in three months time," James replied.

When they returned to Broadlands, James checked in with the builders as Elizabeth discussed some of the arrangements for the planned ball. James had suggested that they hire extra staff for the event and to start the planning straight away.

The next day, James went to Dublin to the fleet offices as was his custom and Elizabeth gathered a basket, gloves and her hat and set off for the parish church to plant roses on James' parents graves as she had offered. As always, she informed Bridget where she was going as she did not want James to be worried when he returned from his daily ride to Dublin and the fleet offices. The walk was a long one and the day was beautiful. She enjoyed the autumn weather and the walk as always. On arriving at the church, she went in search of Father O'Donnell so that he would know she was on grounds. "Good morning to you, Mrs. O'Rourke and what do you have planned this morning?"

"I am going to plant roses on James' parent's graves, Father. I thought it would be lovely for them to have roses all summer once the bushes have taken root," Elizabeth replied.

"What a lovely idea. If you need any help, please let me know and I will be happy to bring our groundskeeper to help you," Father O'Donnell responded.

Elizabeth walked over the cemetery grounds and found the location of her mother-in-law and father-in-law's graves. "I have come to plant some roses for you," Elizabeth told them both. "I promise to take good care of James for you and will love him with all of my heart." Elizabeth had made a habit of talking to her mother and father when she visited their graves and decided to do the same with her in-laws whom she would never know. She bent down to plant the small rose bushes and then her job done, walked around the lovely and well kept cemetery. Behind the larger stones of James' mother and father were smaller graves that marked the graves of children. There were four children buried there ranging in age from infancy to two years old. They were all O'Rourke children. How tragic, Elizabeth thought. All of these children lost and all at such a young age. Then James' mother dies when he is only eight years old. She thought of her own mother dying in childbirth and rather than being frightened of childbirth ahead, made a vow that it would be different for her; she would make herself strong for the labor that lay ahead bringing O'Rourke children into the world.

She heard a carriage pull up behind her and turning saw James at the reins. He had the look of thunder on his face and she wondered what could have happened to upset him. “Please get in this carriage this instant,” James said sharply.

“I was just planting flowers for your mother and father as we discussed, James. Please don’t be cross. What has happened?” Elizabeth asked worriedly.

“We will discuss it at home,” James responded coolly.

Elizabeth gathered her basket and was helped into the carriage by James’ strong hands. When she made herself comfortable in the carriage, James set off at a thunderous speed heading for home. “Are you going to tell me what is wrong or will I have to guess?” Elizabeth asked.

“I said we would discuss it at home and so we will!” James responded sharply.

When the gates of Broadlands approached, Elizabeth was relieved to find that the mystery would soon be at an end. James stopped the carriage and threw the reins to the stable boy. He came to her side of the carriage, lifted her out and took the basket from her hands. When they arrived in the entrance hall, he mounted the stairs to their room, Elizabeth’s hand in his own; pulling her with him.

When the door was closed behind them, Elizabeth looked at James’ furious face and tried to determine what had happened to cause his anger. She sat on the settee and waited for the explanation. It was not long in coming. “Elizabeth, I love your kindness in wanting to plant flowers on mother and father’s graves. It is so like you to think of others before you think of yourself. However, I cannot have you traipsing over the neighborhood all alone and without thought to your safety. Please promise me you will not do so again,” James stated angrily.

For a moment Elizabeth stared at him stunned by his words. She felt that she was back on the dock in Wilmington again receiving a lecture on what she should or should not do. “James, I was not traipsing over the neighborhood as you put it, I was simply walking down to the village and the parish church to plant flowers. Why are you responding in this manner?" Elizabeth was trying to remain calm as she could see that James was genuinely upset, but she couldn't understand why.

"If you had flowers to plant, you could have given them to Seamus and he would have taken them to the church groundskeeper to plant. You didn't have to bother yourself with it. What if something would have happened to you on your way to the village and I would not have known where to find you or how to help you?" James replied.

"Are you thinking about the day in London then?" Elizabeth asked calmly. She was starting to understand the reason for his upset. "It was only the village James and I told Bridget where I was going just as always. You can't get upset every time that I leave Broadlands," Elizabeth replied calmly.

"I can and I do get upset every time you leave Broadlands unless you are with me or with Seamus or one of the other lads. I cannot have you alone when something could happen to you," James replied.

"James, this is not London. You know everyone here and they know us. No one will try to hurt me here not like in London. You can't treat me like a china doll James O'Rourke. I have to be able to walk and breathe and live without your worrying about me every moment of the day!" Elizabeth was starting to work herself up at this moment and was feeling exactly as if she was on the dock in Wilmington again being lectured to by a father substitute.

"I will not lose you, Elizabeth; you have to understand, I cannot lose you." James turned his back then and looked out of the window towards their private beach.

"You won't lose me, James; I am right here." She tried soothing him then placing her arms around his waist and her head on his back.

"I have had a letter from Inspector Flynn. They need us to come to London and testify. Now do you see! We have to go back to London and you have to face the man who tried to kill you. Do you understand why I worry about your every movement without me or one of the lads? What if they try to harm you here as they did in London? And how are you going to face those men in a courtroom, Elizabeth?" James said in anguish.

Elizabeth could see the real reason for the anger. He was angry at Whitfield and Cross and how they had entered their lives and tried to turn them upside down.

"Does Inspector Flynn say when we must come to London?" Elizabeth asked quietly.

"He wants us after Christmas. We must help in preparing for the trial. I have no problem in going myself. I would personally build the gallows if it would mean that those two swung from them. I just don't want you to have to relive that day again," James replied.

Elizabeth took James' hand and led him to the settee. She sat down on his lap then to try to soothe him. "You will be with me in London and the lads on the ship will be there to protect me as well. We have to go, James. You know that. If we were not to testify and those two went free, who knows how many other people that they could hurt. We can't let that happen. You know that I won't go anywhere in London without you. I won't leave the ship unless you and the lads are there to protect me. You truly don't think they would send someone here to harm me do you?" Elizabeth said soothingly.

"I don't know what those two are capable of and I will not take the chance to find out," James replied heatedly.

"How about this; I won't take any walks unless you are with me. If we set a time each day, then I can have my walk and you can come with me," Elizabeth said smiling.

"Why on earth do you need to have your walk? I can place my hands around your waist now," James replied.

"James, when I was at the church yard this morning I saw the graves of your brothers and sisters. You know that your mother died in childbirth and so did mine. You can't wrap me in cotton wool, James. I must be strong to bear the O'Rourke tribe that we will bring into the world," Elizabeth replied.

"Did you truly just say tribe? How many children do you think we are going to have, Elizabeth? Besides, you are the strongest woman that I know." Finally James had seen something humorous in the morning's news.

"Yes, I said tribe. I have to be strong to bear the O'Rourke sons and continue the family line. I don't just mean mentally strong, but physically strong as well. When they call childbirth labor, they are not just using that term lightly. It is hard work and I must be strong to be prepared for it. When I said that I am not going anywhere, James O'Rourke, I mean that I want to sit on our beach and watch our grandbabies playing in the water. I have to be strong so that I can be here for you and for the babies to come," Elizabeth said smiling.

"If you agree to walk out with me each day, then I agree to you taking a walk everyday even if we leave Broadlands. How does that sound?" James replied.

"I like the idea of walking out with my husband. It sounds like we are still courting." Elizabeth had mischief in her eyes when she made the last comment. She placed her arms around James' neck and began kissing him on the ear and neck.

"Elizabeth, do you know what you do to me when you touch me in that way," James said huskily.

"Shush love; you will like it I promise," Elizabeth said laughing. She had used the exact words to James that he had used to her on their wedding night.

James laughed out loud at that moment for the first time all morning. "I am going to torture you until you beg for mercy for that comment," he continued laughing. With that James lifted Elizabeth into his arms and took her to the massive bed.

"James, I have a whole row of buttons remember," Elizabeth said laughing.

"Bridget will find one of your dresses ripped from neck to waist one day all because of those damn buttons," James replied.

"Oh, James; you wouldn't do that? What would Bridget think?" Elizabeth said shocked by his comment.

"I think she would figure it out, Elizabeth. It must be common knowledge by now that I can't keep my hands off my wife," James said kissing Elizabeth's back.

By this time, James had undone enough buttons for Elizabeth to drop the dress to the floor. She stood standing in her chemise and petticoats. James undressed then and was waiting patiently in the bed, his arms behind his neck as if he had all of the time in the world. Elizabeth untied her petticoats and got into bed in her chemise. She resumed kissing James' ear and neck and then started touching his chest with light caresses. "Are you trying to make me forget our argument?" James asked mockingly.

"Is it working?" Elizabeth said laughing.

"It is working all too well. Just so you remember what you agreed to?" James said taking the pins from her hair, working his hands through it and holding her captive with the movement.

"I always remember what I agree to, James darling," Elizabeth replied softly. By that time she had reached his abdomen with her soft caresses and kisses.

"You do know that you could drive a man wild doing that," James said between clenched teeth. At that moment he rolled Elizabeth onto her back and began ravishing his wife. The chemise was quickly disposed of as James began an assault on her neck, her breasts and abdomen. He quickly entered her and began their lovemaking, patient at first but then with greater need and intensity. All of the intensity of the morning was now focused on lovemaking and James was making the most of it. When they had both reached their climax James rolled to his side carrying Elizabeth with him.

"I will not lose you, Elizabeth," James said again quietly.

"You will not lose me James nor I you. We have been destined for one another since that first day on the dock in Wilmington and we are not going to let anyone or anything come between us." She nestled her head on his chest and fell asleep quickly; worn out by the walk, the argument and the lovemaking.

CHAPTER TWELVE

The next few weeks were a blur of preparation for the ball as well as the renovations to the house. James had the builders prepare the dressing rooms for them both and the nursery rooms that completed the family wing of the upstairs. The addition to the main Georgian style home would house renovated rooms for guests. James had promised the house would come back to life and he was faithful to his promise. The window seat in the master suite was the first improvement completed in the planned work. James and Elizabeth made excellent use of that new space. Each evening before bed they would sit on the window seat and talk about the day and what was planned for the next.

Despite the preparations or perhaps because of them, Elizabeth found that she was very tired in the afternoon and had begun taking a daily afternoon nap. James observant as always, asked the builders to work on the guest rooms so that she would not be disturbed. He suspected that the trials of the voyage as well as the London incident had taken more from Elizabeth than she cared to admit and that the shock of the situation was just beginning to catch up with her. He still worried about the upcoming trial, but decided to put it from his mind with the impending ball. He had planned on hiring a groundskeeper who would watch the property and watch for intruders whenever he was away from home. He would take no chances with the safety of Elizabeth and of the household.

Elizabeth received the requested recipes from home and she provided them to Bridget so that some American dishes could also be incorporated into the buffet planned for the night of the ball. Each evening they experimented with the different dishes so that Bridget could obtain confidence in their preparation prior to the big night. James suggested a trip to Dublin for a new dress for the ball which would also give Elizabeth the opportunity to see the repairs to the Alliance.

Everything was in place and ready for the big event. James had sent an invitation to his Uncle Colin to attend, but the preparation for the advent season kept him close to London. He promised to come for the Christmas holidays and to stay until after New Year's Day; as James and Elizabeth had a large Christmas planned as well after the ball was completed.

On the day of the ball, the day rose sunny but cool. All of the decorations were in place, the food was under preparation and Elizabeth was trying very hard to not become nervous at the number of neighbors who would be in attendance. She reminded herself that James would be at her side and as he knew everyone in the county, everything would be fine. She found that she had also determined the reason for her tiredness. She was going to have a baby. She had not yet told James due to all of the excitement of the ball preparations, but planned to tell him the night of the ball. She knew that he would be thrilled as they had talked about starting a family from the time of their honeymoon. In order to get away from the madness at the house, Elizabeth took her normal stroll down to the private beach. She wanted to clear her head before the start of the festivities. As always, she informed Bridget where she was going so that James would not be alarmed if he did not find her in the house. The scare in London had affected both of them so much that they always left notes as to their whereabouts. The letter from Inspector Flynn had heightened that concern and Elizabeth knew that a groundskeeper was now on staff to survey the perimeter of the property and make sure that the household was safe.

The secluded nature of the private beach meant that even when the temperatures cooled, the wind did not penetrate the beach area. The sun on her face felt like the last remnants of warmth for the season. She looked forward to learning how to swim in the summer, but remembered that she would be close to her delivery time and may be too large to enjoy the swimming lessons. As she sat on the bench contemplating all that life had in store for them both, she thanked God again for the happiness that he had provided to them both and the twists of fate that had brought her to yet another beach across the Atlantic from her Wilmington home. She closed her eyes and thought of her former world an ocean away and the joy that she had found from the moment that she planned the trip to London.

After an hour or so, James came looking for her at their usual place. She sat on the bench with her face towards the sun looking as if she was napping. "Mrs. O'Rourke, are you hiding from your guests already?" James said laughing.

"Not a bit of it, Captain O'Rourke; I am sitting here capturing the last bits of warmth from the season and thinking about swimming lessons that I will have here next summer," Elizabeth said laughing.

"I will hold you to that, Elizabeth. Everyone on Broadlands learns to swim just as everyone in my fleet learns to swim. You will not be an exception and besides, we may need to take advantage of this private beach for some private swimming lessons by moonlight next summer," James said kissing Elizabeth.

"If that means what I think that means, I will be looking for a bathing costume in Dublin next spring," Elizabeth said mockingly.

"Why do you think my father created a path to a private beach if not for private swimming lessons by moonlight? You will see; you will come to love it as much as I. Have I ever steered you wrong in the past?" James asked laughing.

"No you have not, my love. I was just sitting here thinking about the twists of fate that have brought me across the Atlantic to my own private beach and the wonderful life that we have here at Broadlands. I could not be any happier James. Thank you so much for our wonderful life together," Elizabeth said smiling.

James kissed Elizabeth and she placed her head on his shoulder as they watched the waves before them and the sun beginning to set. “I know that we could sit here all day Mrs. O’Rourke, but you will want to have plenty of time to get ready for tonight. The whole county will be coming to see my beautiful bride,” James stated.

“I know,” Elizabeth said. “Why do you think I am hiding out here?” she said laughing.

“Come on then, I need you to be ready to dance every dance with your husband. I have to make every gentleman in the room jealous of my beautiful wife,” James replied smiling.

When they returned to the house, Bridget came upstairs to assist Elizabeth in getting ready. The extra help that James had suggested was in place and everything was in order. The only thing left was to get ready and start the receiving line to receive the guests. Elizabeth brought out the new gown that James had purchased for her for the night’s event. There was also a new box on the dressing room table when she arrived there to bathe. She had not yet opened the box, but suspected it was another gift from her wonderful husband for their big night. She had yet to find James a wedding gift but hoped the news that she would be telling him this evening would fit that bill.

When she had the emerald green dress on, she opened the box on her dressing room table and found a pearl necklace inside. James had bought her the necklace to go with her mother’s pearls that she had worn the first night that they had dined together on the Alliance. He thinks of everything, Elizabeth thought as she tried on the necklace. There was a note as well from James. The note read:

My darling wife,

Here is a necklace to match your mother’s pearls. I remember you wearing them the first night that we spent together. You will look beautiful wearing them.

Much love, James.

He is the most considerate man in the world, Elizabeth thought. Bridget saw her smile and thought that the Master had given her another gift just like his father used to do with his sainted mother. If only they could see these two together, Bridget thought, but then again, she was sure that they were all watching over James and Elizabeth. "You will be the belle of the ball, Mistress! No one will hold a candle to you. It is just like the old days when the Master's mother and father would hold balls and parties here at Broadlands. You have brought Broadlands back to life, Mistress just as you have brought the Master back to life. Bless you both," Bridget said crying.

"Thank you so much, Bridget. I am so happy here in my new home. All that I want to do is to make it a real home here for everyone. Thank you for working so hard to make this ball a success," Elizabeth replied smiling.

There was a rap on the door that Elizabeth knew would be James. She called come in and James came in smiling. "So is Mrs. O'Rourke ready to be the belle of the ball?" James asked smiling.

"She certainly is that," Bridget said smiling. "No one will hold a candle to her!"

James gave Elizabeth his arm as they proceeded out of the master suite and down the stairs. Elizabeth knew that she would be fine with James at her side and that she could face the many guests proud of the fact that she was Mrs. James O'Rourke. She was also secretly beaming about the news that she would share with him later this evening about the baby. Her excitement must have shown in her face. James looked at her as they descended the steps and said "I am always amazed that each time I think you are the most beautiful woman that I have ever seen, you surpass yourself time and again," James said smiling.

"Thank you so much for my beautiful gown and for my necklace. I thought emerald green was an appropriate color for tonight. Do you like it darling?" Elizabeth asked.

"I do indeed. I will be the envy of every man in the county tonight," James replied smiling.

James and Elizabeth stood in the hallway and prepared to meet their guests. James as promised knew everyone in the county and Elizabeth was introduced to each person as they came in. She was sure that she would not remember every name, but smiled happy to meet them all and to welcome them into their house. After the guests were assembled, the band began to play the same waltz that had been played when Elizabeth and James had dined at the Carlyle in Bermuda. He led her onto the floor and danced the waltz as they had done that memorable night in Bermuda. The company joined in with the dance, but as he predicted no one could match his Elizabeth.

After several dances, James led Elizabeth over to the buffet table. The delicacies from both the American south and Ireland were laid out for the guests. James spied fried oysters and proceeded to place some on Elizabeth's plate. He brought the plate over to Elizabeth who was seated with Father O'Donnell. "Father you must try some of the fried oysters from the buffet. Many of the recipes are from Elizabeth's family in America," James stated.

"Are they now? Well I must try some of those as well as the other items before us. You certainly set a beautiful table, Mrs. O'Rourke," Father O'Donnell replied.

James set down beside Elizabeth and provided her with her plate. She ate one of the oysters, but left the rest on the plate. "Is something wrong, love? I saw that you left your favorite oysters on your plate," James asked concerned.

"They just didn't taste like they usually do. I think I will have something else for my next plate if you don't mind," Elizabeth replied.

"Not at all, my love," James said smiling. "Let's try some of the other dishes for your next plate."

Father O'Donnell asked James if he might make a toast. "By all means, Father," James replied.

"I would like to ask the assembled guests to be upstanding as I make my toast to our hosts James and Elizabeth O'Rourke. May your life be long; may your children be many and may you dwell in happiness and freedom all of the days of your life. Welcome Mrs. O'Rourke to Ireland and we wish you much happiness in your marriage in the days ahead," Father O'Donnell stated.

"Well said, Father; to Elizabeth," James said smiling.

Elizabeth sat blushing at James and the assembled guests. For the third time she felt that she had found a new home. First she had felt that love on the Alliance with the protective nature of the crew; second in the circle of the O'Rourke men who had loved and protected her since she left Wilmington and now in her new home of Broadlands. It was so much happiness that she shed true tears of joy.

Elizabeth was kept busy answering questions of her guests about America and from the ladies, requests for copies of the recipes which she promised to provide. James captured her for all of the waltzes that were played and the night wore on into the wee hours; a success for both the guests and the hosts. When the last of the guests prepared to leave, James brought Elizabeth over to the door to say goodbye. "You certainly have brought Broadlands back to life," Mrs. O'Neill stated. "It was lovely to meet you and thank you very much for the beautiful night."

James smiled at Elizabeth as they climbed the stairs to their room that night. She was tired, but so happy that she at last had him all to herself so that they could share her news. "Do you need some help with your buttons then, Mrs. O'Rourke?" James said laughing.

"I do, but I need to talk to you for a moment first. Come sit down." Elizabeth had led him to their favorite window seat. Outside the full moon bore down on the grounds at Broadlands and beyond the gardens, to the private beach overlooking the Irish Sea.

"Are you happy, Elizabeth? I think everyone enjoyed themselves and you were of course the belle of the ball as I predicted. Now what is it that you need to tell me, love?" James asked.

"James, I have some news to tell you. I have finally found the perfect wedding gift for you. I am going to have a baby! I wanted you to be the first to know before I told anyone else, but I have nearly burst trying to keep the secret all day long. That is why I was down at the beach, sitting and thinking about the baby and the summers to come," Elizabeth said smiling through her tears.

"My love, I have suspected for some time that you were with child. The naps in the afternoon were the first clue. The fact that you turned down oysters this evening told me that I was right, but I wanted to hear it from you and not take away your wonderful surprise. I am so happy and so proud all at the same time," James said laughing.

"They say that sometimes foods you usually love don't taste the same and that was definitely the case with the oysters. As to the naps, I was trying to keep that a secret from you, but I see that there is no use trying to keep any secrets ever," Elizabeth said laughing.

"What did we say about no secrets between us?" James said pulling Elizabeth onto his lap. "You know that I will always find out!"

"I am so happy, James. I didn't know it was possible to be so happy. And it is all because of you," Elizabeth replied.

"I think it is because of us, because you have made me the happiest man on earth ever since you stepped your pretty foot on the Alliance," James replied.

"I thought I was going to be a lot of trouble?" Elizabeth said grinning.

"Did I say that ever?" James said laughing. "It was before I had my eyes opened and my heart opened as well."

"You must write Uncle Colin tomorrow and tell him the good news. Also, you need to remind him to come down for Christmas and that we will hear no excuses from him for not visiting," Elizabeth replied.

"My darling wife has spoken, so she has and her word is law," James said laughing and kissing Elizabeth.

The next day James let Elizabeth sleep in and went to the study to write to his Uncle Colin in London. There was much news to share and updates to provide to his uncle.

November, 1865

I am writing at the request of Elizabeth. She has asked that I write you and remind you that you promised to join us for the Christmas holidays. We are going to have an old fashioned family Christmas this year here at Broadlands and we would love for you to visit. We won't be travelling this year. As I predicted, Elizabeth is with child and we are not risking bumpy roads or travel by sea until the baby is with us. You were right all of those years ago Uncle Colin. When the right one comes into your life, all of your ideas about domesticity will change overnight. I cannot believe that three short months ago I was on a dock in Wilmington, North Carolina and that my life was about to change forever. Change it has done and most definitely for the better. If the baby is a boy, Elizabeth wants to name him Christopher Colin O'Rourke. I hope that you will agree with us that St. Christopher had something to do with Elizabeth being here with us safe and happy and the Colin is of course for you.

We will need to return to London for the trial of Cross and Whitfield. I will advise Hugh Flynn today that there will be no travelling and no testifying until Elizabeth has the baby. She has been through enough and if they cannot make their case without her, they will have to wait until the baby is born.

I will sign off for now. We look forward to seeing you in December. Love from Elizabeth and from me.

James

His next letter was to Hugh Flynn to inform him that Elizabeth was pregnant and that she would not be able to testify until next summer. James would come after Christmas if that was helpful to Inspector Flynn, but Elizabeth could not possibly travel and he would not consider letting her do so.

After posting his letters in the hallway, he went upstairs to check on Elizabeth. She was sleeping in the center of the huge bed as always. Even if she started on the far left side, she always made her way to the center of the bed by morning to search for him no doubt. He quietly entered the room to see if she was still sleeping. She opened her eyes as he came to the side of the bed. "Good morning, Mrs. O'Rourke. How are you this morning?" he said smiling at his beautiful wife.

"Wonderful, but famished. Have you had breakfast yet?" Elizabeth replied.

"I have and posted two letters so far this morning. I wrote Uncle Colin reminding him about Christmas and wrote Hugh Flynn telling him that you cannot possibly testify until after the baby is born. There is no use trying to change my mind Elizabeth; I will not bend on this point," James said adamantly. He had not informed her that he would be going to London after Christmas as he did not want to upset her in anyway.

"I wasn't going to try to change your mind. I think that Whitfield and Cross should sit in jail until next summer. They should have to think about what they have done. If Inspector Flynn needs my help, I can always help him via letter in the mean time," Elizabeth replied.

"A very sound plan indeed, Mrs. O'Rourke; are you sure that you don't want to try to sleep some more?" James asked tenderly.

"No, I think that I will get up as I need to write some letters also and besides, I will probably need another nap this afternoon. That has been the pattern lately," Elizabeth replied smiling.

"You may need some help with that nap, so don't worry; you won't need to be alone," James said laughing. Elizabeth got up then and went into her dressing room to bathe and dress. She saw the lovely emerald green dress on the hanger as she entered and thought again about the ball the night before. "Will you need any assistance bathing Mrs. O'Rourke?" James said laughing.

"I think that I will be fine, Captain O'Rourke but you can talk to me while I bathe and dress if you like," Elizabeth replied.

"I expect a number of notes from last night's guests. I haven't seen such a crowd here at Broadlands since before mother died," James said.

"Do you think that they have gotten their fill of the novelty of the resident American?" Elizabeth asked.

"I am doubtful of that. Your fame will probably spread throughout the country after last night. I saw several ladies ask you for copies of recipes so they must have enjoyed the American dishes," James replied.

"They were probably just being polite, but I did appreciate the request. James do you think that Father O'Donnell would be upset if we had the baby christened next summer by Uncle Colin?" Elizabeth asked.

"I am sure that he would understand. Do you think that we would take the baby with us next summer then?" James asked.

"I would not consider travelling without him," Elizabeth said.

"So you are sure already that we are having a son," James asked laughing.

"I am indeed," Elizabeth said coming out of the dressing room. "The first baby is always a boy," Elizabeth replied.

"Do I need to remind you that you were the first baby and a girl?" James asked smiling.

"The first O'Rourke baby is always a boy; how about that?" Elizabeth said smiling.

"The wife has spoken so she has; a baby boy O'Rourke for sure and as beautiful as his mother," James replied smiling.

"As handsome as his father," Elizabeth said sitting on James' lap and kissing him.

While James went up to Dublin to check on the repairs to the Alliance, Elizabeth wrote her letters home. Her first letter was to her friend Lavinia Cole. She wanted to let her know how successful the ball had been and that the recipes from home had been well received and requested by several of the ladies in attendance. She also needed to solicit her help. Since Elizabeth knew that she was expecting her first child, she needed to have help from the family midwife and all of the recipes that she would need to recreate for the birthing process far from home.

Lavinia,

I will need a copy of all of the recipes used by Aunt Sally for the child birth process. Since I will be so far from home, I need to know that Aunt Sally is with me in spirit and that all of the secrets that she uses are with me also. I will have to see if there is a local midwife that can help me also. I know that my husband's ship doctor is here, but I will feel so much more comfortable with other women when I give birth. I may have to convince my husband of the benefit of this wisdom, but I know that I am on the right course. Please talk to Aunt Sally and get all of her potions or at least the recipes for them so that I can recreate them here. If there are any ingredients that don't grow here, send me those too and I will keep them for the big day.

In addition, please be so kind to send me recipes for Christmas treats that I can share with my family here. We will be having a family Christmas for the first time in years and I am so anxious to make sure that all goes well. Thank you so much Lavinia and much love to you and your family, Elizabeth wrote.

The second letter was again to Reverend and Mrs. Haynes. As she knew that a trip home was not feasible until the birth of the baby, she wanted to ask them to look out for the family home until next summer when she would be able to schedule a trip home. She also asked that they advise her of any expense that they may incur so that she would be sure that they were reimbursed for their assistance. She placed both letters along with James' letters in the hallway for posting purposes and went to the kitchen for her long awaited breakfast.

Bridget and Seamus were in the kitchen resting from the prior day's events. Elizabeth went to find them and thank them for the wonderful ball. "I just wanted to thank you both so much. I think the ball was a great success and everyone seemed to have a wonderful time," Elizabeth said.

"It was just like old times, Mistress. Everyone in the county is talking about meeting the American, meaning you and of being that happy to see the Captain bring Broadlands back to life again," Bridget replied.

"I guess our next event will be the Christmas holiday. I have already written home and asked for some recipes for traditional southern Christmas dishes so that I can add them to the dishes usually served here. I hope you don't mind Bridget," Elizabeth stated.

"Not at all, Miss Elizabeth; the American dishes were very popular last night and I know that you have been asked for some of the recipes by the guests at the ball. I think it is grand that we have the best of both families for our special feasts. What can I get you for breakfast this morning?" Bridget asked.

"I think eggs and Irish bacon would be wonderful," Elizabeth responded.

After her late breakfast, Elizabeth went in search of James upon his return from Dublin. She went into his library and in his absence, looked at the portraits of his mother and father hanging there. James came in quietly behind her and placed his arms around her waist. "I think that I have thought of the perfect idea for the wedding gift that you have been asking me about," James stated.

"I thought I gave you my surprise last night," Elizabeth said laughing.

"You did, you did; but another thing that I would like is a portrait of you to add to those of my mother and father here in the library. I can contact the painter who did those and ask him to come and paint you. That is the one thing that I would like more than any other," James replied.

"That is a marvelous idea, James; many of the houses at home before the war had portraits of the family members. It would be just like home to have that done. The only problem is it will need to be soon before I start to show," Elizabeth said worriedly.

"As if you would not be even more beautiful when you are with child," James answered. "I will write him now and see if he can come before Christmas."

The letters were on their way requesting recipes, childbirth potions, invitations and a request for a portrait painter. The next thing on the list was the preparation for Christmas. Elizabeth sought out Bridget and Seamus to ask them about Christmas decorations and the schedule for beginning that process. "Mistress we have not decorated for so many years we will need to check on the attic for you to see what we may have. There are plenty of greens on the property here that we can bring in if that would be satisfactory," Bridget replied.

"I don't know if we have ever had one in the past, but I would love to decorate a Christmas tree as well. What about holly and other Christmas greens? Do we have them on the property as well?" Elizabeth asked.

"We do and we will show you where in the garden so that you can let us know what you would like cut for the house," Bridget replied.

Elizabeth had started her list for Christmas preparations; decorations and recipes were underway. The next items would be gifts for James, Seamus and Bridget and for Uncle Colin. She would need to ask for a trip to Dublin to purchase items for them all. She went into James' library again to see if she could find any books on Christmas observance in Ireland. She most definitely did not want to omit a tradition by mistake by not knowing it existed. James came in while she was doing her research. "What can I help you with, love?" James asked.

"I am trying to find a book in your library on Christmas observance in Ireland. I want to make sure that I include all of the customary traditions and then add some from home. I can't find anything that will tell me what I need to know. Is there a library in Dublin that can assist me with that research?" Elizabeth asked.

"Leave it to my brilliant wife to want to know all while she plans our Christmas. Everyone else would put up a tree and call it a day. Would you like me to tell you the O'Rourke family traditions so that you can make a list of those?" James asked.

"That would be lovely, James. Let me get my list of items and we can add to it. James sat down in his library chair and motioned for Elizabeth to come sit on his lap. "James O'Rourke, you know full and well if I sit there we will lose our concentration and start thinking about everything in the world except Christmas. I will sit across from you and ask you questions and you can tell me the family customs and I will make a list of what we will need," Elizabeth said primly.

"Very well, Mrs. O'Rourke; ask me your questions and I will tell you what you will need to know," James responded smiling.

"What is your greeting at home for Christmas?" Elizabeth asked.

"The Christmas greeting is *Nollaig Shona Duit*; which means basically, Happy Christmas," James answered.

"I will need you to write that down for me as I have no idea how to spell it. I may just need to say Happy Christmas. What kind of decorations do I need to plan for the Christmas holiday?" Elizabeth asked.

"There will be holly and ivy wreaths for the graves. We have holly and ivy in the gardens so that can be cut for you to make the wreaths. Oh and we will need a crib," James replied.

"I know we will need a crib, James; but that will be for the baby's room. I am talking about Christmas," Elizabeth responded.

"I am speaking of Christmas also, love. A crib is Irish for a nativity scene. There should be one in the attic from years ago. If not, we can get one in Dublin when I take you Christmas shopping," James said smiling.

"Are you taking me Christmas shopping, then? I was hoping so, but wasn't sure yet. That will be wonderful so that we can get whatever we will need that I can't find here. What about the Christmas holiday itself? Do we observe Christmas Eve and Christmas Day and New Year's only?" Elizabeth asked.

"We will start with mass on Christmas Eve and have the grand feast on Christmas Day. St. Stephen's Day will be December 26 and 27th and family visits will extend until Little Christmas on January 6," James replied.

"What traditional items do you serve for your Christmas feast?" Elizabeth asked.

"We should have turkey, goose or ham or all three if you like and Christmas pudding. That will be something that you have probably not tasted before, but Bridget will know what to do. On Christmas Eve we should have fish. Now anymore questions for your teacher, Mrs. O'Rourke?" James asked mockingly.

"No, Captain; I think that should be sufficient for the day. Thank you very much. I will ask Seamus to bring down whatever we have in the attic and then I can take inventory and determine what we will need to shop for in Dublin. Thank you, darling. You are an excellent teacher as always!" Elizabeth added mischievously.

"Oh, you have no idea, Mrs. O'Rourke. Now then, give your teacher a kiss and we will go on your walk. Then we may need to plan that nap that you talked about earlier," James said with a wink.

CHAPTER THIRTEEN

The next few days were brimming with Christmas activity. Seamus brought all of the available decorations from the attic so that Elizabeth could inventory and see what would be needed in Dublin to complete the Christmas décor. A historic crib or nativity was brought down and placed in the location of honor beside the Christmas tree which was cut from the garden. As soon as Elizabeth saw the crib she was reminded of the crib that was needed for their little one and thought to ask Seamus about any furniture that may also be in the attic after Christmas was over. She intended to keep her baby secret within the immediate family until after the holidays.

Holly and ivy were brought in from the garden as well to decorate the staircase and mantels and for Elizabeth to fashion into wreaths for her in-laws graves. James was the ever hovering presence after returning from Dublin each day to make sure that she was not doing too much in any given day. As soon as he would return from the fleet office they would go on their walk, have lunch and then a special nap as James referred to it.

On the 5th of December, the portrait painter arrived at Broadlands and Elizabeth revised her schedule to include time sitting for the portrait in the morning while James was in Dublin. Mr. O'Toole agreed to keep the final portrait a surprise for Elizabeth to provide to James on Christmas morning. She wore her emerald ball gown and the pearl necklace in the portrait as a thank you to James for his thoughtfulness. She thought to ask Mr. O'Toole if it would be possible to do a portrait of James as well, but since he was never still for long, she would have to determine a way to have Mr. O'Toole do the portrait without sittings, if that was feasible.

Once the Christmas decorations were completed and the wreaths placed in the cemetery, Elizabeth turned her attention to the list for the Christmas shopping. She also needed to find a date and time that would work with James' schedule for the promised Christmas shopping outing in Dublin. The shopping for the baby she decided would have to wait until after Christmas when James returned from London. Every time that she thought about James' London trip, she would place it in the back of her mind. Since August, the two had not been separated for more than a few hours and she knew that she would miss him horribly. She thought it might well be a good time to visit with the local midwife while James was gone. It might be the only opportunity that she would have to ask the questions that she needed to ask and become prepared for the baby's coming. She decided to broach the idea of a trip to Dublin this afternoon when they took their daily walk.

When James' returned from Dublin, he found her in the master suite dressing room changing from the portrait session in the morning. "Elizabeth, are you ready for your walk? We need to try to get one in before the rain starts," James said through the dressing room door.

"I will be out in a moment," Elizabeth called.

James as always thought it amazing that his beautiful wife was still shy about changing in front of him. He put it down to another mystery of Elizabeth that he may never solve. He was happy that the dressing rooms were one of the first improvements put in place after their return to Broadlands. That and the nursery which he was also glad to put to use in short order. Whenever his mind turned to Elizabeth delivering the baby, he had to put away the thought. As thrilled as he was about the pregnancy, the specter of child birth chilled him. He was serious when he had told Elizabeth that he would not lose her. Whatever it took to have her deliver their baby in the safest way possible would be his mission. When he was in London, he thought to search out the best specialists in this area and ask for their advice and counsel.

"Darling, when should we go to Dublin to do our Christmas shopping?" Elizabeth asked coming from the dressing room. "And after you answer that question, what would you like for Christmas?"

"The same thing that I wanted for my wedding gift; I want my beautiful wife and I need her in my bed. Other than that, I am a contented man," James replied smiling.

"Well there must be something that you would like. What about some cigars for your after dinner smoke?" Elizabeth asked.

"I have all that I need, but I thank you for the thought," James replied.

"Well, we need to get a gift for Uncle Colin and what about Bridget and Seamus?" Elizabeth asked.

"Bridget and Seamus are easy. On St. Stephens Day they receive a bonus like the English do with their Boxing Day. Uncle Colin may prove to be more difficult. Like me he is a man with few wants and needs. I will have to give that one some thought. Would you like to go up to Dublin tomorrow if the weather cooperates?" James asked.

"That would be lovely. Thank you, darling husband," Elizabeth said kissing James' cheek.

The weather did not cooperate and set in for several days of rain. Elizabeth's portrait project moved along very well, as there were multiple hours that could be devoted to the project. The Christmas shopping was temporarily placed on hold until there was a break in the weather. In the interval, letters were received from America and Elizabeth added some additional items to her list for the special dishes that she wished to make for Christmas. The items for the birth of the baby she placed in her dressing room until she could read and study them uninterrupted.

When the weather did improve, James and Elizabeth went up to Dublin to complete their Christmas shopping. Elizabeth was in love with the decorated store windows and the beautiful decorations. She also experienced her first snow while they were in Dublin and thought the city looked just like a picture post card. She bought cards with *Nollaig Shona Duit* emblazoned upon them to send to Lavinia Cole and to Reverend and Mrs. Haynes. Although James was always at her side, she managed to do some secret shopping for him and for Uncle Colin. The day was a merry one and Elizabeth could not remember such a Happy Christmas since before the war when her mother and father were alive and with her.

Returning in the carriage, Elizabeth felt the customary sleepiness come upon her and remembered her special present that was the cause of the afternoon naps. She placed her head on James shoulder and slept until they returned to Broadlands. As they pulled up to the house, Elizabeth woke up and saw the lovely wreath that she had placed on the front door and the candles at the windows welcoming the Christ child. The light snow had made the whole scene look like a Christmas card. She felt well and truly home at that point and could not wait to celebrate her first Christmas with her husband in her new home. “James, the house looks just like a picture from a Christmas card with the snow and the candles. I can’t wait for our first Christmas together,” Elizabeth exclaimed.

“I was thinking as we pulled into the lane that I have not looked forward to Christmas in the same way since I was a child. This is all because of you, Elizabeth. You have brought life back to Broadlands and Christmas back as well. I am truly blessed to have you in my life; thank you, darling girl. Let’s get you upstairs so that you can hide that secret Christmas gift that I saw you buy for me,” James said laughing.

“Oh, James; you did not see it. I was so very careful to make sure that you didn’t. Thank you any way for the beautiful compliment, darling,” Elizabeth replied.

The next week was Christmas week and Father O'Rourke would not be arriving until St. Stephens Day so that he could complete services for his congregation. James would pick him up from Dublin on the 27th and they would celebrate a family Christmas on that date. Christmas Eve and Christmas Day would be spent with Elizabeth and James at home. The community would be welcomed on the 26th for Boxing Day and the rest of the holiday would be spent with Uncle Colin. All was in place for the holiday season.

The portrait that James had requested was finished the week before Christmas. Mr. O'Toole stated that he had tried to capture the life and vitality of Mrs. O'Rourke in his work and he hoped that he had accomplished that very thing. He would be anxious to hear the response from Captain O'Rourke when it was presented on Christmas Day.

Christmas Eve arrived and James went to Dublin to spend a few hours with the crew members and to dispense their Christmas bonuses. Elizabeth placed the wrapped gifts under the tree so that James and Uncle Colin would be surprised. Elizabeth had found a pair of cuff links for James and a decorative bible for Uncle Colin. For Bridget and Seamus she had found chocolates and tea that she hoped that they would enjoy along with the St. Stephen's Day bonus. Everything was set and ready.

James arrived home in time for luncheon. He was as excited as a schoolboy. "The lads all appreciated their Christmas bonuses. They send Happy Christmas wishes to the Mistress and hope you are doing well. They are of course all still in love with you. I am the lucky man who comes home to you and gets to spend my Christmas holiday worshiping my beautiful wife," James stated kissing Elizabeth.

"Thank you, darling. You say the sweetest things. Don't worry I won't tell anyone and ruin your reputation," Elizabeth said laughing.

"Don't you think we should take one of our special naps after luncheon so that we are ready for the Christmas Mass this evening?" James said with the wicked look in his eye.

"I think that is a capital idea, Captain O'Rourke as I would not want to fall asleep during mass this evening. I hope I will not be so sleepy all through the pregnancy," Elizabeth replied.

"You may sleep everyday my Sleeping Beauty if it brings you well and happy on the other side," James stated.

"I will be James; you wait and see. Everything will be fine and I will be stronger than before," Elizabeth responded smiling.

That night during Mass, Elizabeth sat thinking about the Holy Mother. She thought that all expectant mothers must think the same when they are pregnant during Christmas. She placed one hand outside her muff and rested it on her stomach, cradling the baby within. That night when they went to sleep, James leaned over and said "Happy Christmas, darling girl." He kissed her and her stomach saying "Happy Christmas, Christopher Colin. You are going to love your beautiful mother when you are born."

The next day was Christmas. James and Elizabeth shared a Christmas breakfast and then opened their presents. James loved the portrait and said that the artist had captured Elizabeth's beauty and the fire in her eyes that made her so special. He loved the cuff links and put them on immediately. For Elizabeth there was a pearl bracelet and ring to match her mother's earrings and the necklace from November. She was developing the second set of jewelry to remind her of her love of James, as if she needed that reminder. The day was spent with much food and much Christmas spirit.

The day following was St. Stephens Day or Boxing Day in England. Gifts were provided to Seamus and Bridget and the community was invited to stop in for punch and good cheer. Father O'Donnell joined the family and admired the new portrait of Elizabeth. "He certainly has captured Mrs.

O'Rourke. She has such spirit and has touched the lives of everyone here in the village and beyond. I wish you both many blessings now and in the future," Father O'Donnell stated.

The community Open House meant that friends from the county would stop and share punch and refreshments. All who saw the portrait thought that it had captured Elizabeth and asked if the Captain would be sitting for a portrait as well. "I am not one for sitting, but maybe someday we will do another portrait to match Elizabeth's," was James' reply.

The next day with the continuation of St. Stephen's Day, Father O'Rourke arrived to celebrate the holiday with James and Elizabeth. James picked him up in Dublin and they talked about all of the improvements that had been made since his last visit. Father O'Rourke could not believe the changes at Broadlands. "It is a real home again, Elizabeth, and James tells me that we have you to thank for that. If it is at all possible, I believe that you are more beautiful than on your wedding day. I would not have believed it possible, but it truly is the case. Bless you for making James so happy and for inviting me to a true family Christmas for the first time in many years." Like the friends and family who had visited, Father O'Rourke admired the new portrait of Elizabeth and said that it so matched the original. At dinner that evening, after the blessing Uncle Colin gave a toast to Elizabeth and James. "On your wedding day, James; you looked as though you had been handed the moon and the stars. Today I see you even happier than that day. I know that it didn't seem possible then, but that is how it is when you find the one that makes your life complete."

James rose then and said "Uncle Colin, she takes my breath away every day."

Elizabeth sat with tears in her eyes. "It is so wonderful to have family together for Christmas. It feels like it did before the war when mother and father were alive. Next year God willing, we will have a new baby with us for his first Christmas and it will be even more special," Elizabeth stated.

"So it is a boy for sure then?" Father O'Rourke said mischievously.

"All O'Rourke men have boys first, so it will be a boy," Elizabeth answered emphatically.

"My wife has spoken, so she has and so it shall be," James said smiling.

The remaining days of the Christmas holidays were spent happily playing charades, walking and reading on the cold, snowy days that followed. All too quickly it seemed the threesome was popping a cork for the New Year's festivities or *Oiche Chinn Bliana* as the O'Rourke men informed Elizabeth. She had not realized when she came to Broadlands that she would be learning so much about her new country's customs and traditions. It was something that she embraced wholeheartedly to make her adopted country her own.

*****

All too soon the holidays were over and reality for Elizabeth and James returned to their lives. James would be travelling back to London with Father O'Rourke for their meetings with Inspector Flynn. It was not a task that he relished, but was happy to substitute for Elizabeth until the baby was born. Elizabeth realized it was the first time that they had been apart for more than a few hours since their meeting last August. She didn't mean to feel emotional, but her pregnancy and their leave taking were having that affect.

The night before James' departure he had told her that he wanted her to stay at Broadlands and not to come to Dublin to see them off. "I don't want you on the roads alone, Elizabeth. We can say our goodbyes here in the morning and then I will know that I will leave you safe," James stated adamantly.

"I know that it seems silly, James but we have not been apart but for a few short hours ever since we met. I will miss you dreadfully you know," Elizabeth replied.

"I know that, darling girl. I will miss you just the same. But think about what a wonderful homecoming that we will have on my return. The special nap may take all day!" James said laughing.

"I will hold you to that, my darling," Elizabeth said smiling through her tears.

When Elizabeth awoke in the morning, James was just ready to leave. "You don't have to come downstairs, love; I can say my goodbyes here," James said.

"I want to come down and say goodbye to Uncle Colin as well James. I will be just a moment," Elizabeth replied. She ran into her dressing room and quickly put on a morning gown and left her hair down around her shoulders. She grabbed a shawl and was with James again in short order.

"Let me check those buttons, Mrs. O'Rourke," James said laughing. "I know that you will have missed some trying to dress so quickly." He kissed her then and despite himself, felt the same yearning that he always felt when kissing Elizabeth. It did not help that she was returning his intensity in the kiss. "If we are not careful, love, I will be late for the ship and will never hear the end of it. I love you, darling girl. Stay on the estate until I get back. Seamus has been given instructions to walk with you down to the village so that you can go to church and see Father O'Donnell. Before you know it, I will be home and we will plan for the baby's coming together." The tears were in her eyes again, but she was putting a brave face on it.

"I will follow those orders because they are given by James and not by Captain O'Rourke," she said with the same old mischief in her eyes.

"They will be followed regardless of who gives them," James said with an arched brow, but broke into a smile despite himself. "You are the only one who is not intimidated by my orders you know," James replied.

"I know, darling but only because I love you so much and can see how sweet you are!" Elizabeth responded archly.

"There is that word again. Please don't let that word go beyond these four walls or I will never live it down," James replied smiling.

Elizabeth walked down the stairs with James and met Uncle Colin ready for departure. "Thank you so much my dear for the lovely Christmas. I have not enjoyed myself so much since I was a lad in this house. You have truly made it a home again, Elizabeth and you have made my nephew a happy man," Father O'Rourke stated.

"Amen to that, Uncle Colin. Goodbye, my love; I will be back so soon that you won't have time to miss me," James stated.

James kissed her on the forehead then, causing Uncle Colin to laugh and say, "Give her a real kiss, James; one that will last until your return."

"I always listen to my Uncle, Elizabeth." He kissed her then as he had in the master suite and caused the tears to return to her eyes. She stood on the porch watching them go and felt as alone as she had the day she set foot on the Alliance and watched Wilmington in the distance as she began her odyssey that led to Broadlands. Going back upstairs, Elizabeth decided that she could not feel sorry for herself and needed to take this time to put her plan in action to find a local midwife and make preparations for the baby's birth in keeping with her own vision for childbirth. She prepared properly for the morning then and decided that she would ask Seamus to walk with her to the parish church after breakfast. She knew just who to enlist on her mission and how to accomplish it.

Seamus and Elizabeth found Father O'Donnell ready to hear confession. She asked if she might speak to him so that they could have private time together. Elizabeth entered the confessional. "Father I have something that I would like to speak to you about," Elizabeth started.

"Of course, my child would you like me to hear your confession?" Father O'Donnell asked.

"Not exactly, Father. I would like to know if you could introduce me to a local midwife that you would recommend as you see Father; I am going to have a baby," Elizabeth replied.

"That is blessed news indeed. I am sure that Captain O'Rourke will be over the moon when he hears the news. Have you told him then child?" Father O'Donnell asked.

"I have Father and he is over the moon. He only wants the best care for me given his mother's passing and mine in childbirth. I would like to think that I could allay his concerns by talking with a midwife that you might recommend so that we can assure that all will go well when the time comes," Elizabeth replied.

"I will send Mrs. O'Brien to the house to speak with you. She is the most experienced around and will address all of your worries. Now don't think another thing about it, Elizabeth. You will be in good hands when the time comes and we will see that baby into the world in no time at all," Father O'Donnell replied.

When they left the church, Elizabeth knew that she had enlisted the aid that she needed and the confessional silence of Father O'Donnell in the bargain. On returning home, she started to review the directions for tea and salve that Lavinia Cole had sent from home. She would make her list of ingredients needed so that they could pick them up when they next went shopping in Dublin for baby things.

As Elizabeth was making her birth plan, Father O'Rourke and James were returning to Dublin and from there onto London. Uncle Colin noted that James was quiet all of the way to Dublin and even quieter as they boarded the Alliance. In order to calm his mind, James took control of the wheelhouse as they left Dublin Bay behind them. His thoughts as always were on Elizabeth. He knew that she would be safe during his journey, but like her he was suffering from the fact that they had not been apart for three solid months. Not that he had needed convincing, but any thought of returning to the sea full time was erased on that morning as they left Dublin. The thought of leaving Elizabeth behind for months on end held no appeal to him. He would consider travelling if she was with him, but would not consider a return to his old life. He laughed for the first time then since leaving Broadlands. How could one so slight have turned his life upside down, he asked himself? He was not sure how it happened but knew that he was not unhappy at the change.

CHAPTER FOURTEEN

When James and Father O'Rourke returned to London, the berth was close to the previous berth of the Alliance two months ago. So much had happened since they left London that fateful day. James had to remember life without Elizabeth and found that it was a memory that brought him no joy. Upon arriving in London, James said goodbye to his uncle and told him that he would pick him up the next day for his meeting with Inspector Flynn. James would be heading there first thing this morning to begin the preparation for the trial that had been delayed until the summer after the birth of their first child.

Hugh Flynn's offices in Scotland Yard were located at 4 Whitehall Place off of Great Scotland Yard. James remembered so well his first visit to Hugh's office in search of answers about Benjamin Whitfield and Charles Cross. He had so hoped that he was wrong then, but knew now from harsh experience that he was right about them and their plans for Elizabeth. James arrived in Hugh's outer office and was shown into the Inspector's offices upon arrival.

"James it is so good to see you. Thank you for the invitation to visit Broadlands for Christmas. I promise to take you up on one next year. This year we have been at sixes and sevens about this Whitfield and Cross case and sorting out the number of victims of their crimes. The case has grown even more complicated in the past several months. One thing is for sure, the attempt on your life and on Elizabeth's life as well as the kidnapping of Father O'Rourke and admission of guilt by Whitfield are the strongest pieces of evidence we have going for us. Father O'Rourke of course will be a very strong witness as a priest of the church testifying to his treatment. I hate to have to drag her into the whole sordid affair, but Elizabeth's testimony will also be critical to the outcome. The judge and jury will be horrified by an attempted murder of a client and especially when that client is a female. You will be able to testify what you heard Whitfield state as you came into the church. My lads will be able to do the same as they heard Whitfield's confession before taking him down in the church," Hugh stated.

"The key thing for you, James will be to keep your temper when you are in the courtroom and confronting Whitfield and Cross. I know that you would like to take them apart limb by limb for what they tried to do to Elizabeth. Remember you must stay calm and recite the facts only. No elaborations and nothing that the newspapers will seize upon to make this case more salacious than it already is. We were able to keep it out of the papers when it occurred, but I am sure that we will not be so lucky this time. Your whole family must be prepared for the way the press will magnify the sordid details of Whitfield and Cross's intensions especially as they pertain to Elizabeth. Do you think that she will be up for it old friend?" Hugh asked worriedly.

"If there is anything that I have learned about Elizabeth in the past months it is that she will be up for any challenge. I on the other hand will be a wreck worrying about her until this whole thing is over. I appreciate your understanding that she could not testify until after the baby was born. I won't have her go through that especially if it could put the baby and her in danger. She has gone through enough of that in her young life."

"I see that the past two months have only added to your wedded bliss. Congratulations, James; I couldn't be happier for you. If only she had a sister at home, I would send for her immediately," Hugh said laughing.

"She is a one of a kind and a treasure. When this is all over, I am going to take her back to Bermuda where we fell in love and then onto her home in Wilmington so that we can sell her house and so that I can meet her friends. If I see any single southern belles there who fit the bill, I will see what I can do to encourage them to come to England," James said laughing.

James' next visit was to the offices of London doctors that his Uncle Colin had told him about. He wanted to obtain as much information as he could to take back to Elizabeth. Although he was not in favor of bringing her to London to have their baby, his hope was that he could take information to her that could help her and Dr. Wilkinson when the big event occurred. He admitted to himself that he felt strange trying to learn such information for his wife, but put it down to the new life that he was carving out for Elizabeth and himself.

That night he invited Uncle Colin to the Alliance for dinner. He wanted to brief him on his meeting with Hugh Flynn and prepare him for his own meeting the following day. He shared with Uncle Colin the thoughts of Hugh about the upcoming trial. "It appears that they think you and Elizabeth will be the strongest witnesses, as the word of a priest will be unchallenged and of course, the judge and jury will be in love with Elizabeth as soon as she enters the courtroom. Such is the charismatic effect of my beautiful wife," James said laughing but without mirth.

"Whatever it takes to put those two bastards away, I am all for it," Father O'Rourke replied. "We are a blunt family, James as you know. Had it been in my power on that day, I could have easily forgotten the church's teachings on thou shall not kill. They are villains James and need to never see the light of day again. I will give the judge and the jury a piece of my mind on that front," Uncle Colin stated.

"I hear what you are saying, Uncle Colin; but Hugh has already warned me that our famous O'Rourke tempers are not to get the best of us. We have to stay calm when in the witness box and recount what we personally heard and experienced. Elizabeth will no doubt be the most convincing witness. I just wish that we didn't have to put her through reliving that horrible day. As she has told me, Uncle Colin we can't let them go and place more people in harm's way because of it. She always puts others before herself, Uncle Colin. It is one of the things that I love most about her and one of the things that terrifies me most about her. I have sworn to protect her and protect her I shall. I told Hugh today that I would take her and the baby back to Bermuda after the trial is over. It is where we first fell in love and of course we need to go back to Wilmington and sell her house and visit with her remaining friends there before returning to Broadlands for good. I know just from this short time away from her that I will not return to the sea unless she is with me. I am miserable without her, although it pains me to say it. How such a slip of a girl changed my life is beyond me, but it has happened and there it is!" James said smiling.

Uncle Colin laughed at that last admission. "Are you by way of giving me confession, nephew because if you are, I can't feel sorry for you. Many a man would change places with you in a minute. Take her with you if you have a hankering to see the world again. She is a real corker as you said and would probably love the adventure. Unless I miss my guess, young Colin will be the same with the blood of both of you in him. I of course will reserve the right to call him Colin although I know his first name will be Christopher and I know why. You and Elizabeth have been protected by the angels from the first, so you have, and are two pieces of a missing whole. God love you, James; enjoy every minute of your happiness as there is precious little of it in the world around us," Uncle Colin stated. James agreed with that admission and looked forward to his return to Elizabeth and to Broadlands.

The next day James visited again with Hugh Flynn and took Uncle Colin with him for a meeting as well. They had lunch and then James took off to do some shopping for Elizabeth and for the baby. Even if the whole idea of childbirth was beyond him, he promised to pick up some of the latest books on the subject and to take them home to

Elizabeth for her to digest. He would be returning to Dublin the next day and could not wait to see his beautiful wife and their home. That night he dreamed of Elizabeth as he had done while they were on the voyage from Bermuda. This time the beautiful mermaid was carrying a beautiful baby boy who looked just like his mother. He seemed to smile at him as he and his mother swam by the ship. When he awoke James shook his head and said that Elizabeth had even entered his dreams, a sure sign that he needed to get home.

*****

While James had conferred with Hugh Flynn over the trial and the needed testimony, Elizabeth had met with Mrs. O'Brien, the recommended midwife. She had been sent by Father O'Donnell to meet with Elizabeth and confer on Elizabeth's pregnancy. Mrs. O'Brien met with Elizabeth in the master suite. "I am so pleased to meet you, Mrs. O'Rourke. You and I will be close partners in the weeks ahead. You have nothing to worry about. You are a strong girl I hear and will do just fine." Elizabeth explained to Mrs. O'Brien about the tea and salve that her Aunt Sally had used in America. Although Mrs. O'Brien was not familiar with either, she was happy to assist any mother to avoid discomfort during childbirth. She explained to Elizabeth about the birthing chair and that she could have the baby here in her room. They agreed to meet monthly so that Mrs. O'Brien could answer questions that Elizabeth might have and to plan for the big event.

Elizabeth slept in the middle of their huge bed while James was away and felt as if her other half was missing. She did her best to keep herself busy during the day, but the nights were the worst for Elizabeth. It had been that way when her mother died and again when Robert and her father died. The night brought with it too much time to think and to pine for the one not in her midst. She reminded herself that James would be back shortly and would hopefully not need to go away again until they both returned to London for the trial. Before that horror was the joy of preparing for the baby and the birth itself. There was much to look forward to in 1866, even though a portion of the year would be spent confronting Whitfield and Cross again.

The next day, Elizabeth reviewed the information sent from Lavinia Cole so that she could make sure that she had access to the necessary herbs and other ingredients needed to make the tea and salve that Aunt Sally had sworn by for years. She would review this information with Mrs. O'Brien on their next meeting in the event that she could assist in obtaining the herbs needed. She knew from experience that midwives had used all sorts of recipes in the past to assist mothers during the worst time of their labors and she had no doubt that the two together would soon have the matter sorted.

Elizabeth knew that James would be home on the following day so she did all necessary to keep herself busy. The final task during their separation was the most difficult of all. Elizabeth sat down and reviewed the statements that she had prepared at the time of the shooting by Whitfield. Hugh Flynn had been so very kind at such a difficult time and had sat with her for over two hours taking down everything that she could remember about that horrible day. He had told her then to write a copy for herself so that she could remember every detail. Even with an amazing memory, such a shocking experience could lead to a faulty recall in the future, as the mind tried desperately to block out the ugliness of what had occurred.

Elizabeth had always kept a diary and on the most exciting trip of her life to Bermuda and onto London, she had kept a detailed account of the places that she visited, meeting James, being infuriated at James and ultimately falling in love with him. In that same diary, sadly; she had to record what had taken place that fateful day in October when Whitfield had tried to kill James and ended in shooting the one person he claimed to want to protect. She reviewed those diary entries and the one that she had prepared at Hugh's suggestion noting each and everything that Whitfield had threatened on that fateful day. As hurtful as the memories were, she knew that she would want to discuss them with James on his return and to learn any additional preparation that she needed to do prior to the trial and the testimony that she would be compelled to provide. She reviewed the diary entries over and over until she had them committed to memory and knew that she would be doing the same again each month of her confinement to make sure that she was prepared for the most important court appearance of her life. After that exercise, Elizabeth called for Seamus and asked if he could accompany her on her daily walk. She needed that distraction to clear her head and to remind her that James would be returning the next day and that all was better when he was near.

Elizabeth dressed carefully the next morning looking forward to the return of James from his London visit. She hoped the voyage from London to Dublin would clear his head, as every mention of the Whitfield attempted murder placed him in a rage. She knew that his meeting with Hugh Flynn would bring back all of the memories of that terrible day. She had relived them herself alone with the diary and the statement that Hugh had requested her make. She took comfort in the fact that James would soon be back and with him at her side, she knew she could face anything.

She went downstairs for breakfast and as casually as possible asked Bridget if the carriage had been called for to pick up the Master at the docks. "Don't you worry, Mistress; the Master will soon be home and you will have the roses back in your cheeks. The lads have gone to fetch him now so I expect he will be back within the hour." Elizabeth blushed with happiness at that remark and went to James' library to wait for the sound of the carriage wheels on the drive. His library always reminded her of James, as it had that masculine smell of cigars and after dinner whiskey.

Try as she might she could not concentrate on the book that she was trying to read in anticipation of James' return. She thought then what it would be like to have him away for weeks or even months and decided that she did not want to think about it at all. If the voyage was to a location that she would like to see, she would ask James if she and the baby could go along. She had proven herself to be seaworthy even during a hurricane, so she hoped that he would not consider her too much trouble as he had once suspected. Considering how that voyage ended, she hoped James would see the wisdom of taking her along on future trips.

At long last she heard the carriage wheels on the drive and went to the front door and out onto the drive to await his return. There had been a snow the night before so the drive was blanketed with snow. She was glad that she had her shawl around her and knew that James would soon be keeping her very warm indeed. James was driving the carriage as always and threw the reins to the lads. When he saw her on the drive he smiled that smile that always made her weak in the knees and ran up to greet her. Casting dignity aside, Elizabeth threw her arms around his neck and James laughed and kissed her then despite the watching eyes of the lads. "I have missed you, Mrs. O'Rourke," James said laughing.

"I have missed you too, Captain O'Rourke and am glad to see you in good humor. Come in before you catch your death of cold," Elizabeth said smiling.

"I have some presents for you, but we will get to them later. Come with me, Mrs. O'Rourke," James said.

James took her hand and climbed the steps to the master suite. He had many things to tell her and needed her all to himself before sharing her with the rest of the household. As soon as the door was closed he gave her a proper kiss and carried her over to their favorite window seat. "How was your trip, darling? Did everything go well?" Elizabeth asked with concern.

"First let me look at you and then we will talk about London. Are you ever going to start showing with our son?" James said laughing.

"Well I do have to keep my figure for my husband," Elizabeth replied with eyes shining.

"Don't worry about your figure, love; you just worry about staying healthy with our boy. The figure will sort itself out later. As active as you stay, your figure will not be a problem," James said with a wink.

"Tell me about your meeting with Inspector Flynn and Uncle Colin," Elizabeth said.

"Well the meetings went as well as you can expect having to plan for such a thing. Hugh says the evidence against those two rascals is as strong as he can make it. He believes the testimony by Uncle Colin and by you will have the strongest impact on the jury. Are you up for that then, love?" James asked worriedly.

"I reviewed my diary entries and the statement that Hugh had me prepare after that horrible day. I will be ready when the time comes James to do what we need to do to put those two away," Elizabeth said earnestly.

"I don't think they will be put away, love. I think it will be the gallows for them both. They have at least two murders on their hands and three attempted murders to answer for. I have thought of little else but those two villains for three days. I would like to think about my beautiful wife and nothing else at this moment. Come and show me how much you missed me while I was gone," James said smiling.

"How do you know that I missed you while you were gone? Don't you believe that to be a bit presumptuous, Captain O'Rourke?" Elizabeth said teasing.

"The best evidence was you wrapped in a shawl standing on the front drive in snow waiting for me to come off the carriage. Do I need to provide further evidence, Mrs. O'Rourke?" James said huskily.

"You have been around too many inspectors for your own good, James O'Rourke. I admit it; I missed you terribly. It was the longest that I have been away from you since we met and I don't mind you knowing that even though it will give you a big head," Elizabeth replied placing her arms around James' neck.

"Then I will tell you a secret, Mrs. O'Rourke; you even entered my dreams while I was away. So I believe we missed one another equally. How is that for fair? Now, give me a real kiss and show me how much you missed me," James said huskily.

"In broad daylight, James?" Elizabeth said laughing.

"In the broadest of daylight and for God and everyone to see; I love you Elizabeth O'Rourke and I don't care who knows it!" James replied.

CHAPTER FIFTEEN

The next few weeks and months were like a dream for both James and Elizabeth. The tasks leading to the birth of the new baby occupied both of their worlds. James took Elizabeth up to Dublin for shopping for the baby and as the weather improved into spring, work on the nursery outfitting began in earnest with everything standing in ready for the birth of the baby. As the weather improved, James also reminded Elizabeth about their swimming lessons that he had first told her about on her arrival to Broadlands. Still getting accustomed to the weather in cooler climes, she asked that they delay that event until the weather was warmer. By the month of June, the weather was cooperating and James decided to hold Elizabeth to her promise. The full moon was shining that night and James thought it a perfect time to begin her lessons. They continued through the month of June and into the month of July when the cooling water was blissful to Elizabeth in her final month of pregnancy.

At the end of July, James and Elizabeth went to their private beach with a blanket, snacks and towels for their usual swimming lesson. Elizabeth had been reluctant all day when the subject of the swimming lesson was broached. At nine months pregnant, she did not consider that swimming as the best activity for her at this point, but at James' urging, she decided to go along. The day was wonderfully warm and she thought the water would feel so cool. She would find some way to convince James that skinny dipping was not in the cards for a woman of her advanced pregnancy.

When they arrived at their beach with the full moon shining on them, James quickly stripped off his clothes and ran into the water. Elizabeth started smiling and covered her eyes at his display. "Why are you covering your eyes Elizabeth, I am the one naked?" James said laughing.

"I cannot believe that you have me out here at nearly nine months pregnant to learn to swim, James much less skinny dipping," Elizabeth said laughing.

"What is skinny dipping?" James asked.

"It is going swimming without clothes on, James. It is a term from home, my love," Elizabeth replied.

"And how would you know about skinny dipping, Mrs. O'Rourke?" James said mischievously.

"I don't know about it, James I only know the term. I have been bathing before, but wore a swimming costume and only with my family. My swimming costume covered my arms and legs and I wore a hat as well. You are truly incorrigible you know," Elizabeth replied.

"Haven't I been telling you that all I need is a little encouragement, like the smile from my beautiful wife? Come here and let me teach you how to swim. You will like it I promise. Have I ever steered you wrong in the past?" James said huskily.

"I am coming, but I am leaving my chemise in place," Elizabeth said laughing. She stepped into the cool water and instantly felt the relaxation. She hated to admit it, but it did feel wonderful and she felt buoyant as well, which was quite a feat at nine months pregnant.

"Now, darling girl, put your arms around my neck and let me lift you up," James said. "I am going to lay you down in the water and hold you up so that you can experience the feeling of floating in the water. Isn't that grand now? Did I steer you wrong?" James said smiling.

"No, James; it feels wonderful just like you said it would."

"Wouldn't you like to take off that chemise so that you could feel the full effect?" James said huskily.

"Are we still talking about swimming, James?" Elizabeth said looking up at him and laughing.

"We might be talking about swimming and we might not be," James said with the look of mischief in his eyes. James lifted Elizabeth into his arms again and held her in place.

"Put your legs around my waist, love." Slowly he took the pins from her hair so that it fell around her shoulders. She was his mermaid again returned to her natural element. James slowly kissed her, lightly at first and then passionately as she responded to him in her customary matter. Within moments, both were carried away by the water, the moonlight and their passion for one another. James held Elizabeth against his hardness, carefully at first so as to not hurt her and then with true intensity. Elizabeth looked at him with the misty look of passion that he had seen for the first time aboard the Alliance. Suddenly they were both transported back to that night and to the first time that they had kissed and to the first time they made love on their wedding night. Despite her pregnancy or perhaps because of it, Elizabeth was not shy about her responses to James. Her responses to his overtures brought an intensity to the lovemaking. They were soon shaking with need for one another. When at last they met their climax, both were out of breath and holding onto each other. James kept kissing Elizabeth and holding her as he carefully carried her out of the water.

The next morning Elizabeth awoke to a vague sensation of cramping. James was already up and out as was his custom, so Elizabeth was alone in the huge bed. She quickly got up and dressed and proceeded down to the kitchen. "Bridget, I am going to take my walk down to the beach. I will take a light breakfast with me as I am not sure, but I think my time may have come," Elizabeth said quietly.

"Oh, Mistress, that is grand news. Shall I have the lads go to Dublin to pick up the Master?" Bridget asked.

"Oh no, I want to wait for a while to make sure that I am right. I don't want James to start pacing and waiting if it is a false alarm. I know from the books that James brought back from London that it will take longer with the first baby. I want to keep walking and not get into the birthing chair until I need to. Would you ask Seamus to contact Mrs. O'Brien and put her on notice that today may be the day? Oh please also brew the tea that we will need so that everything is ready," Elizabeth requested.

Elizabeth set off down the path to the private beach thinking all the way that James must have helped her reach her time. Mrs. O'Brien had told her that making love was one way to bring about delivery and it certainly must have worked. She would have to remember to tell James that later, much later in the day after Christopher Colin O'Rourke made his appearance in the world. For now, she tried to concentrate on staying calm and making herself eat the light breakfast that Bridget had fixed for her. She knew that she would need her strength for the day ahead.

Mrs. O'Brien was alerted and came to wait at Broadlands until she was needed. She expected a long wait, as this was the first baby for the Mistress, but thought it best that she stay close at hand to oversee the arrangements. The tea that Elizabeth had requested was brewed and cooled. The salve that Aunt Sally had recommended had been prepared and was waiting in Elizabeth's dressing room. Bridget went down the path several times that morning checking on the Mistress. She continued to walk and tried to stay calm. The cramping had not stopped, so she was sure that she was right. The baby would be born this day. She did not want to alarm James yet however and would wait until his midday return to the house.

Several hours later, Bridget's visit to the Mistress told her that things had moved along well enough that she needed to be moved into the house. Her water had broken and the contractions were coming at a closer rate. Bridget ran up the path from the private beach in a dead run on the track of the Captain. Elizabeth's time had come for certain. Her water had broken while she sat on her favorite bench and now the entire house would be alerted. Elizabeth sat calmly waiting for the household to explode with activity. She was ready to set her plan into action and was calmly waiting James' arrival down the path.

In short order, Elizabeth heard footsteps arriving at her favorite place. “Darling girl, Bridget came to find me. Let me carry you to the house,” James stated worriedly.

“James, I am fine. I just need your arm to lean on. The walk will do me good, darling,” Elizabeth replied.

“I am not hearing another word, Elizabeth. You don’t weigh more than a sack of potatoes, Elizabeth O’Rourke; you never have. Not one more word.” James lifted Elizabeth in his arms and carried her to the house and the master suite. Bridget was there waiting for them.

“Bridget, please help the Mistress get into bed and I will get the doctor,” James stated.

James ran from the room then. Bridget and Elizabeth exchanged glances. “Is everything ready, Bridget?” Elizabeth asked.

“Everything is in your dressing room and we are ready. Are you sure Mistress that the Master won’t be angry?” Bridget replied.

“I think the Master will be over the moon after meeting his son for the first time,” Elizabeth said smiling. “I am going to change into my chemise if you will be so kind to help me into the next room.”

Mrs. O’Brien was waiting in the dressing room. “Let me help you, Mistress. I have the salve that you made and we are ready with everything that you asked for. The birthing chair is ready and the stool as well.”

“I am going to keep walking as long as I can. Aunt Sally swears by it. She didn’t know about the birthing chair but thinks that is a wonderful idea also,” Elizabeth replied.

“Let me check you Mistress and I can tell you how far you are along,” Mrs. O’Brien stated with authority.

“I waited as long as I could and didn’t dare wait any longer,” Elizabeth said. “Aunt Sally says we all need to wash up with this strong soap before we start and then use her special salve to prevent tearing.”

"Mistress, you are a wonder," Bridget said. "How can you keep so calm? I am a nervous mess and I am just helping."

"The Mistress is right; it's the most natural thing in the world. All this fuss and bother by these men. Women have known what to do for hundreds of years. There is nothing more natural in the world then bringing a baby into it," Mrs. O'Brien answered.

When Elizabeth was checked, Mrs. O'Brien smiled. "It won't be long now, Mistress. We will have that baby born, swaddled and you back in bed before the Captain returns."

Elizabeth was clearly in the last hour of her labor and the contractions were very close together. Bridget continued to put cool cloths on her forehead and to wipe away the perspiration.

"Here is the tea you asked for. I have never used it myself before, but will be anxious to see how it works," Mrs. O'Brien stated.

"Thank you, Mrs. O'Brien. It is so cool and soothing. Aunt Sally said it will keep me calm during the worst of the contractions." Elizabeth was amazed at the quick action of the tea. She had eaten little, so the tea quickly affected her. She became very tranquil and slightly sleepy. Between contractions she started to doze and think lovely thoughts about James and their time together.

Her first memory was standing on the dock and meeting James for the first time. Sparks flew in many ways and they started their courtship dance.

"Mistress, I need you to start to push now. Mistress, are you alright? Can you hear me, Mistress?" Mrs. O'Brien asked anxiously.

"Yes, I was just dozing from the tea. May I have some more please?" Elizabeth replied.

Her next blurred memory was walking towards James on their wedding day. He looked so handsome waiting at the altar.

"Mistress, I think it won't be long now." The words entered into her dazed mind as she drifted in and out from the effects of the tea.

Her next image was a recent one. Just last night she and James had gone for a swimming lesson at their private beach. She was too shy to skinny dip as she told James. He loved the term and her in her chemise coming to swim. She knew that making love could bring on her labor and sure enough, it had worked. She would have to remember to tell James. He would love that part of the story. That lovely memory was violently interrupted by a very intense contraction.

"Not long now, Mistress. Stay with us and start to push hard now. That's it; you are doing very well, Mistress. The salve is working. Not much longer now. Push Mistress, push," Mrs. O'Brien stated anxiously.

Elizabeth felt as if she was in the middle of the worst pain of her life, but she knew it wouldn't be much longer. Just like the pain of her wedding night times one thousand.

"He's coming Mistress; he's coming." Within a matter of minutes the final push and release. "You've done it, Mistress; a beautiful baby boy!" Mrs. O'Brien stated happily.

Bridget took the baby from Mrs. O'Brien to be washed and swaddled. He was lustily crying, so they all knew that he was healthy. Mrs. O'Brien stayed with Elizabeth checking her and completing the birthing process.

"Now, Mistress; let me help you bathe and cool down. You have done it, Mistress. You have a beautiful boy. Let's take care of you now and get you back into bed before the Master gets home," Mrs. O'Brien stated.

Elizabeth let Bridget and Mrs. O'Brien help her bathe, change, and get back into bed.

"The young Master wants his mother, Mistress," Bridget said, tears in her eyes as she spoke.

"Let me see him, Bridget," Elizabeth replied.

Bridget passed the baby onto Elizabeth who was in bed leaning back on the pillows in the huge bed.

"Did you need me to find you a wet nurse Mistress?" Mrs. O'Brien asked.

"Oh no thank you, Mrs. O'Brien; if all goes well, I hope to be able to nurse him myself," Elizabeth said smiling. "He is so beautiful. He looks so like James," Elizabeth said cooing to the baby. The baby's hungry cries were soon ending as Elizabeth began to nurse him.

"You are a natural at this, Miss Elizabeth. You were meant to be a mother," Bridget stated.

"I so wish my own mother was here but you both have been so wonderful to me. Thank you so much," Elizabeth replied with tear stained eyes.

"Now, Mistress; there you are looking too beautiful to just have had a baby. You make sure that you tell the Master that I said no paddy fingers for six weeks and not before," Mrs. O'Brien said with authority. "Sure I will be using that salve and tea going forward. Your Aunt Sally knew what she was about."

"She delivered all of the girls of my acquaintance and all of their babies plus had ten of her own. She is an expert to be sure. Thank you again for all of your help," Elizabeth said smiling.

Elizabeth sat with Christopher Colin O'Rourke; Christopher for the St. Christopher medal that had saved her life in London; Colin for Father O'Rourke. Her beautiful boy was nursing for the first time and she felt blissfully happy and as tired as if she had just run from the parish church. She couldn't wait for James to get home and see her darling boy and his darling girl.

Bridget peeked around the corner at her Mistress sitting up in bed with the new baby. "The dressing room is in order Mistress and the birthing chair and stool are put away and the room is tidy again."

A half hour later, Elizabeth heard footsteps coming up the main staircase and the door thrown back on its hinges. James was standing at the door with Dr. Wilkinson in tow. He looked at her in disbelief. "Elizabeth, what has happened? We were delayed by an accident on the road," . . . he stopped then as he saw the bundle in her arms.

"James, meet your new son, Christopher Colin O'Rourke," Elizabeth said smiling.

"How . . . what . . . how did you do this on your own?" James was so stupefied he could barely get the words out. He sat on the edge of the bed and could not take his eyes from his beautiful girl and their new baby boy.

"Would you like to hold your son, James?" Elizabeth asked proudly.

At that moment, Dr. Wilkinson came panting up the steps having run all the way from the carriage. "Mrs. O'Rourke, have we missed the big event then?" Dr. Wilkinson said smiling.

"Would you like to check the baby first?" Elizabeth asked smiling. "We have our first boy," Elizabeth said proudly.

"He looks a fine lad," Dr. Wilkinson said smiling. "I will take a quick look and then check on you next."

James sat gazing at Elizabeth stupefied. It was as if she had conjured the baby by magic given his response. "How are you really, darling girl?" James asked worriedly.

"I'm just tired, darling, but so very happy. He is beautiful. He looks exactly like you."

Dr. Wilkinson returned with the yawning baby Christopher. "He is perfect Mrs. O'Rourke. Well done indeed. If Captain O'Rourke has no objections, I will check you now as well."

"I will step into Elizabeth's dressing room and get to know my new son," James said laughing.

When James stepped out, Dr. Wilkinson briefly examined Elizabeth. "I know you weren't able to perform this miracle all on your own, despite your many talents. Did Bridget and Mrs. O'Brien lend a hand?"

"They did indeed, Dr. Wilkinson. Everything went very well. I am fine and just tired," Elizabeth replied.

"You are indeed, Mrs. O'Rourke. Now, lots of rest and try to limit physical activity for the next several weeks."

"No paddy fingers then doctor?" Elizabeth said smiling.

"Right, exactly so Mrs. O'Rourke. Good day and well done," Dr. Wilkinson said upon taking his leave.

James came back into the room then holding his new son. "He is so beautiful, Elizabeth. Now, tell me the whole story!" James asked.

"There is not much to tell. Mrs. O'Brien and Bridget were here and Christopher came into the world with very little fuss and bother," Elizabeth stated smiling.

"What aren't you telling me, Mrs. O'Rourke?" James asked raising one eyebrow.

"James, I am awfully tired. Can we talk further later? I need to take a nap when our son is taking a nap. You look as though you could do with a nap also. I am to pass along the message however; no paddy fingers, Captain O'Rourke; not at least for six weeks," Elizabeth said smiling.

James smiled from ear to ear at that comment. "I told you the word had got round that I can't keep my hands off my wife. I promise naps only for six weeks. You have done very well my clever wife."

When Elizabeth woke from her nap, James was with her in the huge bed for once and not out and about. He was looking down at her with shining eyes waiting for her to awaken. "I didn't want you to wake up all alone. I wanted to be here in case our boy woke up also," James said holding her.

"Isn't that a wonderful sound darling; our boy. He is so beautiful; he looks just like you," Elizabeth said smiling.

"Are you truly alright, darling girl? Are you in any pain?" James looked so anxious when he asked the question that Elizabeth sought to allay his fears.

"For an hour or so, the pain was so overwhelming. I had my recipes from home to help me through and I was just fine," Elizabeth calmly replied.

"What recipes, darling; what helped you?" James asked anxiously.

"Aunt Sally from home delivered all of us and she had special teas and salve to help women through childbirth," Elizabeth replied.

"Was the tea to help with the pain, Elizabeth?" James asked.

"Yes. It relaxes you and calms you so you can get through the worst pain," Elizabeth responded.

"What is the salve used for?" James asked.

"Well, the salve," Elizabeth said shyly, "it helps to keep you from being injured when the baby is born."

"How did you learn about all of these things, darling girl?" James continued.

"Why I learned them from Aunt Sally of course. She delivered all of the babies of our acquaintance and all of my friends babies and had ten of her own," Elizabeth responded.

"Baby girl, I thought all of your family had passed, but you call her Aunt Sally?" James continued confused.

"Everyone calls her Aunt Sally, but she isn't our relative. She works for Lavinia Cole's family," Elizabeth replied.

"She is an old family retainer then?" James asked.

"Yes until a few years ago, she was owned by the family," Elizabeth responded.

"She was a slave then, darling?" James asked.

"Oh yes. What she doesn't know about delivering babies, no one knows," Elizabeth replied shyly. "Aunt Sally did not know about the birthing chair, but I am sure that she would totally approve had she had the chance to see one. It's like I told you, love, I knew I needed to be strong to bring O'Rourke boys into the world also."

"The tribe," James said smiling.

"Just so, the tribe indeed. If they are all as beautiful as Christopher, we will be rearing a tribe to be reckoned with," Elizabeth said smiling.

At that moment, they heard their new son crying from the dressing room. Elizabeth had moved the crib closer so that she could hear him when he needed her. “It sounds like someone is hungry,” Elizabeth said smiling.

“Are you sure that you don’t want me to engage a wet nurse, love?” James asked with concern.

“No, darling; Aunt Sally swears by it and with good reason,” Elizabeth replied.

“What would that reason be love?” James asked.

“You will see in due time,” Elizabeth said mischievously.

James lay in bed listening to Elizabeth coo over the baby as she nursed him. Could there be any greater bliss, he thought? A loving wife, a beautiful son; it was more then he thought he deserved, but he was happy to receive it. The only dark spot was the coming trial. When that was over, he would take his family back to Bermuda to celebrate their love and back home to Wilmington for his darling girl to see her friends and show off her new baby boy.

*****

The next weeks sped by quickly. They fell into the routine that a new baby brings to a house and prepared for the upcoming trial. James still walked out with Elizabeth each day and she grew stronger by the day. Christopher was, all agreed, a genius, as he seemed to love nothing more than to sleep and coo and be the happiest baby in Ireland as Bridget had named him.

At last the six week interval had passed. Mrs. O’Brien came to the house and pronounced the Mistress fit as a fiddle and the new baby a hearty and healthy lad. For James’ sake, Elizabeth had the same examination by Dr. Wilkinson with the same results provided.

Elizabeth had teasingly told James to mark the date on the calendar. To him, it was the longest six weeks of his life. Returning to his paternal nightly kisses was not a pleasure, but a pain. He held Elizabeth each night dreaming of the end of their imposed isolation.

On the evening of her medical release, Elizabeth teased with her husband that she would like another swimming lesson at their private beach. James was slow to catch on at first, but then grasped the meaning behind her words. As a full moon was forecast for the night and the weather warm, the stage was set.

Elizabeth nursed Christopher after dinner and put him down in his cot. She was not only feeling maternal this evening. Tonight she would return to her husband and she had been counting the days; not that she would tell him that. She dressed in a chemise and long robe and met James in the library along with a bag and a blanket. James looked up with a smile on his face when she came in. "Ready for a swimming lesson then?" James said smiling.

The two walked hand in hand down the path to their own private oasis. When they arrived there, James stripped off his clothes as was his custom and splashed into the water. "Are you covering your eyes again, darling girl?" James said mischievously.

"Not this time, darling. I want to see my handsome husband in all of his glory," Elizabeth said laughing.

Elizabeth spread out the blanket, took off her robe and let down her hair. James watched mesmerized waiting to see what she would do next. She slowly unbuttoned her chemise and let it fall to the ground then shook out her hair. Standing before him, the mermaid of his dreams was replaced by a goddess; and a goddess who was walking toward him. She's a goddess and she's all mine, he thought possessively.

When Elizabeth reached James she looked up at him with shining eyes. "Did you want me to put my arms around your neck?" Elizabeth asked quietly.

"I have one question first, Elizabeth," James said worriedly.

"What is it, darling?" she answered pressing her body against his.

"Did Mrs. O'Brien say you were fine?" James said kissing her absently.

"Yes, darling," Elizabeth replied running her fingers across his chest.

"Did Dr. Wilkinson say you were alright?" James asked more urgently than before.

"That's two questions and yes he did," she said laughing.

James picked her up then and held her against him drinking in her neck, her breasts and running his fingers through her hair. "I don't think we are going to have a swimming lesson this evening," James said through clenched teeth.

"Perhaps later on," Elizabeth said smiling.

"I missed you so much," James replied.

"I missed you too, James. Please love me now," Elizabeth replied quietly.

James needed no further invitation. His passion for his wife burned as brightly as on their wedding night. That night she had been a voluptuous young woman, but now she was a goddess and he made sure that she knew he approved of the change. How she could have this beautiful body after only six weeks was beyond him, but he had to remember to thank Aunt Sally when they met in the fall. James carried Elizabeth to the blanket so that he could make love to her properly without drowning. It was his last conscious thought. His passion for her knew no bounds and her shyness to him was lost. For Elizabeth and James experienced the pent up passion of the last six weeks, coupled with a mixture of bliss not yet experienced. Their lives were so complete that at times they could not imagine life without the other. Elizabeth could not get close enough to James and James cherished his wife as never before. When at last they reached their climax,

James rolled to his back carrying Elizabeth along with him. The full moon shone down on them and on the water creating a magical appearance to the night. He had his Elizabeth back for sure and could face whatever the world threw their way; even the impending trip to London.

CHAPTER SIXTEEN

The next day, they started packing for London. James was engaging a nanny to help Elizabeth with Christopher while they travelled, so they needed a larger ship than the Alliance; one with more cabins on the Captain's side to house Elizabeth and James, a dressing room for James and a room for the nanny and baby. The Triad would fit the bill. They would leave out of Dublin, sail to London for the trial and collecting cargo in London; sail onto Bermuda and lastly to Wilmington.

Mr. Pearson would be back with them and Dr. Wilkinson. Many of the lads from the Alliance had asked to sail on this trip so that they could help the Captain keep Miss Elizabeth and the baby safe. Inspector Flynn had promised Scotland Yard support when they reached London. As before James would take no chances.

They all set off the next day for Dublin with luggage packed for a two month's trip. The Triad was ready and waiting for them when they arrived at the docks. James was excited to sail again, but apprehensive of the upcoming trial. Elizabeth for her part was excited to be at sea again with James and looking forward to the chance to see Bermuda and Wilmington again. London was a trial that must be met first however.

When all of the gear was placed below, James in control of the wheelhouse sailed out of Dublin Bay heading for London. Whatever thoughts and worries he may have felt he kept to himself. Elizabeth was waving to Bridget and Seamus on the dockside both who promised to keep Broadlands safe during their voyage.

Once in open waters, James came below to their cabin. Elizabeth was starting another travel diary just as before. "What are you doing, love?" James asked.

"I am starting my travel diary just as I did when we left Wilmington," Elizabeth replied smiling.

"You must let me read it sometime. Am I a character mentioned in your diary?" James said curious.

"You are definitely a character and you are definitely mentioned. I don't need you to become any more arrogant than you are already by reading my diary," Elizabeth said laughing. "I see you moved the huge bed into the Triad from the Alliance," Elizabeth said mischievously.

"I always sleep in the huge bed, Mrs. O'Rourke. As you are aware I need room to maneuver when I am coming alongside my prey," James said huskily.

"You sounded just like a pirate then, Captain O'Rourke. Would that make me your mermaid again?" she asked teasingly.

"That would make you my goddess," James said kissing her passionately.

That night they arrived in London and pulled into the same docks where they had berthed in October. They would meet Father O'Rourke for dinner and stay on board for security reasons as they had previously done.

"It seems so strange to be here again, James. Broadlands seems so far away that you can almost block out the ugliness that we faced here. I am glad that we can face Whitfield and Cross together and end their reign of terror," Elizabeth said.

Arriving at the church for dinner Elizabeth had mixed emotions of one of the happiest days of her life coupled with the worst day of her life. The joy would be in seeing Uncle Colin again and for him later to see his namesake great-nephew. The carriage carried them from the ship to Chelsea Old Church for dinner. They would have dinner on the Triad the following night so that the Uncle and great-nephew could meet. The day after would be Colin's christening in the same church where his parents had been married.

Arriving at Chelsea Old Church, Elizabeth and James went directly to the Rectory, bypassing the church for now which seemed like the best approach for all concerned. Uncle Colin had presented a lovely table for his guests as always.

He warmly greeted Elizabeth and congratulated her on his new great-nephew. "You wait until you see him, Uncle Colin. He is beautiful and looks just like James," Elizabeth said smiling.

"Is she saying you are beautiful now, James?" Colin said mischievously.

"Ignore him, Elizabeth; he likes to get my goat with his comments which are very out of character for a priest I might add," James said smiling.

"We are going to keep our spirits up until this dreadful business of the trial is over, Elizabeth. A family sticks together and we will stick together through this, my girl; make no mistake. Then onto more pleasant concerns like young Colin's christening. Keep focused on that Elizabeth in the days to come and all will be well," Uncle Colin stated.

On the way back to the Triad, Elizabeth placed her head on James' shoulder. Both were dreading the day before them, but avoiding all discussion of it. James had tripled the guard just in case any untoward activities were planned. Hugh Flynn had inspectors surrounding the Triad and James and Elizabeth wherever they went. Security outside the courtroom was not an issue. Facing men who had tried to kill James and Elizabeth was quite another matter altogether.

As they returned to the Triad and the master cabin, Elizabeth remembered the day that she had asked James to make love to her to block out the ugliness of the attempted murder. She would do the same tonight and have James' strong arms block out the hatred that had almost overwhelmed them both. While James changed in the adjoining cabin, Elizabeth looked in on the baby and kissed his dear head. She thought of all the joy that she had known since leaving London; exploring Broadlands and the village, the ball, the Christmas holidays and best of all the baby and James; all of which could have been wiped away by the senseless act of two mad and power hungry men. All of this would have been denied them if Whitfield had succeeded in his mission to destroy them both.

When she returned to the master cabin she quickly changed into her trousseau gown and robe and thought again of the many changes since her wedding night. She lit candles all around the room and twirled the bottle of champagne she had asked for along with the two glasses. She would seduce her husband this time if needs be. Although if she admitted to herself, she doubted that would be necessary. She let down her hair and brushed it until it shone. She heard James checking in on Colin as well and knew he would soon join her.

When James came into the cabin he saw Elizabeth sitting brushing her hair and as always his breath held in this chest. "Are those candles that I see, Mrs. O'Rourke?" James said casually.

"They are indeed," Elizabeth replied calmly.

"And is that champagne and glasses I see on the table?" James said again casually.

"It is, darling," Elizabeth replied.

"Are we celebrating something then?" James continued casually.

"You could say we are celebrating the anniversary of when we first met or our night at the Carlyle . . ." Elizabeth continued.

"Or of me breaking down your cabin door . . ." James said laughing.

"Or that," Elizabeth said smiling.

"Are you planning on seducing me then, Mrs. O'Rourke?" James stated with mock sincerity.

"Well, I was hoping to block out the ugliness we are about to face with the beautiful memories of one year ago. It doesn't seem possible, James that all of the beauty that we have known together over the past year could have been destroyed by Whitfield and Cross," Elizabeth said passionately.

"The important part is that they didn't succeed and we are here together as we were meant to be with the most beautiful boy in Ireland sleeping in the room next door. And where are they Elizabeth but where they deserve to be; in a cold lonely cell facing an uncertain and hopefully temporary existence on this earth. Now why don't you come over here and seduce me, Mrs. O'Rourke. I promise you I will like it. Have I ever steered you wrong?" James said huskily.

"You have not, Captain O'Rourke and I intend on letting you tell me everything that will please you," Elizabeth replied.

"I like the sound of that, darling girl," James responded.

With that Elizabeth brought James a glass of champagne and one for herself. She drank the cool bubbles and remembered the warmth she had felt on her wedding night. She filled both glasses again and then slipped off her robe. James lifted her into his arms and brought her across his lap. Elizabeth kissed his eyes, his mouth, his ears and neck and returned again to his mouth. The kisses were light at first then became more intense and demanding with each moment. Her hands circled his chest as James removed her gown. He cupped her breasts and she placed her arms around his neck drawing from him his strength, love and support as she had in the past. James' fingers traced her inner thighs and then within her inner recesses. Elizabeth's hand dropped from his neck to his abdomen. His head dropped to her neck with a deep growl in the back of his throat.

When he came within her, the effect was wondrous, bringing with it all of the love, laughter and happiness of the past year. They both drew their strength from each other and together they could face whatever life would bring. When they reached their climax, the words of endearment that followed proved the seduction had been a joint one; an indication of their mutual love and passion for each other.

When Elizabeth awoke in the morning, James was still with her. He looked down at her lovingly. "Did you sleep well, love?"

"I did, James; I always sleep well in your huge beds," Elizabeth said smiling.

"I always sleep well when my beautiful wife is sleeping with me in my huge bed; that is when we get around to sleeping," he said laughing and kissing Elizabeth. With that he threw back the covers and started to the door to wash and dress in the adjoining room.

"James you may want to put on your robe, darling. You don't want to terrify Nanny," she said laughing.

"I have a surprise for you, darling girl. After you have bathed, wait before dressing." Elizabeth was curious then and gathered her robe to proceed to bathe and dress.

James came walking in with a huge box and a smaller box on top. "These are for you to wear today, love. I shall be so proud of you; always remember that. You will need some help getting into it. It has a new fangled closing to the back; no buttons," James said laughing.

The new dress was sapphire blue to match her jewelry parure which she would wear with it today. The back had ties like a corset so that the dress would be fitted snugly at the waist. He is showing off my new figure, she thought smiling. The smaller box had a matching sapphire blue hat with a very seductive veil. She would be dressed like a queen when she entered that courtroom today. She knocked on Nanny's door to ask her to make up the laces in the back. She wanted to be ready when James knocked for her.

His knock came an hour later. She was dressed and ready. When he opened the door, the glow in his eyes told her all that she needed to know. "You look like a queen, my love. Are you ready to go?" James asked.

The trip to Fleet Street involved three carriages; one for James, Elizabeth and Uncle Colin; the chase vehicle by the Triad lads and the third carriage with the Scotland Yard escort. James held Elizabeth's hand in the carriage. The usual O'Rourke banter and laughter was not in evidence. They were all focused on the trial today and all that lie ahead for each of them.

When they reached the Old Bailey, off of Newgate Street, Elizabeth could feel her stomach tighten. The three were separated, as they were not allowed to hear the other's testimony until each had testified in open court. James would be called first, followed by Uncle Colin and Elizabeth last. James had obtained Hugh's promise that he would not leave Elizabeth's side and that promise would be kept. Hugh led Elizabeth to a witness room reserved for the members of the aristocracy. The room was lovely like Elizabeth, Hugh thought. Hugh was clearly smitten and planned to ask Elizabeth if she had any friends in Wilmington who would consider coming back on the Triad with them. If she was an example of an American woman in general, he was ready to sign on.

"We can wait here, Elizabeth. It is a more genteel space than the usual waiting space for male witnesses," Hugh stated. He provided Elizabeth with a glass of water and tried to make polite conversation until she was called to testify. "Do you have a large circle of friends in America, then?" Hugh asked casually.

"I have a large circle of lady friends, Hugh. A great many of the men were carried off in the war. There are whole towns where very few men survived the war. It is very sad; a great number of widows, orphans and of course unmarried ladies," Elizabeth replied.

"Is that so, Elizabeth? Well that is sad indeed. I did not realize that; very sad." Hugh decided to make a mental note of that fact and pass it along to James when next they spoke. "How do you find Broadlands then, Elizabeth?" Hugh asked.

"Oh I so love it, Hugh. James has made some wonderful improvements in the family quarters. We have also redone the guest rooms in the guest wing. You must try to come and stay with us this Christmas. Uncle Colin truly enjoyed his visit with us. We had an old fashioned family Christmas that everyone seemed to love; just like the old days when James' parents were alive," Elizabeth replied smiling.

"I appreciated the invitation, Elizabeth. All of the preparation of these trials kept me in London last Christmas but I promise that I will take you up on an invitation for this coming Christmas," Hugh replied.

They chatted about family, Elizabeth explaining that she had no family remaining in North Carolina, only her family here. Hugh talked about growing up in the county around Dublin and going to school with James as boys.

"Was he always such a tease then, Hugh?" Elizabeth asked.

"I will be honest in saying that I have never seen James as happy has he has been in the past year since before his sainted mother died. He is a changed man for sure; Elizabeth and I put that down to you. For anyone who knows him, they can see the man he was and the man he is now," Hugh replied.

"That is so kind of you to say, Hugh. We were just talking last night about all of the changes that have happened in our lives in the past year and all of the happiness. If Benjamin Whitfield and Charles Cross had had their way, that happiness would have ended before it began," Elizabeth replied wistfully.

"I know this is hard on you, Elizabeth. Don't let them rattle you today and just tell what happened as you told it to me the day after. It will all be fine and you will soon be off to Bermuda for your second honeymoon," Hugh said smiling.

Their chat continued; both trying to keep up their end of the conversation and avoid the unpleasantness that lies ahead. An hour and a half later, a knock came to the door and a bailiff asked Elizabeth to join him to be escorted into the courtroom. Elizabeth glanced at Hugh and smiled and proceeded to follow the bailiff. Hugh went up the stairs to the galleries where he knew James and Father O'Rourke would be waiting to watch the proceedings.

As Elizabeth walked into the courtroom, she steeled herself for the moment that she would see Benjamin Whitfield and Charles Cross for the first time in nearly a year. She remembered what James had told her; she looked like a queen and he would be so proud of her. She vowed to find him in the galleries so that she would know where he was at all times and gain her strength from his presence.

The bailiff called out "Elizabeth Majors O'Rourke; come into court," and Elizabeth was escorted into the witness box. She was sworn in and prepared for the questions that would follow. As the barrister rose from his desk, she scoured the galleries for James and found him, Uncle Colin and Hugh now standing with them. She focused on the barrister and tried not to look for Whitfield and Cross in the courtroom.

"Elizabeth Katherine Majors O'Rourke; you are a citizen of the United States of America; is this not true?" the barrister asked.

"Yes sir, I was born and reared in Wilmington, North Carolina," Elizabeth responded.

James watched the jurors sit forward in their seats. They had apparently not been prepared for a female witness and decided to angle for a better view. Next to him a journalist from one of the London newspapers was starting a sketch of Elizabeth which would appear in the next day's paper. He was not sure how he felt about that, but kept his opinions to himself.

"Will you tell the court, Mrs. O'Rourke why you travelled to London in 1865 from the United States of America?" the barrister continued.

"I travelled to London to settle the estate of my late father which was being handled by Hilary Cross," Elizabeth replied.

"Can you tell the court how you came to be acquainted with Mr. Charles Cross?" he continued.

"Mr. Charles Cross came to handle my father's estate due to the failing health of his father, Hilary Cross," Elizabeth responded.

"Can you tell about your first meeting with the accused?" he continued.

"I met with Mr. Cross regarding the status of my father's estate as it proceeded to probate. The matter had been probated in New Hanover County in the state of North Carolina, but due to the ending of the war and the disruption that resulted, I was unsure if the correspondence that I had sent had been received. I had not received a response to any of my letters to Mr. Cross," Elizabeth replied.

"Did you have siblings or other male family members who could settle the matter for you?" he continued.

"No sir; my mother and father are both deceased and my brother died before the end of the war. There were no other male family members to complete the probate and indeed no other family members at all," Elizabeth responded.

James in watching the jurors could see that they were impressed by Elizabeth's cool responses and that she was not flustered by the questions coming to her by the barrister. He continued to watch the sketch evolve next to him as he listened to Elizabeth's testimony.

"Could you tell the court when you first came to meet Benjamin Whitfield?"

"Yes, I met Mr. Whitfield on board the sailing ship the Alliance upon leaving Wilmington, North Carolina. He departed the Alliance in Bermuda which was our first stop on the way to London," Elizabeth replied.

"Did you have reason to meet Mr. Whitfield again, Mrs. O'Rourke?"

"Yes, I had reason to meet Mr. Whitfield in the Chelsea Old Church on October 3rd, 1865," Elizabeth responded.

"Can you tell the court why this date is significant to you?"

"On that date, I went to Chelsea Old Church to meet with my uncle by marriage, Father Colin O'Rourke. I had received a note which I believed written by him inviting me for tea. When I arrived at the church, it was to discover that the note that had brought me to the church was not written by my uncle, but by Mr. Whitfield," Elizabeth replied.

"Your Grace, I enter into evidence the note in question as exhibit number 20. Your Grace will see as you read the note that it was written in such a way as to appear to be from the witness' uncle by marriage; Father Colin O'Rourke, when in reality it was written by Benjamin Whitfield."

The jurors and galleries exchanged mumbled comments about that piece of evidence. The attention on Elizabeth was rapt. She continued to calmly respond to the ongoing questions.

"Can you tell the court, Mrs. O'Rourke; what occurred after you arrived at the Chelsea Old Church?"

"I entered the Chelsea Old Church seeking my Uncle Father O'Rourke. He was not to be found. I called for him, but there was no response. I was preparing to leave, but Mr. Whitfield had entered the church without my knowledge," Elizabeth responded.

"Can you tell the court what next transpired, Mrs. O'Rourke? Please take your time in explaining to the court."

"Mr. Whitfield proceeded to tell me that Uncle Colin had not written the note, but that he had written the note in order that I might come to the church," Elizabeth continued.

"It was written under false pretenses then?"

"That is correct, sir," Elizabeth replied.

"What happened next?"

"Mr. Whitfield told me that Uncle Colin, Father O'Rourke was being detained. Mr. Whitfield then started to speak about Mr. Cross and the fact that he had been directed by Mr. Cross to eliminate me and my husband. Mr. Whitfield had been sent by Mr. Cross to do that task," Elizabeth responded.

"When you say eliminate, Mrs. O'Rourke; did you mean murder?"

"Objection your honor; I object to this line of questioning."

The jury and galleries was ignited by that objection. The judge hit the gavel and called for order in the court.

"The objection is overruled. Please proceed my dear and tell the court your story," the judge replied.

James smiled at that response from the judge. Elizabeth has done it again; the judge is smitten with her. He was pleased that she had an ally in that courtroom. He noticed that she had not yet made eye contact with Whitfield or Cross and was keeping her attention on the barrister before her.

"Thank you your Grace. Mr. Whitfield proceeded to tell me that Mr. Cross had directed him to eliminate both my husband and I due to the fact that my father's estate was in the hands of Mr. Cross and that some of the funds in the estate were now missing and I was not to know that this had occurred. As I had no family members, if I were to die and my husband as well, the proceeds of the estate would remain with Mr. Cross and Mr. Whitfield," Elizabeth continued.

The courtroom ignited again with sounds of shame coming from the galleries. Again the judge hit the gavel and demanded quiet. The journalist sketching Elizabeth stopped at that moment taken in by the testimony provided by the lovely American.

"Please proceed, my dear. I know that this is taxing for you and if you need to stop at any time, we will advise the bench to take a break," the judge stated.

"Thank you your Grace. Mr. Whitfield continued to tell me that it was not his intention to kill me, but only my husband. Mr. Whitfield stated that it was his intention that I be spared provided that I agreed to . . . well . . . to become his companion," Elizabeth continued quietly.

The courtroom erupted again with jurors shaking their fists and the galleries shouting down shame again to Whitfield and Cross.

"By companion, Mrs. O'Rourke, and again I apologize for the indelicacy, did Mr. Whitfield mean that he would replace Captain O'Rourke in your affections after he had cold heartedly killed him in your presence?"

"Objection; I object to this line of questioning your Grace!" The defense barrister was on his feet and angrily noting his objections. "Mr. Whitfield and Mr. Cross are both officers of the court. To hear them libeled in this matter is too much."

"Objection overruled. Mr. Stanley-Smyth, you have stood in this very courtroom and heard members of Scotland Yard testify to these very facts. You have heard similar testimony by the witness' husband, Captain O'Rourke. The witness has tried to delicately tell this tale as she is clearly a lady. Would you have her continue to be placed through these objections of yours? Sit down, sir; sit down! Please continue," the judge stated.

"Thank you your Grace. Now then, Mrs. O'Rourke, what did Mr. Whitfield next say?"

"Mr. Whitfield said that Mr. Cross had directed him to eliminate my husband and myself, but that he could not bring himself to kill me. He said that if he killed my husband, then I was to be his reward," Elizabeth continued quietly.

The courtroom again erupted; cries of, "Monstrous simply monstrous," was heard coming from the gallery. The judge again silenced the courtroom.

"Mr. Whitfield stated that my uncle was being held against his will and that the men who were holding him would be in the church shortly to dispense with me," Elizabeth continued.

"Did you make any comment to Mr. Whitfield?"

"I told him that I thought he had no intention of actually harming anyone, but perhaps only trying to scare us. I told him that if he would carry through with his threats, that he would be the responsible party and that Mr. Cross would simply walk away and leave him to hold the blame," Elizabeth responded.

"What was Mr. Whitfield's response to that statement?"

"Mr. Whitfield said that he had thought of that and that his only concern was my husband. He said that he had no intention of harming me because if it had not been for my husband Captain O'Rourke, I would be on his arm now. He further stated that once my husband was out of the way, we would have the opportunity to get to know one another and that I would find him a considerate person and willing to take care of me," Elizabeth continued.

"Can you relay to the court the next series of events, Mrs. O'Rourke?"

"I could see a small crack in the door which was the entrance to the church. I could see that my husband and members of his crew had come into the church while Mr. Whitfield continued to speak and to threaten me. When my husband Captain O'Rourke spoke, Mr. Whitfield began to threaten him as well," Elizabeth continued.

"When you say threaten, Mrs. O'Rourke; can you describe the nature of the threats for the court?"

"Mr. Whitfield stated that he would kill my husband Captain O'Rourke and that I could then be his . . . companion after my husband's death," Elizabeth continued.

The courtroom erupted again with jeers and screams of shame coming from the galleries. James could see the affect the testimony was having on the jurors. The judge again banged the gavel.

"Silence; I will have silence in the court and if I must I will clear the galleries! Pray continue, my dear," the judge stated.

"Mr. Whitfield then came closer to my husband who was directly in front of him. Mr. Whitfield then pulled a gun from his jacket. I then screamed. Two shots were fired at that time," Elizabeth continued.

"Can you tell the court Mrs. O'Rourke, to whom those shots were fired? I am sorry if this is difficult for you."

"Objection; the prosecution is leading the witness," the defense counsel stated.

"My lord; my concern is for the testimony that you will now hear which will be difficult, nay nearly impossible for the witness to provide. I pray your forbearance my lord."

"Objection overruled; pray continue," the judge stated.

James could see that the judge was on their side and without being biased, was as disgusted by the need for Elizabeth to relive that day as was James, Uncle Colin and Hugh. Although hardened to crime by the nature of his work, Hugh had been sincerely touched by Elizabeth's bravery in the face of attempted murder and injuries sustained at the hands of Whitfield.

"The two shots were fired at me, sir," Elizabeth stated quietly.

Mumbles were heard throughout the courtroom with that statement. The artist standing next to James continued to sketch away and was also sketching Whitfield and Cross while this testimony was given. Both men had gone quite pale as the testimony continued. They knew both the judge and the jury had been moved by Elizabeth's brave testimony. They knew as did James that the court would be more moved by Elizabeth than by all of the other witnesses combined; especially with the evidence yet to come.

"The two shots were fired in your direction, Mrs. O'Rourke. Could you describe what occurred next?"

Elizabeth then continued, "I felt the impact of the first shot and then pain of the second shot as it hit my left arm. I remember falling at that point and my husband Captain O'Rourke rushing to my side."

"My lord I submit into evidence exhibit number 21; a St. Christopher medal. Mrs. O'Rourke can you tell the court the significance of this item to this case?"

"Yes sir. The St. Christopher medal was worn by me on the day in question. The St. Christopher medal caught the first shot that was fired at me. The St. Christopher medal was around my neck on that day," Elizabeth replied.

"Around your neck Mrs. O'Rourke and over your heart is that not correct?"

"Objection my lord; the prosecution is again leading the witness," the defense counsel stated.

"Objection overruled; where else would it be if it was around her neck? Pray continue my dear," the judge replied.

"The St. Christopher medal was around my neck and above my heart. The medal captured the first bullet that was fired at me by Mr. Whitfield," Elizabeth stated quietly.

"Pray tell the court the location of the second shot."

"The second shot hit my arm. I remember feeling the shot and then seeing the blood . . . the blood started to flow across my chest," Elizabeth continued.

"My lord; I now submit into evidence exhibit number 22; which is the dress worn by the witness at the time of the shooting. My lord and members of the jury; Mrs. O'Rourke has not seen this dress since the day of the shooting. I note that it may be difficult for her to see it now. I pray the court's indulgence in the submittal of this evidence however difficult to the court's attention," the barrister stated.

The St. Christopher medal captured by Hugh on the day after the shooting was shown to the members of the jury and to the judge as was the dress that Elizabeth had worn that fateful day. The entire bodice on the left side of the dress was coated in blood. For the first time, Elizabeth could understand James' reaction when he had come to her aid. For the first time Elizabeth could understand James' terror for her safety ever since. As the medal and dress were shown to the members of the jury and to the judge, Elizabeth looked up to the gallery and found James. Their exchange of glances said it all. James hands were white from grasping the rail surrounding the gallery. Elizabeth's hands were the same as she grasped the railing of the witness box. Elizabeth saw Uncle Colin place his hand over James' hand in a show of solidarity. He winked then at Elizabeth as if to say, everything will be fine.

"Mrs. O'Rourke, can you confirm to the court that the medal shown to the jury and the dress marked as exhibits numbers 21 and 22 are indeed the medal and dress worn on the fateful day of October 3, 1865 in Chelsea Old Church?"

"Yes, sir; that is my medal given to me by Father O'Rourke and my dress worn on the day of October 3, 1865," Elizabeth responded calmly.

The court erupted again with a woman in the gallery fainting at the sight of the dress. James thought to himself, this woman faints at the sight of the dress and my Elizabeth has to relive the day and stands calm and composed. She is a marvel, James thought and she looks like a queen standing in that witness box.

"My lord; I have no further questions for the witness."

The defense then rose to begin his questioning of Elizabeth.

"Mrs. O'Rourke; you have testified that you went to Chelsea Old Church upon receiving a note marked as exhibit 20 by the prosecution. Are you certain that you did not go to the church upon some pre-arranged assignation with the defendant; an assignation that went horribly wrong when your husband appeared on the scene?" he stated.

Cries of shame went up from the gallery. The support of the court was behind Elizabeth and the crowd knew it. She stood ramrod straight and calm at the question posed by the defense. Hugh had warned her that they may try to rattle her and her story. She would have none of it. James saw the flash of color in her cheeks and knew that she was about to do battle.

"No, sir; Mr. Whitfield was a Yankee, sir. I have lived through an invading army during the War of Northern Aggression. I have lived through the occupation of my home city by an invading army before the end of that war. My father died bravely fighting for the Confederacy at Union hands. I assure you, sir I would not have had words or an assignation with a Yankee under any circumstances. In addition, sir, I was married to Captain O'Rourke not two days before the day in question. No sir; under no circumstances would I have had an assignation with Mr. Whitfield or any other man. I received a note which I believed to have been sent to me by my uncle through marriage, Father O'Rourke. I went to the church to see him and no one else. As I was not familiar with his handwriting, I had no idea that the note that I had received had been forged by another to lure me to Chelsea Old Church under the pretense of meeting a family member and a priest."

The gallery erupted again with cries of hear, hear. James heard an older gentleman say from behind him, "She's a little one, but she's got spirit. She will tell that so and so what's up in short order!" Even Father O'Rourke had to laugh at that comment. It was his first laugh of the day.

"Your, Grace; I have no further questions of this witness. The witness may be excused," the defense counsel stated.

At those words, Hugh raced down the stairs, followed quickly behind by James and Father O'Rourke. They had all made a pact that they would meet Elizabeth as soon as she was excused from the witness box so as to protect her from the press that they knew would surround her as soon as she had completed her testimony. This was a salacious trial, as the men on trial were both officers of the court. Add to that fact that an American whose life had been threatened and a priest kidnapped in the bargain and the newspapers would have a story that went on for days. When the shooting had occurred, the press was not informed of the matter. In the early days of the case when Whitfield and Cross were taken into custody, more momentum had followed the story. James and Elizabeth were then safely in Ireland and at Broadlands. The impact of the story now would be huge and Hugh, James and Father O'Rourke had conspired to protect Elizabeth from the affect of the trial if they could not protect her from having to testify and relive the day's events.

Because they were racing to Elizabeth's side, they had not seen the look that Elizabeth only then exchanged with Whitfield and Cross. It was a look of contempt at two men who had tried to steal both her inheritance and her life. It was the very look that the press had been waiting for and they captured that information greedily for their afternoon columns. Elizabeth let go of the railing at that point, hoping against hope that her legs would work and that they would carry her from this place. The jury, judge and galleries were not disappointed. Elizabeth turned on her heel and floated from the witness box as she was indeed the queen that James had described. She would let no one see the effect that this morning had had upon her. She only wanted to find James and to have his arms around her, assuring her that everything would be alright.

When she emerged from the witness box and courtroom, the bailiff was standing beside her. By pre-arrangement with Hugh, he would remain with her until Hugh, James and Father O'Rourke could encircle her and take her back to the witness room. Within minutes they were by her side. Hugh and James all but lifted her, one arm each to get her away from the crowding press that they knew would bombard her within moments. Hugh led the way back to the witness room reserved for the aristocracy with Father O'Rourke bringing up the rear. They had succeeded in spiriting her away from the hungry members of the press. Hugh would go out and answer questions of them while James sought to calm Elizabeth from the effects of this morning's testimony. Father O'Rourke closed the door to give them a moment of privacy before the world again descended.

"Oh, darling girl; I am so proud of you. I told you that you looked like a queen this morning and not only did you look like a queen, you behaved like one as well. I know that it was difficult, but you were amazing, my love. You had that jury and judge in the palm of your hand. It didn't hurt of course that the judge was smitten with you; probably half of the jury as well; what am I saying the entire jury!" James said smiling.

"Oh, James; please hold me. I am shaking like a leaf. I was fine while I was in the courtroom, but now I am shaking all over. I think it was the fact that I finally looked Whitfield and Cross in the eye only after the judge had told me that I was dismissed. They look like broken men, James. They didn't even look like the men that I had seen last October," Elizabeth replied.

"I know, love. Their fate has been sealed and they both know it. Hold no sympathy for them, Elizabeth. Their evil deeds have caught up with them. I know you have a forgiving heart but Elizabeth; those men nearly succeeded in killing you!" James replied passionately.

"I know, darling. I had not seen the St. Christopher medal until today or the dress. I understand now why you would get that look in your eye every time that you thought I could be in danger or going out on my own. I am so sorry James that I ever worried you in any way," Elizabeth replied through tears.

"You have nothing to apologize for. How were you to know? I was trying hard not to have to tell you everything that occurred and how it looked when I came to your side. I thought for sure that I had lost you and it was all that I could think of then and ever since. Now, Mrs. O'Rourke; raise that veil so that I can give you a proper kiss. My heart is racing as fast as yours for what you have been through this day," James replied.

Elizabeth raised her veil and kissed James long and hard; a real kiss as he would say and one that held with it the release from all that Elizabeth had just experienced. Elizabeth started to cry then softly at first and then stronger. "What's wrong, darling? It's all over now you don't have to face them ever again," James asked.

"I know, James; I can always get through the worst of things; it's when they are over that I fall apart!" Elizabeth replied.

James started to laugh in spite of himself. "If that is all, I can fix that. I will just kiss you until you stop thinking about it. How's that? Think on me instead," James started kissing Elizabeth for real and proper at that moment; holding her as if he would never let her go. Father O'Rourke stuck in his head at that moment and started to laugh.

"There is a time and a place for that, Jamie boy. How is our girl doing; alright Elizabeth?" Father O'Rourke said smiling. "Hugh is trying to hold off the hoards of reporters out in the hall that want nothing more than to descend on you both. I will be minding the door out here in case anyone is interested," Uncle Colin stated.

Elizabeth started to laugh then through her tears. She felt safe and loved as she always did by the O'Rourke clan. Had James not told her that she would be at the center of the family? She certainly felt that way now. The only thing missing was baby Colin and she would have hold of him soon enough.

"If you are holding forth then Uncle we will leave you to it. Close the door and I will get on with making Elizabeth feel better in here," James said laughing. The easy banter between the two had returned and Elizabeth was starting to breathe again after the agony of the courtroom and the witness box. "The press will want to accost you as soon as you leave this room, love. That is why we came to collect you and get you in here as soon as possible. Uncle Colin is going to stay here with you while Hugh and I go back inside and hear the summation, verdict and sentencing. We don't want you to have to go back in there, darling girl. We promise to tell you everything that is said, but we don't want you to have to face that or them again," James said earnestly.

"I understand, James; Uncle Colin can keep me company while I wait here," Elizabeth said quietly.

"Just don't go after asking him questions about me when I was growing up. That is all that I ask," James said with a wink.

"I wouldn't think of such a thing, darling," Elizabeth said smiling. They had gotten their banter back again also and that was a very good thing in James' eyes.

"One last kiss and I will go out and retrieve Hugh. We will see you when this is all over, darling girl. Just stay strong and know that I love you. I will let you know how much when this is all over." With that James kissed Elizabeth again and held her until she could barely breathe again. He was off again to rejoin Hugh and Uncle Colin came in to sit with Elizabeth.

"I told you the O'Rourke family sticks together, Elizabeth. We were all that proud of you, James the most of all. I told him he had found his match with you and so he has. Now are you alright, darling girl? What shall we talk about to get your mind off of this bad lot, then?" Uncle Colin asked.

Elizabeth was starting to regain her composure and her smile. "Well, we could start with your stories about James growing up," Elizabeth said smiling. "Come and tell me all of your stories about our James," Elizabeth continued smiling.

James met up with Hugh in the outer hallways. The reporters were filing back into the courtroom having gotten their questions answered by Inspector Flynn. They still wanted to meet with his star witness, but he was having none of it. Just the facts Hugh had given them and he was not about to give them salacious details such as Whitfield's apparent lust for Elizabeth. As Hugh was now aware, every man who met her fell in love with her. Whitfield had the misfortune of being a Yankee and as Elizabeth had told the court that was the end of any chances Whitfield could have had.

As Hugh and James returned to the gallery, the courtroom had again calmed and the prosecution was giving his final summation to the judge and jury.

"My lord, members of the jury, you have heard the testimony provided by Scotland Yard, by the only victims of these two men remaining alive, Captain James O'Rourke, Father Colin O'Rourke and Elizabeth Majors O'Rourke. They paint a picture of depravity so extreme as to have resulted in the murder of two individuals, the kidnapping of a third and the attempted murder of two additional individuals remaining to tell the tale. All this with but one root in mind; the accumulation of wealth through the embezzlement of funds belonging to the parties in question. We are too late for those two murdered individuals. Fortunately, Mrs. Elizabeth Majors O'Rourke lived to tell the tale of these men who through their greed and unscrupulous behavior did conspire to end the life of a young woman, new to our shores, a lady who came to this country for the sole reason of trying to settle an estate left in trust to her through the hands of these murderers, kidnappers and embezzlers. I ask the jury for the verdict of guilty and for the sentence of hanging for these two men before you. An eye for an eye for their two victims who were not lucky enough to survive their clutches. I ask also that the assets of these two men be sold so that the surviving victim Mrs. Elizabeth Majors O'Rourke be provided restitution for her pain, suffering and for the rightful inheritance which these two men sought to steal from her and from her family."

The defense rose to make his final statement as well. He knew the case was against him. He knew the opinion of the court; judge, jury and public were also against him. His final summation told the tale when he asked only for mercy to be shown to his clients as officers of the court.

At the conclusion of the summation, the judge placed upon the jury their responsibility for the verdict in this matter. "Mr. Foreman, you have heard the evidence presented in court. I ask that you render your decision in the fate of Benjamin Whitfield and Charles Cross," the judge stated gravely.

The jury quickly assembled and discussed their views on the case. The decision was swift, having been made within fifteen minutes of the judge's instructions.

"My lord, we have reached a verdict," the jury foreman stated.

"Mr. Foreman, pray rise and read the verdict," the judge replied.

"My lord, the jury finds Benjamin Whitfield and Charles Cross guilty of the crimes of murder, kidnapping, attempted murder and embezzlement," the foreman stated.

"Thank you Mr. Foreman and the members of the jury for your service. Benjamin Whitfield and Charles Cross; please stand for the rendering of sentence. You have heard the verdict of this jury. You have been found guilty of the heinous crimes of murder, kidnapping, attempted murder and embezzlement. I sentence you both to death for your crimes. I further direct the bailiff to sell your estates and chattel so that the remaining victim, Mrs. Elizabeth Majors O'Rourke may be provided restitution for the estate of her father, Robert Majors in the amount of 50,000 pounds. May God have mercy upon your souls. Bailiff, take them away."

The courtroom erupted in cheers at the fate of Whitfield and Cross. Hugh looked at James who stood in shock at the amount of the estate read by the judge. "It is not enough that you marry the most beautiful woman in London, but an heiress as well? Are you not the luckiest man in Ireland, James O'Rourke?" Hugh said slapping James on the back.

"I had no idea, Hugh; truly I didn't. I don't believe Elizabeth had any idea either. She was just trying to do what she knew to be the right thing and get the damn estate settled.

She came all this way, nearly got herself killed and had no idea that she was an heiress of that magnitude. We have to go find her in hopes that the reporters don't try to besiege her," James replied worriedly.

"I think she is safe for now. They have run back to their offices to write this story and the verdict and sentence. We will let the courtroom clear and then bring her and your uncle out of hiding. The quicker we can get them back to the Triad, the better," Hugh responded.

After some minutes, Hugh and James went back to the witness room and knocked on the door. Father O'Rourke went to the door, opened it a crack and let them both in. "It is all over, Elizabeth. They have been found guilty and sentenced to death. Further their estates are to be sold to provide restitution to you for the embezzlement," James stated.

Elizabeth looked from James to Hugh who stood shaking his head yes. It was unbelievable to Elizabeth. It was all over after so many months of worrying and waiting.

"You are an heiress, darling girl. Cross and Whitfield both knew that and of course hoped that you would never know the truth until they could either control you or . . ." James stopped at that point.

"Or murder you . . ." Hugh had completed the sentence.

Elizabeth sat still in shock by the news provided by her husband and Hugh Flynn. She knew that the events of today would register in her mind at some time in the future. For now, it was all too much to take in. All she wanted to do was to return to the Triad, hug her son and try to process all that she had learned today and all that had taken place during their prior visit to London.

As if he had read her mind, James interrupted her train of thought. "Let's get Elizabeth back to the Triad. I don't know if a celebration is in order, but we definitely all need lunch and I for one, need a drink, a large stiff one."

"I second that motion," Father O'Rourke said smiling at James.

The trio set off again, as the protective circle around Elizabeth. James took her hand and didn't let go of it again as they hailed the cab which transported them back to the Triad. The protective detail from the Triad followed behind as well as the escort from Scotland Yard.

Once they had returned to the Triad, Elizabeth asked to be excused so that she could check on Colin and give him a long, much needed hug. At this point, she was unsure whether she needed the hug more than Colin. She would also nurse him which always gave her a sense of calm and purpose beyond the insanity that had been her day.

James, Hugh and Father O'Rourke went into the master cabin and poured drinks all around. "We need to drink a toast to Elizabeth when she joins us," Father O'Rourke said. "She is the most extraordinary woman, James. I don't know how you could have found another like her."

"Hugh seems to believe that all American women are like her, Uncle Colin. I think he wants me to kidnap one for him and bring her back on the Triad. Hopefully we can find one of Elizabeth's friends who won't be too frightened of the sight of him to at least exchange letters first," James said laughing.

"Well I did think it worth a try, James. You have to admit, you have never met anyone like Elizabeth on this side of the Atlantic or any other ports of call that you may have visited," Hugh said smiling. The three sat drinking their whiskeys and taking in the events of the morning as well.

"On the matter of tomorrow's christening, James; have you thought of a godfather for young Colin?" Father O'Rourke asked.

"Why I select Hugh of course, Uncle Colin. Who better to watch over our boy then the best friend a man could have? We couldn't have gotten through this without you Hugh and that is for sure," James responded.

"Thank you, James; I would be proud to be young Colin's godfather. You just have to find me the godmother in America to complete the job," Hugh replied smiling.

"We will put Elizabeth to the task. She will soon have it sorted won't she, Uncle Colin?" James stated smiling.

"Well she certainly got you sorted, James; so yes, I think she is up for the challenge," Uncle Colin responded.

The three continued to exchange jokes and good humored banter until Elizabeth joined them. She came walking in with young Colin. Her eyes were shining then and James knew that she had put away the events of the morning for the time being with Colin the center of her attention.

"Hugh, Uncle Colin; May I introduce your great nephew Christopher Colin O'Rourke," Elizabeth said smiling. "Colin, may I introduce the O'Rourke circle of protection. You could not be better protected by these three men. I should know; they have protected me now for almost a year now." Elizabeth was smiling through tears again. James could tell that she was very near her breaking point, but still she smiled on. That was his Elizabeth; the calming eye of the storm of life that surrounded her.

"So this is my great-nephew, Colin. Bless you, darling boy and your mother who brought you into the world. Aren't we hearing that you are a beautiful boy who looks just like your father? Is that by way of saying your father is beautiful then?" Uncle Colin said laughing.

"I have heard him called many things, Colin; but never beautiful," Hugh said laughing.

"Something tells me you two have many stories about James that I will need to hear," Elizabeth said looking at James.

"I think it is time for more whiskey and some lunch. Elizabeth, are you having a glass of champagne, my love?" James said closing the subject.

"Have you introduced her to good Irish whiskey, then?" Colin asked.

"No, my wife is partial to champagne. Isn't that so, darling?" James said with mischief in his eyes.

"Sounds like a bad habit that James would have introduced her to," Colin said smiling.

"Hugh has agreed to be godfather to baby Colin," James said trying to change the subject again.

"That is wonderful news, Hugh. Thank you so much. Now we have to do something about the godmother," Elizabeth replied.

"That is what I said, Elizabeth. You see, she will have it sorted just like Uncle Colin said," James said laughing.

"Have what sorted? Why do I feel like I am missing information from this conversation?" Elizabeth said coming to sit next to Uncle Colin and smoothing the baby's hair.

"You have no idea, lass. We will fill you in on all you need to know over luncheon," Colin said looking meaningfully at James.

"Where is Jones with the luncheon?" James said again changing the subject.

The banter went on through luncheon and beyond. The O'Rourke circle was trying their best to raise Elizabeth's spirits and keep her mind from that courtroom and all that had taken place today. James knew that the two would have to talk out this day's revelations for days and weeks to come. For now, he was fine in keeping her smiling and focused on baby Colin and the O'Rourke circle. There would be time enough for conversations on the window seat between London and Bermuda.

Luncheon went into late afternoon and late afternoon into supper. The O'Rourke clan joined forces to raise up Elizabeth and they were bound to that task. At last Father O'Rourke got up to leave and Hugh at the same time. "James and Elizabeth; you show hospitality fit for a king whether at sea or dry land. That is only fitting as we are in the presence of the O'Rourke queen. Thank you Elizabeth for your hospitality and for bringing life to this family again. I will see you all tomorrow morning for the christening of young Colin. God bless all here," Uncle Colin stated.

"Goodbye James and Elizabeth," Hugh said. "I will share a carriage with Father O'Rourke and see you both in the morning along with my godson Colin."

When the door closed behind them James opened his arms and Elizabeth gladly went into them. "I believe Colin and Hugh are in their cups, darling girl. I can't abide men who can't hold their whiskey," James said meaningfully.

Elizabeth thought to herself that James had matched them glass for glass, but kept the opinion to herself. It had been quite a day. "Elizabeth, I am going to get you drunk. I am going to fill your champagne glass until you are unable to stand," James said smiling.

"James, darling; although I think that a sound plan on its face; how will I possibly nurse Colin if I am too drunk to stand?" Elizabeth responded logically.

"Ah, a good point; very sensible of you as always. I have a second plan, darling girl. You go check on young Colin and when you come back there will be a surprise waiting for you," James replied with a wink.

"What kind of surprise, James?" Elizabeth responded smiling.

"Now, if I told you that then it wouldn't be a surprise, now would it? That's not at all logical is it?" James replied mischievously.

"No, darling; I expect not. I will go check on the baby and give you time to get your surprise ready; alright darling?" Elizabeth replied.

"Capital idea," James responded.

Elizabeth went down the hall to check on the baby and nurse for the evening. When she had finished, she changed his nappies and left Colin cooing in his cot. What a perfect boy, she thought, and we made him together. Now for the father, she thought smiling.

She closed the door on Colin's room and started down the hallway. James stopped her at his dressing room door crooking his finger to her and placing his finger over his mouth to whisper. "What are you up to?" Elizabeth said smiling.

"My surprise of course; ready?" James answered.

Elizabeth came into the dressing room and found lit candles surrounding a giant bathtub which had been filled with hot water and rose petals.

"James, where did you get this giant tub? It is nearly as huge as our bed," Elizabeth said laughing.

"Not quite, love; but the floor has been reinforced to hold the weight just in case," James replied.

"Are you serious?" Elizabeth said laughing.

"Shush love and yes. You have to be quiet so you don't wake baby and Nanny," James said with a wink.

"I know. She is going to think we are mad and we haven't left London yet," Elizabeth responded.

"Here is your champagne, darling girl. Let me help you with the new fangled closings on your gown. I brought your robe and mine. You see; I thought of everything," James said smiling.

"You have indeed, darling as always." Elizabeth turned towards James to have him undue the laces of her beautiful new dress. He gently untied the outer corset laces and as the laces came away caressed and kissed Elizabeth's back at each opening. As the dress was undone James held it as Elizabeth stepped out of it. There was another sea of petticoats, an inner corset and chemise beyond.

"Elizabeth, you have more layers than a wedding cake," James said laughing.

"Don't be discouraged, James, not many more to go," Elizabeth said smiling.

He sat drinking his glass of whiskey watching the layers disappear. The warmth and steam from the tub rose up to surround them both. The smell of roses was in the air and for James, the smell of roses meant only one thing; his Elizabeth.

When she reached her chemise he took off his shirt and pants. Elizabeth stood looking at the tub still skeptical about the weight. As if he had read her mind, he said laughing "I will get in first. If we don't land in the cargo bays, we are safe because you don't weigh more than a sack of potatoes." With that said he splashed into the tub. Everything held without creak or groan, so Elizabeth felt it safe to continue. James sat watching his beautiful wife undue her chemise and slip into the tub in front of him. James sat down his whiskey glass and picked up a sponge and Elizabeth's rose scented soap.

"Do you mind smelling like roses, James?" Elizabeth said quietly.

"I have smelled nothing but roses for over a year, my love. I will never smell a rose again without thinking of you. How could I mind that? Lean against me love and let me help you relax and wash away the day," James said lovingly.

Elizabeth leaned against James and felt the tension of the day fade away from his caresses and the warmth of the water.

"Let me take care of you, darling girl. Close your eyes and just feel," James said.

Elizabeth did as she was bid and let James massage her shoulders and wash every inch of her body. He did so slowly and tenderly with the promise of the lovemaking that was to follow. When he had finished his hands came to caress her breasts. She raised her arm to trace his beard and neck. His hands ran down her side over her stomach and into the recesses of her womanhood. James continued his ecstatic torture of her until she came apart in his arms and found her release. At that point, he whispered into her ear. "Are you ready for me, my love?"

Elizabeth turned rather than spoke. James lifted her onto his lap and his hard arousal as he caressed her breasts with his lips and her bottom with his hands. Both were lost in their own trance of love. Their mouths mated as did their bodies. No words were exchanged and none were needed. Their bodies matched the age old rhythms of life. The climax when it came was magical for them both. They held onto each other blocking out the world and all of its demands. The moment was theirs; their love stronger with each passing day and each challenge that they faced together. They sat for a long time, drained of energy, and seeking only the love, strength and support of the other.

CHAPTER SEVENTEEN

The next day was Christopher Colin's christening. James had left instructions that Elizabeth was not to be disturbed unless or until needed by Master Colin and only then. These were his instructions for the remainder of the trip as well. He knew the toll that the trial had taken on Elizabeth and he knew it would take her a while to process and to recover from that experience.

At the first sound of Colin's cry, Elizabeth was awake and ready to jump out of bed. "I will bring him to you, love. Just lay back and relax," James stated.

A few minutes later James came into the cabin holding Colin. He had his little finger in Colin's mouth quieting him until he could bring him to Elizabeth for nursing.

"That is such a beautiful picture," Elizabeth said smiling. "My two favorite boys in the entire world. Could I possibly be any happier?" Elizabeth said through tears.

James handed Colin onto his mother. "I will start bathing and dressing love while you put a smile on young Colin's face."

Elizabeth cooed and talked to Colin as he nursed. "Today is your big day little one. Everyone will come to see Uncle Colin christen you. Uncle Hugh will be there even though he is not your real Uncle; but close like family and the lads from the Triad; all to see you, baby boy," Elizabeth cooed.

James came to the cabin door with shaving cream on his face. "Are you talking to the lad then and does he understand every word?" James said smiling.

"It doesn't matter if he understands; he just likes to hear the sound of my voice; don't you beautiful boy?" Elizabeth smiled at James, her eyes shining.

"Now that's a picture love; my darling girl and our boy," James replied.

The christening was at 11:00. The lads from the Triad had shaved and were presentable just as on Elizabeth and James' wedding day. Elizabeth and James with baby Colin travelled by carriage. Hugh would meet them at the church.

"I see that you are no worse for wear from yesterday's luncheon," Elizabeth said smiling.

"Oh you mean the drink?" James said laughing. "Any Irishman who can't hold his whiskey has no business calling himself an Irishman! You will see; Hugh and Uncle Colin will be fresh as a daisy."

James was as true as his word. Hugh and Uncle Colin looked as if they had attended a tea party the day before instead of the wake that it had become. Elizabeth may not have understood it, but she knew she loved her O'Rourke clan and the circle of love that they provided to her.

Colin was the perfect baby at his christening just as his mother predicted. When Uncle Colin sprinkled his head with holy water, baby Colin just cooed and laughed. Elizabeth and James just beamed at their brilliant boy.

After the christening, Uncle Colin hosted a luncheon for the party at the Parish Hall. It was the scene of their wedding reception and brought back beautiful memories for Elizabeth. Colin was by this time fast asleep, so Elizabeth could enjoy herself with the O'Rourke clan once more.

"I have something for you, Elizabeth. Here is a replacement for your St. Christopher medal and one for my namesake when he is old enough to wear it. We all know what you have been through, lass. Don't let the past color the future. You have a good man and a treasure of a son. Enjoy your life and keep exploring," Uncle Colin stated.

"Thank you, Uncle Colin. I will treasure it and keep this one for baby Colin until he is old enough to wear it," Elizabeth replied.

James said to Hugh as he clasped him on the back "Have you placed your order with Elizabeth yet?" Hugh blushed then and gave James the evil eye.

"What's this about an order?" Elizabeth asked confused.

"Hugh here is in search of a bride, Elizabeth. He has decided that I did very well with my American wife and wants us to find one for him as well," James replied winking.

"Oh, I see," Elizabeth replied with mischief in her eyes. She was trying to keep from laughing so kept her composure. "So by order, you wanted to tell me if he preferred a blond or red head or brunette; short or tall etc. Is that about it?" Elizabeth said winking at James.

Uncle Colin joined in at that point. "Now Hugh here being such an ugly lad he couldn't be as particular as our James had. What did you call him, Elizabeth; was it beautiful then?"

Hugh decided to join in the fun at this point. "I happened to mention in passing that I liked the spirit of the American and this is what happens to me. Take pity Elizabeth and rescue me."

"Perhaps we could start by you giving me your address here in London. That way I could pass it along to any of my friends who may want to engage in a correspondence first," Elizabeth said with mock sincerity.

"Of course Elizabeth because what Hugh here wants is a correspondent," James said laughing.

"I will put my mind to it Hugh and promise to give it a good deal of thought when we get to Wilmington. I still haven't heard your order, however," Elizabeth said smiling.

"If you can find him someone that makes him half as happy as our James here," Uncle Colin interjected, "you will have done a good day's work."

"Well said, Uncle Colin," James replied.

Elizabeth smiled shyly and reached her hand across the table and pressed Uncle Colin's hand. "I have a different sort of question, Uncle Colin."

"Thank heavens," Hugh said in exasperation.

"How did you get from Ireland to London for your church work?" Elizabeth asked.

"So many of our lads were leaving Ireland, Elizabeth, that I thought I could do better work here. The boys coming off the ships here needed consoling and direction. There's a priest for every church in Ireland, but not as many here where they were needed. On occasion I got to see my nephew when he was back from the sea for a week or so. Of course I see him now more in one year than in a decade before," Colin said laughing, "and that of course is due to you also," Father O'Rourke replied.

All too soon, the party broke up and the O'Rourke circle began their return to the business of life. Hugh gave Elizabeth his address in London. Uncle Colin hugged Elizabeth and kissed his namesake, baby Colin. Elizabeth received commitments that both would be at Broadlands for Christmas. "We will see you both in five to six weeks, Uncle Colin and Hugh," James stated.

"Try to keep him from kidnapping anyone for Hugh while you are there," Uncle Colin said with a wink to Elizabeth.

"I will let you know when the matter of the estate funds has been sorted," Hugh said to James. "It will be next on our list to resolve."

"Thank you Hugh for everything," James replied.

"Thank you so much, Hugh for all of your help to James and especially to me. From now on we can meet under happier circumstances. Don't worry; I will not forget your request." Elizabeth kissed him on the cheek then making Hugh blush red.

CHAPTER EIGHTEEN

The next day the Triad headed out for Bermuda. James as always was at the helm for the start of the voyage. He had brought a sleeping Colin into their bed in case he was to awaken when James would be above decks. That way Elizabeth would only have to roll over to see her beautiful boy.

James had not yet discussed the matter of the estate proceeds with Elizabeth. He thought to raise the issue today as she would have had a day or so since the trial to process some of what had occurred.

When they were in the open sea again, James gave the helm to Samuel Pearson and went below to check on his family. He loved the sound of that word and the fact that Elizabeth had so embraced the O'Rourke clan of himself, Uncle Colin and Hugh. That was a trinity worthy of the name. They would protect her and baby Colin with their lives and they had proven that trust again and again.

The scene before him when he opened the cabin door made him catch his breath. His beautiful wife had her mermaid hair around her shoulders and was making Colin squeal with her kisses on his chubby cheeks and feet. They were rough housing on the huge bed.

"I can't believe how he has grown, Elizabeth. He will be walking by Easter," James said smiling.

"Oh don't tell me that, James. If only he could stay this size for a little longer," Elizabeth replied smiling.

"There will always be the next one remember darling girl," James said winking.

"The beginning of the tribe," Elizabeth said laughing. "All this happiness in one year's time, James. Thank you for that and so much more."

"Thank you, Elizabeth. What would I do without you? You take my breath away every day," James said kissing her.

Colin squealed again then and Elizabeth laughed saying "He doesn't want to be left out; do you baby boy?" He received a kiss from both parents; one on each cheek for his trouble.

"Darling girl, after you put the baby down, I need to talk to you about something," James stated.

"Of course, James; I will be right back." She took Colin to his little cot, changed his nappy and left him laughing and cooing.

"What is it, my love?" Elizabeth asked.

"When you were in the witness room with Uncle Colin, you did not hear all components of the judge's sentence of Whitfield and Cross. You know that they were found guilty and sentenced to hang," James stated.

"Yes, darling; I remember," Elizabeth said quietly.

"There was more, love. The judge ordered that Whitfield and Cross' estates were to be declared forfeit and the proceeds returned to you as restitution for the embezzlement of estate funds. The proceeds of your father's estate equal 50,000 pounds which would equate to about $100,000 American dollars," James stated.

"James, that couldn't be possible. How could I have inherited that much money?" Elizabeth asked.

"I don't know, love. Perhaps we can put the pieces together between London and Wilmington. Hugh is responsible for the sale of assets and restitution under a writ proceeding. He will have the records that reflect those proceeds in order to complete the necessary accounting. This means, Elizabeth; that you are a wealthy woman. That is the reason that Whitfield and Cross pursued you in the manner that they did. I understand now, Elizabeth. That is the reason that they were so dangerous. It was all about lust for money and by its receipt, power. I will advise you to place the money in trust, love. We certainly don't need it," James stated earnestly.

"It would be nice to have money to buy my husband a wedding gift or Christmas gift without having to use his own funds to do so," Elizabeth replied smiling.

"You know I would buy you anything you ever wanted, darling girl," James responded.

"I have everything I could ever want, James; a wonderful husband, a beautiful baby boy, a beautiful home and a circle of friends that I haven't had for years. What more could I ask for?" Elizabeth replied with her eyes shining.

"Well perhaps another member of the O'Rourke tribe could be in the offing?" James said winking.

*****

The voyage to Bermuda was as uneventful, as the trip to London had been dramatic a year before. Their days were spent with young Colin and making plans for Bermuda and Wilmington. James saw the wisdom of Uncle Colin's suggestion that James, Elizabeth and baby Colin travel the world together. James would have the joy of the sea, but would have that experience enhanced by the chance to show the world to his wife and young son.

When at last they arrived in Bermuda, the Triad berthed in St. George as they had nearly a year before. James and Elizabeth were having dinner at the Carlyle and Samuel and Nanny were to be left in charge of the Triad and young Colin.

Elizabeth dressed in the turquoise silk dress that she had worn a year earlier. As James had noticed on their private beach, the birth of Colin had made her more voluptuous, which meant the turquoise silk dress reflected that change. She wondered if James would notice. The final touch was the pearl earrings from her mother and the pearl necklace, bracelet, and ring from James.

As James knocked on the door, Elizabeth was ready for their night out. When James entered the room she saw that he had very quickly noticed the change in the fit of the dress. "I may not have to protect you from the crew tonight, but I may still need an extra escort for you in that dress. I don't think it quite fit like that last year, darling girl. Do you need me to check the buttons, Mrs. O'Rourke?" James said with a wink.

They took a carriage to the Carlyle Hotel where they had dined last year. The same restaurant staff showed them to their table where champagne was chilling. "This is such a beautiful room, James. I remember being so overjoyed to be here, drinking champagne and having dinner with you last year," Elizabeth added shyly.

"A great many changes in one year, love. I remember wondering how I was going to keep my hands off you in that dress. I still wonder about that, so I guess not everything changes," James said laughing.

Elizabeth smiled over her glass of champagne. "At least you won't have to break down the cabin door tonight."

"I will if you want me to," James replied laughing.

When the orchestra started playing a waltz, James took Elizabeth's hand to lead her to the dance floor. As he placed his hand on her waist, he had the same response that he had nearly one year ago; how will I keep my hands off her on the dance floor. At least I won't have that worry later, he thought smiling.

The dinner of local fish and seafood was fresh and delicious, the champagne chilled to perfection and the love of the two diners visible to all who bothered to watch. Although Elizabeth was easily the most beautiful woman in the room and the subject of sideways glances from both men and women, James noticed that Elizabeth only had eyes for him. He was inwardly arrogant about that last point and possessive as always of his own private goddess.

When the dinner had concluded, James ordered a carriage to tour the island. "I had wanted us to take this tour last year, and let you see the island by moonlight. Whitfield's men interrupted that plan. Tonight I will show you the beauty of St. George by moonlight," James stated.

As they toured the island, James allowed himself the liberty that he could not engage in one year ago. His arm around Elizabeth he kissed her forehead, her eyes and mouth as he used to do in his paternal role as her protector only. His fingers traced her neck and his hands caressed her back and sides. He decided he needed to stop for now as he wanted this evening to last and to make another beautiful memory for his wife. When he saw her swollen mouth, he decided he needed to delay and take in the passing beauty of the island. He wanted this evening to be very special. Elizabeth put her head on his shoulder as she had wanted to do one year before.

When they returned to the Triad, James took Elizabeth's hand and helped her from the carriage. They walked up the gangplank arm in arm, each lost in their own memories of the prior year's visit. No threats to them this time, only we two and of course baby Colin sleeping below, she thought.

The major difference between the two visits was lying in his little cot when they went below. Elizabeth stopped in to nurse Colin, change his nappy and put him to bed for the evening. James had gone along to the master cabin. When Elizabeth came into the suite, James arose from the window seat where he had been sipping a whiskey. "One year ago, we ended our evening with a kiss on the hand do you remember love?" He kissed Elizabeth's hand then as he had done a year before. "What I would like you to see this evening is what I had dreamt of one year ago, particularly after your nightmare and our kiss."

James took Elizabeth's face in his hands and kissed her deeply. His mouth slanted over Elizabeth's mating with her tongue as he did so. When he pulled himself away, Elizabeth's lips were again red and swollen. "If I had done that last year what would you have thought, love?" James said huskily.

"When you kissed me last year, James it was the first time I had even been kissed. I had no idea what would follow or what could occur between a man and a woman," Elizabeth said quietly.

James turned Elizabeth around at this point and started to unbutton her dress. "This is what I dreamt about last year, love," James said huskily. He took off his jacket and slowly unbuttoned Elizabeth's dress, kissing her neck and her spine as he did so. He felt Elizabeth shiver as he did so and she felt and heard his husky groan. He helped her step out of her dress. James took off his shirt at this point laughing as he did about the sea of petticoats in front of him. "I had no idea of the layers last year, Elizabeth. It took less time in my dream," James said laughing.

"What else was in your dream, James?" Elizabeth asked.

By this time James had reached the final petticoat, corset and chemise. The layers dropped away like shaved snow. When at last he reached her chemise, James slowly unbuttoned each button of her chemise and took the pins from hair. When he had finished he pulled Elizabeth up to his chest placing his hands around her waist as he did so.

Elizabeth put her arms around James neck and he picked her up and placed her in the middle of the huge bed. At that point, James finished undressing and spread himself on Elizabeth punishing her mouth with his kisses. He traced hot kisses down her chest, abdomen and lastly at the base of her abdomen and into the dark recesses of her womanhood. Elizabeth let out a moan.

James said huskily, "Shush, darling; you will like this; I promise," James proceeded to tease Elizabeth with his fingers and his lips until Elizabeth came apart in his arms. James then lifted her hips and entered her quickly, capturing her soft cry with his mouth and tongue. The affect on them both was magical as always. When Elizabeth found her release, she called James' name and he called hers a few moments later.

Both lay still trying to recapture their breaths. James rolled onto his back pulling Elizabeth into his side. She rolled to her side and placed her head on his still heaving chest. When she could again speak Elizabeth said to James "I didn't know that you could even do that, James. Was that really in your dream last year?" she asked shyly.

"Oh that and much more, darling girl; we are just getting started," James laughed.

"Is that why you were always in such a bad mood around me James?" Elizabeth said smiling.

"I was trying to maintain my self control and that turquoise dress and you in it didn't help any. I waited for you Elizabeth longer than I ever waited for another woman. It was certainly worth the wait. As you can see, I am a lot happier these days," James said laughing.

"I love you to be happy, James," Elizabeth replied.

"You do a brilliant job, love. If I were any happier I couldn't stand myself," James said again laughing.

*****

The next morning they set off for the most sentimental portion of the trip. James planned to be very careful to watch Elizabeth's reaction to the return to Wilmington. She had spent twenty-two of her twenty-three years there and he only hoped that Broadlands, he and Colin would be sufficient to make her want to return to Ireland. He was sure of the answer, but only wanted her to be happy.

As they entered the mouth of the Cape Fear River at Southport, Elizabeth had asked if she could join James on deck. Normally she stayed below during the day and spent time with the baby. Today she was coming home and she wanted to see all. The marshland, even the smell of the water reminded her of home. She wondered how she would feel seeing it all again after everything that had come to pass during the year away.

James smiled at her along the rail. She had on her sun hat and gloves against the strong North Carolina sun. He was curious to see how Elizabeth would tell the story of the past year to her friends. Knowing her as he did, he thought she would edit out the attempted murders and the trial. Elizabeth was nothing if not a positive person and he did not believe that part of their history would be discussed. When they passed into the built sections of Wilmington proper, James gave the helm to the river pilot and went to stand with Elizabeth as she pointed out landmarks. She told him about the dram tree, the Spanish moss hanging from the trees and about the spires of the various churches in the distance.

"Will we be going to the house first, James?" Elizabeth asked.

"I will see the harbormaster about renting a carriage. It won't be like Bermuda and London with cabs and carriages waiting quayside. I remember walking to most of my destinations in the past. That would have only included Water and Front Streets then," James replied.

"I was never allowed to go to Water Street, except for one fateful day in August, 1865," she said smiling up at James.

"That was the day that changed both of our lives," James said smiling back. "Once we have the carriage, I will send a lad to Lavinia Cole's house with a note so that she will know you are home and would like to visit."

"If it is alright with you, James; can we stay aboard the Triad tonight? I don't have a huge bed in the house. I want to make sure you are comfortable, my love," Elizabeth said smiling.

"We are comfortable, love. I think young Colin likes his cot well enough also," James replied.

"He has been so good this whole trip. I think he enjoys travelling, James. He is just like his father," Elizabeth responded.

"I think his mother enjoys travel also," James said placing his arm around her waist.

When they had docked, James made arrangements with the harbormaster and came back up the gang plank. Elizabeth was struck by the fact that they had met on this very dock over one year ago.

"Why don't we leave young Colin with Nanny until we see the lay of the land, love?" James asked.

"Alright, James; I will check in with him, get my purse and be right with you," Elizabeth replied.

When Elizabeth returned to the deck she had a flashback to their first meeting. James was standing on the dock looking at her with mischief in his eyes. He was no longer holding a bull whip, but holding out his hand to help her down the gang plank. "Your carriage awaits, love," James stated.

Once she was seated, James took the reins and they headed down Water Street. "You will want to turn left here James onto Market Street," Elizabeth said. "We will go up to Fourth Street and then turn right."

For Elizabeth it was all so familiar, yet so strange. Being away for over a year, she was seeing the city with fresh eyes. The Union occupancy was still in evidence. James remembered Elizabeth's reference to that during the trial and knew how the words had been spoken with bitterness which was so foreign to Elizabeth's true character. He well understood how an occupation army could affect the citizens under that occupation day in and day out.

Elizabeth pointed to the turn for Fourth Street and James turned the carriage onto the tree lined street. He could visualize the teenage Elizabeth walking these beautiful streets to church and school. Elizabeth pointed to the lovely house that had been her family home. He remembered then to thank Reverend Haynes for the assistance in upkeep of the property. James helped Elizabeth down and took her hand as they climbed the stairs to her house. She handed him the key which he used to gain access to the house.

The house had the stillness that comes from long term closure. James watched Elizabeth walk from room to room in the nearly empty house. “We sold furniture and silver to make ends meet during the war, James. There is so little left to pack. It seems so much smaller than I remember it after Broadlands,” Elizabeth said wistfully.

“It is a pleasant house on a pleasant tree lined street. I can see you living here, Elizabeth. It is an elegant house which produced an elegant lady. Anything that you want to pack and take with us; just remember we have plenty of room in the hold even with the cargo,” James said tenderly. “We can have the lads come up and pack everything that remains and you can sort whatever you want to keep when we get home.”

“It seems so strange, James; like a former life as I walk through these rooms. When you said we would sort things when we got home, I suddenly became homesick for Broadlands, James, and Bridget and Seamus and Father O’Donnell,” Elizabeth said quietly.

“That’s what I hoped you would say, Elizabeth; but I didn’t want to pressure you. I wanted you to reach that conclusion on your own,” James replied.

“I think your plan is sound, James as it will shorten the time we need to sort out the house here before we can offer it for sale,” Elizabeth stated.

“Let’s go back to the Triad and get the lads started. We will rent a wagon and get everything packed and loaded. We had better inform Reverend Haynes so he doesn’t think your home is being robbed,” James responded.

Elizabeth went next door and knocked on Reverend Haynes’ door. The Reverend and his wife had received Elizabeth’s letter and were waiting for her return. “The lads from my husband’s ship will be loading up my belongings.

We will be placing my home for sale before we return to Ireland. I wanted to make sure that you knew so that you would not be alarmed. Thank you so much for your wonderful assistance in looking after the house this past year," Elizabeth stated.

Elizabeth returned back to the house after consulting with the Reverend and his wife. "After we check with the lads, James; I would like to visit my parent's graves before we return to the Triad tonight."

"Of course, Elizabeth," James replied.

Once the lads were sorted and the packing had begun, James drove Elizabeth to Oakdale Cemetery to the grave sites of her parents. When they arrived at the site, James lifted Elizabeth out of the carriage. She took his hand and led him to her mother and father's gravesite. October roses were still growing on the rose bushes that Elizabeth had planted. James thought back to the day that she had planted roses on his parent's graves and he had chastised her for traipsing over the countryside by herself. So much had happened in one short year; so many memories in one year and so many more memories to make.

"Mother, father, this is James. He is my husband. We have a new baby named Colin. He looks just like his father and is the happiest baby in Ireland." James watched her talking to her parents and was not quite sure of the protocol. "I always talked to them, James and I talk to your parents also. Don't be alarmed; I haven't had too much sun. It is just my way of connecting with them," Elizabeth explained smiling.

"I understand, love better than most. It is hard when you are the last member of your family," James replied tenderly.

The two walked hand in hand around the area of Elizabeth's family graves. The adjacent group of graves had surnames of Roberts and Foster. "Are these graves of family members also, Elizabeth?" James asked.

"Yes, James; these are my grandparents and great grandparents. The family business was named for them. My father retained the name until the war; Roberts-Foster Cotton Exchange," Elizabeth explained.

"Elizabeth, I transported cotton for your family before the war. That is why we came to Wilmington. That is why I was here a year ago," James replied.

The circle between the two of them had just been closed. It was as if the two of them had been meant to be together all of their lives. Their lives had been intertwined before they had even met.

"I told you that I was never allowed to go to Water Street. The first time I went there was the day we met. You may have met my father before the war, James!" Elizabeth stated.

"Not only before the war, love. We transported items for the blockade runners and off loaded outside of the blockade lines. That is the answer, Elizabeth. Your father had the proceeds from the business, but also the secret business during the war. That accounts for the fortune," James replied.

"I never knew, James," Elizabeth stated quietly.

"You wouldn't have known, as your father was off fighting in the war. We brought in medicines and all the items that had become hard or next to impossible to obtain after the blockade was established," James replied.

James walked back to Elizabeth's parent's graves. "I promise to take care of your, darling girl. She is as dear to me as she was to you. She is safe in my hands, sir. I will protect her with my life," James stated.

Elizabeth looked at James with tears in her eyes. "Let's go back to the Triad and see if your lads have been able to make contact with Lavinia Cole and her family," she replied.

A note was waiting for Elizabeth when they returned to the Triad. It was from Lavinia Cole inviting James and Elizabeth to lunch the next day. All of Elizabeth's remaining possessions had been loaded into the hold while they were gone. Samuel reported that Miss Elizabeth's home was now empty and ready for sale. James thanked Samuel and headed below. Elizabeth was in with Colin, so James sat on the window seat thinking about the events of the day. Elizabeth's father and James' father had done business together. If Elizabeth had been allowed to walk to her father's business, he could have met her earlier and avoided years of searching for the love of his life. She had literally been five blocks away from him all this time.

But what if her father had not approved of her travelling halfway across the world to marry an Irishman and a mariner to boot, he thought? Things happened when and where they are intended to happen, James thought to himself. Suppose I had not been ready to be a husband and a father and had broken her heart.

When Elizabeth came from Colin's room, she was unusually reflective and quiet. "Have you thought about the fact that I could have met you years ago and we could have started our happiness before now?" Elizabeth asked.

"I was sitting here thinking the same thing, love. But would your family have allowed you to move to Ireland with a wild Irishman and a mariner to boot? I have my doubts, love," James replied wistfully.

"I suppose everything happens for a reason, James and when it was meant to happen. As we have seen, everything happens when it is fated to do so. So, my love: what shall we take as a hospitality gift for luncheon tomorrow, James?" Elizabeth asked smiling.

"If her husband likes whiskey, I am sure he would like the real thing from Ireland. What do you think?" James replied.

"I am sure that Robert would enjoy it. I am not sure about Lavinia," Elizabeth responded.

"If it is like it was during the war years, a bottle of whiskey may be the kind of luxury that would be hard to come by," James stated.

"Do you have plenty, darling?" Elizabeth asked.

"I travel on a ship, love; I always have room in the hold for private stock," James replied smiling.

*****

The next day, James, Elizabeth and baby Colin set off for Fifth Avenue and the home of Robert and Lavinia Cole and their family. When James knocked at the door, it was answered by Robert Cole. "Elizabeth is that you?" Robert said wide eyed.

"It is Robert. How lovely to see you. This is my husband, Captain James O'Rourke and this is our son Colin," Elizabeth responded warmly.

"Please come in and make yourself comfortable. Lavinia is in the basement finishing luncheon," Robert replied.

"We brought you a hostess gift, Robert. It is from James' private stock," Elizabeth stated.

"Thank you both. There aren't many luxuries available still with the occupation continuing," Robert responded.

"Are things any better Robert or just the same?" Elizabeth asked.

"A little better, Elizabeth; but you know the drill. I think I hear Lavinia. She may be ready for us and luncheon. Lavinia is that you?" Robert asked.

"It is. I am ready for everyone if you will come through," Lavinia replied.

"Lavinia, this is Captain James O'Rourke, Elizabeth of course and their baby Colin," Robert stated.

"It is nice to meet you James and look at baby Colin. How are you Elizabeth?" Lavinia asked.

"Oh I am fine thank you, Lavinia. Thank you so much for having us. Will Aunt Sally be joining us?" Elizabeth asked.

"She stays pretty much to herself in the cabin out back. She wants to see you right after luncheon though. Please sit down and make yourself comfortable. You can put Colin here in the bassinette until the luncheon is over. Bobby and Lee are upstairs in their room so they won't bother us at luncheon. So tell us; how did you two meet?" Lavinia asked.

"James was the Captain of the ship that transported me to London last year. You remember when I wrote you last autumn?" Elizabeth replied.

"Oh, yes; so much goes on with the boys, I have a hard time keeping everything straight. So you have only the one ship, James?" Lavinia asked.

"We have a fleet of ten based in Dublin," James replied.

"And you have a cottage nearby?" Lavinia asked.

"Lavinia, you remember Elizabeth's letter; they have an estate outside Dublin," Robert interjected.

"Oh yes; that's right. When were you married?" Lavinia asked.

"We were married last October in London," Elizabeth interjected. "James' uncle is a priest who married us."

"Oh that's right. I remember now. When was Colin born then?" Lavinia asked.

"He was born in July, Lavinia. Don't you remember my letters?" Elizabeth responded frowning.

"I just don't understand why I am expected to remember all these details of other people's lives," Lavinia responded heatedly.

Elizabeth sought to change the subject to something less controversial. "How is Aunt Sally doing, Lavinia?"

"She is as difficult as always. She is always telling me how to live my life and raise the children. I don't know why I put up with her interference!" Lavinia replied heatedly.

It seemed that there was no subject that was without controversy. James tried next. "Robert has the cotton crop come back since the war? I used to transport cotton from Wilmington to London before the war," James said.

"How on earth could the cotton come back with no one to work the fields?" Lavinia replied impatiently.

James and Elizabeth exchanged glances at that point. Robert saw the exchange and sought to intervene. "Lavinia, didn't Aunt Sally make a dessert for the day? I am sure that Elizabeth and James would enjoy some pecan pie."

"Oh we definitely would, Robert. I haven't had any since last year aboard the Alliance," Elizabeth stated smiling at James.

"Is that one of your ships, James?" Robert asked.

"It is indeed. As I mentioned we have ten in total. We are on the Triad for this trip. It is a tad bit roomier for a growing family," James said smiling at Elizabeth.

The dessert was provided and the luncheon ended more quietly than hoped for by Elizabeth. "May I help you with the clearing up, Lavinia?" Elizabeth asked.

"Oh no, Elizabeth; I am sure that you have help to do so at home. I wouldn't want to inconvenience you," Lavinia replied.

"If agreeable then, I would like to take James and Colin out to meet Aunt Sally," Elizabeth replied.

"That would be fine, Elizabeth. I don't know why you bother though. She is so disagreeable these days," Lavinia answered irritably.

Elizabeth and James took baby Colin out to the cabin behind the main house. An older lady sat at the entrance rocking her chair. She had the look of a woman who had seen much and experienced more. She was Aunt Sally who Elizabeth had told James about so vividly. Born into slavery, she had been freed by the Emancipation Proclamation, but like some had chosen to remain with the family that she had worked for prior to the Civil War. She lived in the tiny cabin in the post war years. She looked expectantly at the young woman coming towards her. She knew that Elizabeth was due to visit today and had waited for her to come and see her after the luncheon. "Let me see my Lilliebeth; all grown up with a baby of her own," Aunt Sally cried.

"Aunt Sally, this is my husband, Captain James O'Rourke and this is my baby boy, Colin. His full name is Christopher Colin O'Rourke and everyone says that he is the happiest baby in Ireland. Now I think he is the happiest baby in the United States as well. I wasn't sure about the travelling, but he has taken to it like a duck to water," Elizabeth replied smiling.

"Look at that little face. I think he could be a scamp, Lilliebeth. I bet his father was a scamp when he was that age," Aunt Sally stated laughing.

James looked at Elizabeth and smiled. "She tells me that Colin is my image, so I think that may be true, ma'am."

"Aunt Sally, what has happened to Lavinia? We tried all through luncheon and could not find a conversation that didn't cause Lavinia to bristle like a cat on a hot tin roof. I would not have known her if I hadn't been in her house," Elizabeth stated.

"Don't you listen to Miss Lavinia, baby girl. She is not a happy girl like you and she makes everyone else unhappy because of it. Miss Lilliebeth was always a good girl, Captain. She was always good to me. Are you a good man, Captain James?" Aunt Sally asked searching James' face.

"I am a better man, Aunt Sally for knowing your Lilliebeth," James said his eyes shining.

"Do you love my baby girl, Captain?" Aunt Sally continued.

"Yes ma'am; I love her with all my heart," James replied gazing at Elizabeth.

"That's all that matters. You two will be fine. You take care of my baby girl and give her lots of babies, Captain. That is what she always wanted. I knew my baby would be a good mother. Look at this angel she gave to you, Captain and always remember what she went through to get him born. Baby girl, I wrote down all of the recipes I could think of. They are all here for you. You are the only one to ask for them. You take care of them and take care of yourself and this baby. Captain, you take care of them all," Aunt Sally stated firmly.

"I will, Aunt Sally; I promise I will. It was a pleasure meeting you, ma'am. Thank you for bringing her into the world for me," James replied smiling.

When Elizabeth and James came back into the house with Colin, James asked to speak with Robert for a few minutes. The two went out on the porch to smoke and speak privately. James intended to ask Robert if he would oversee the sale of the Majors family house for a commission. Robert was glad to do so and appreciated the offer by James.

While they spoke, Elizabeth and Lavinia chatted in the parlor. "How did you find Aunt Sally?" Lavinia asked.

"She looks very well I think. She never changes," Elizabeth replied smiling.

"She is such a know it all and is always trying to interfere. She tries to tell me I should change my mind about Robert, but I tell her to mind her own business." Elizabeth did not want to pry so she said nothing. Lavinia continued "I have decided there will be no more babies in this house, Elizabeth. I have made up my mind and my wishes are known to Robert so he is clear on the subject."

Elizabeth did not know how to respond to that statement. "I would love to meet your two boys, Lavinia," Elizabeth stated at last.

"Children are better not seen and not heard mother always said. I follow that advice. They are forever getting into mischief all the day long. They are a strain on my poor nerves," Lavinia replied.

"I am so sorry, Lavinia. I hope our visit wasn't a burden to you," Elizabeth responded.

"Not at all, Elizabeth; I know my duty," Lavinia replied sternly.

At that moment, James and Robert came in from the porch having finished their cigars and their quiet talk.

"Are you ready to get our young lad back to the Triad, Elizabeth?" James asked smiling.

"I am, James. Thank you both for the lovely luncheon and for the chance to catch up. I will write again soon," Elizabeth replied hugging Lavinia.

When Elizabeth and James were back in the carriage and Colin comfortably situated, Elizabeth sighed audibly. “I am so sorry, James. I had no idea that luncheon would be so disagreeable. Lavinia is not the person I remember.”

“I know, love. Robert filled me in while we were smoking our cigars. She holds onto the past and can’t fathom that her life won’t be as it was before the war. She is bound to be unhappy with that kind of thinking,” James replied.

“That isn’t all, James. I will share the rest this evening when we are alone. I understand Aunt Sally’s comments now. I fear Lavinia will never be happy again nor will Robert; not ever again.” Elizabeth looked so distressed that James decided not be pry further at this time. He drove them back to the Triad. He would get Elizabeth and Colin settled then supervise the remainder of the loading to make sure that they were ready to leave in the morning.

When all was completed above decks, James went below to talk to Elizabeth. They would have an early night tonight. James had already made arrangements with Jones for dinner for the two of them. He wanted something special for Elizabeth after the trials of the visit.

Elizabeth was sitting on the window seat when he came into the cabin. She was clearly deep in thought. “Colin went right out for his nap, James. He is the best boy in the world,” Elizabeth said then returned to her worried look.

“Now,” James said sitting down beside her, “tell me what is bothering you.”

“I am so sorry about the luncheon, James. Lavinia is definitely not the person I knew,” Elizabeth replied.

“I know, love; so you said. But that is not what is worrying you; is it?” James responded.

“I’m worried about Aunt Sally. She can’t be happy there James,” Elizabeth replied worriedly.

“Would Lavinia let her come with us to Ireland?” James asked.

"Oh thank you James for thinking of that. But Aunt Sally would never leave her family to go that far away. James, I was thinking; if I could borrow some money until the estate is settled I would get it to Aunt Sally to make sure she has enough to get by on. I know Lavinia and Robert are struggling and I want to make sure that she is alright," Elizabeth replied.

"What have I told you before, love? What is mine is yours. Of course we can help Aunt Sally. I talked to Robert about handling the sale of the family home. I wanted him to have the commission for his trouble," James replied.

"Oh that is good of you, James. Robert is a good man. Lavinia seems to want to make the whole family unhappy," Elizabeth responded.

"You told me there was more to the tale when we left their house," James stated casually.

"It seems that Lavinia has decided that she doesn't want any more children and has told Robert the same. How does someone stop wanting to be with their husband, James?" Elizabeth asked worriedly.

"Oh sadly it happens, love; not to us of course in case that is your worry, but it does happen." James put his arm around Elizabeth with the last comment and pulled her onto his lap. "Let me ask you a question; when you made the comment about the O'Rourke tribe, it was because you thought you would be pregnant every year into the foreseeable future; am I right?" James asked tenderly.

"Well yes, James; I love you and would never tell you I didn't want to be with you in all ways," Elizabeth said blushing.

"That is just one of the reasons I love you, Elizabeth," he said kissing her. "When the time comes that you need a break from having babies, there are ways Elizabeth that we can prevent that," James replied.

"There are, James? But how?" Elizabeth replied wide eyed.

"I will show you rather than tell you when the time comes love. Rest assured this problem will never become our problem. We are too well matched in love, passion and temperament if the truth be told," James said nuzzling Elizabeth's ear.

"I can have a frightful temper at times, James," Elizabeth confided worriedly.

"Only when barristers rile you on the witness stand," James said laughing. "I can have a fearful temper when someone tries to hurt someone that I love."

"I am so happy that we found each other, James," Elizabeth stated.

"So am I, my love; right on this very dock a little over a year ago. You know; I have asked Jones for an early night this evening to celebrate our happiness and the anniversary of our first meeting. What do you think of that idea?" James asked smiling.

"I love that idea, James. Thank you for being so considerate," Elizabeth stated placing her head on his shoulder.

"And sweet; don't forget about sweet," James responded mockingly.

"Oh always sweet, James. I think I hear our son waking from his nap. I will bring him in for a few moments for a bit of a romp. I like children to been seen and heard and loved and kissed especially if they are a bit of a scamp like their father," Elizabeth said smiling.

"Agreed love; agreed," James replied.

After their romp, Colin was put down for the night and Elizabeth changed and bathed in anticipation of their time together. Elizabeth had decided to show James how much she appreciated his constant love and support. She used her rose soap and changed into her trousseau nightgown and robe.

James was sitting on the window seat with a whiskey in his hand when she came into the cabin. The table had been set, champagne was chilling and supper laid out for them both. James smiled when he saw Elizabeth changed for the night. "I approve of the change in costume," James said with mischief in his eyes.

"Thank you my love for being the most understanding man in the world," Elizabeth stated with her eyes shining.

"Thank you for being my beautiful wife who loves me very much, even if I am a scamp!" James replied teasing.

"That's right. I love you very much and would never close my bedroom door to you," Elizabeth replied.

"That's right, love only because you know I can break it down if needs be," James said laughing.

"That's only because you thought me in danger, darling," Elizabeth responded with mock sincerity.

"That's true, but I could certainly think of other reasons as well," James said nuzzling Elizabeth. "I think we better have dinner before it gets cold, love," James said kissing Elizabeth.

After dinner James drew Elizabeth over again to the window seat so they could talk further. It was their favorite place on the Alliance, at home in the master suite of Broadlands and now on the Triad. In their window seat, they had had many excellent conversations over the past year and James knew they could resolve any issues their marriage would face in the future.

"I have something to discuss with you, love," James said earnestly.

"Of course, James," Elizabeth replied.

"I have been giving a great deal of thought to returning to the sea again, Elizabeth," James stated.

Elizabeth was silent for a moment. "Of course, darling; it is only natural. The sea has been your whole life since you were eighteen years old," she replied.

James noticed that Elizabeth was quietly wringing her hands which was in stark contrast to what she had just calmly stated.

"I don't think you fully understand, love. If I return to the sea again, it will only be if you are with me. I love the sea Elizabeth, but I love you more. If I take a voyage, Elizabeth it will be of my choosing and a place that I think you would want to visit. I have been many places, love but I would not want to return to all of them and certainly not take you to see many of them," James replied.

"Oh, James; would we take Colin also?" she asked smiling.

"Of course, love. Do you think I would separate that little boy from the mother he loves? I told you that you would be the center of our world. You are the center of the O'Rourke clan, love; you, me, Colin, Uncle Colin and now God help him Hugh as well," James said smiling.

"Speaking of Hugh, James; I thought of a possible candidate for him," Elizabeth said smiling.

"Oh really?" James said laughing.

"Yes, I went to the St. Mary School with Kathleen Sullivan who now lives in Savannah, Georgia. I could write her to see if she would like to visit us at Broadlands. Would we be leaving on our first voyage before Christmas or after?" Elizabeth said with excitement.

"Oh after Christmas, love; a Broadlands Christmas is now again a tradition. Did you just say that you went to the St. Mary School here in Wilmington?" James asked.

"Yes, darling; why?" Elizabeth asked.

"I always wanted to marry an Academy girl. And now I can say that I have," James said laughing. "So do you want to write a letter to your friend in the morning? We can post it before we leave. And would you like another glass of champagne, darling girl?" James asked smiling.

"What a good idea; thank you James. I think I shall have another glass of champagne," Elizabeth replied.

"Shall we drink to our new voyages?" James asked.

"Oh, yes James; please. Have you ever been to France and to Normandy?" she asked excitedly.

"Of course, darling girl; it is right across the Channel. Wherever there is an ocean, I can take you," James replied.

"Colin will love to travel, James. He has been so happy on this trip," Elizabeth replied.

"He's happy anywhere, love. He is the happiest boy in Ireland remember? I suppose he will be the happiest boy in the world," James said smiling.

"Let us drink to that then, James; to the happiest boy in the world and to our new adventures, my love!" Elizabeth replied.

"And to his brother as well," James replied gazing intently at Elizabeth.

"What brother, James?" Elizabeth asked.

"The next baby, love. He will probably be due next July. He and Colin will be Irish twins," James said laughing.

"Do you think so, James?" Elizabeth said her arms around James' neck.

"I am just following Aunt Sally's direction; am I not?" James said laughing.

"So you are, James. Thank you for Colin and for Broadlands and for all of our happiness," Elizabeth replied.

"Why don't you show me love rather than tell me?" James replied huskily.

James lifted Elizabeth then into his arms and carried her to the bed and placed her carefully in the center. He kissed her gently and untied her robe removing it with one quick gesture. Elizabeth pressed against James until he was lying on his back. She started kissing his mouth, his neck and down his chest to the deep V lying at the base of his abdomen. As her hands and lips travelled down his chest and abdomen, James clenched his teeth in anticipation. Dear God, he thought what is my sweet wife up to now? James' jaw began to twitch in anticipation. "Elizabeth, love; what are you doing?" James said through clenched teeth.

"Well, James; I am not quite sure," she answered shyly. "I thought you might help me to please you or at least teach me how you like to be pleased, James," Elizabeth responded.

"Come here, my love," James said tenderly.

Elizabeth moved to lie in James arms and when she saw his shining eyes, she knew all would be well. "Did I do something wrong, James?" Elizabeth said quietly.

"Oh no, love; just the opposite. When I make love to you, I want the sensation to last as long as possible. When you do that to me, I am aroused so quickly that it won't last. Do you understand me, love?" James continued tenderly.

"Oh yes, James. I just want to please you in every way that you please me," Elizabeth replied.

"I know that and I love you for it. God knows I love you for it. Now, let me show you how I make our love last," James replied. "I kissed you first on the hand like a suitor," James then kissed her hand. "Then on the forehead like a brother or a father," James kissed her there next.

"I know, James; I didn't think you cared for me then; only as a brother or a father looking out for my welfare because you were afraid of what would happen to a wee bit of a thing on her own," Elizabeth replied smiling.

"Oh no, my love; I was only exerting self control. Then next I kissed you on the lips and heaven help me self control was lost after that," James said laughing.

After that kiss and many more there was no more talking, but only touching and caressing and stroking and all of the elements of their love that extended their lovemaking. James' last logical thought was that he was only following Aunt Sally's directions and giving Elizabeth the babies she always wanted. Colin and the new boy would be great chums and only one year apart in age.

*****

The next morning Elizabeth finished her letter to Kathleen Sullivan in care of Savannah, Georgia and provided it to James to post before they left Wilmington. She came above decks to watch them leave her hometown, just as she had the year before. After they had left the dock and headed down the Cape Fear River, James came to stand at the rail with Elizabeth who was watching her hometown from the decks of the Triad. "Is it hard to leave then, Elizabeth?" James said worriedly.

"No, James; it was my home for twenty-two years, but it is only a town filled with ghosts for me anymore. If there is only one person left that you will miss, it is not your home anymore. My home is with you and Colin wherever we may be," Elizabeth replied.

"And don't forget the new baby, my love!" James said smiling.

"The new baby; oh, James; do you think so?" Elizabeth replied with her eyes shining.

"Oh yes, love. I will always follow Aunt Sally's direction. I will always love her Lilliebeth, protect her, and give her lots of babies because that is what she has always wanted," James said with a wink.

Elizabeth put her head on his shoulder and watched the Triad move into the open ocean. They were headed for their next adventure and would do so together.

THE END

NOTES

- The Yellow Fever Epidemic of 1862 – The referenced Yellow Fever Epidemic of 1862 which took the life of Elizabeth Major's Brother Robert; was a historical event of significant impact to Wilmington, North Carolina. Not only was there significant loss of life, but Wilmington as the principal port city supplying the Army of Northern Virginia, significantly impacted the supply lines of the Confederate Army when the port was shut down by the epidemic. Blockade running ships were quarantined for thirty days, especially those coming from the Bahamas where the illness was believed to have been transported to Wilmington's shores. People fled the city in droves and those who remained were in grave danger of the epidemic. Only the frost of 1862 brought an end to the spread of the illness. Elizabeth witnessed a major health crisis during her residency in the city as well as the loss of her brother to the dread disease.

- Chelsea Old Church – All Saints – As in the novel, a church by this name is located only a few yards from the Thames River where James' ships the Alliance and the Triad would have docked. It is an Anglican church currently, but would have been a Catholic church until the days of the Reformation during the reign of Henry VIII. As early as the 8th century, there was a church at this location, with major additions in 1528 when it was rebuilt as the private chapel of Sir Thomas More and later in 1670. The church experienced major damage during World War II and was rebuilt and reconsecrated following the war.

- Broadlands – The inspiration for Broadlands, the home of James O'Rourke in the book, is Newbridge House, outside Dublin. A Georgian era house that sits in 370 acres of rolling Irish landscape; has been the residence of the Cobbe family, whose roots date to the 15th century. The remaining aspects of the grounds, such as the private beach; were writer's imagination of a home lived in by a mariner family.

- Scotland Yard – The workplace of Hugh Flynn in the novel, Scotland Yard is the headquarters of the London Metropolitan Police which services the city of London and the Greater London area. The force was created in 1829 and called "bobbies" after Sir Robert Peel, Home Secretary who was credited with introducing the bill that originally created the force. The starting location of the force was 4 Whitehall Place, the back of which opened on a courtyard called the Great Scotland Yard. The name derives from a palace where Scottish royalty were entertained while in England.

- Old Bailey – The Old Bailey was the sight of the courtroom where the trial of Whitfield and Cross was held. It was named after the street on which it was located, off of Newgate Street and next to Newgate Prison in the western part of London.

- St. Mary School, Wilmington, NC - The St. Mary School was begun in 1869, but for purposes of our novel, both Elizabeth Majors and her friend

Kathleen Sullivan were graduates of the school which was an adjunct of the St. Mary's Catholic Church in Wilmington. It continues providing education to both boys and girls in Wilmington today.

- My thanks to my readers who inspire me to begin each day working on a new book, editing an existing book or completing research for future books. Thank you for your comments and your support in this adventure called writing.

- Thanks also to my beta reading team of Bill Hammond and Pamela Swartwood. I love to receive your comments and to see my characters and books through your eyes. Many thanks for your time and patience.

- This book represents a second edition of *In the Eye of the Storm*. I had not included historical notes in the original version and always wish to differentiate between the writer's imagination and factual information.

- My thanks to the people of Wilmington, North Carolina who inspired this story. I worked there for ten years and began this book during my tenure. I was pleased to have the opportunity to complete it over twenty years later and to continue my writing adventure. I will be releasing a tenth book this autumn of 2016 and a sequel to this book which features our friend Hugh Flynn in the main role and Elizabeth and James O'Rourke as minor characters. Father Colin O'Rourke will also be along for the story, as well as baby Colin who will be joined by a new baby brother in the upcoming sequel which is tentatively titled *Storm Chaser*.

- Follow me on Facebook at Deborah Hammond and on twitter at @DeborahHammon18. I also have an Author Central page on amazon.com.

SOURCES

- Chelsea Old Church Web-site.
- Smithsonian.com.
- The Old Bailey Web-site.
- St. Mary's School Web-site – Wilmington, NC.
- Historic Houses of Ireland Web-site.

Made in the USA
Middletown, DE
04 May 2022

64986234R00166